By VICTOR J. BANIS

A Deadly Kind of Love

Published by DSP PUBLICATIONS
www.dsppublications.com

A DEADLY KIND OF LOVE

VICTOR J.
BANIS

DSP PUBLICATIONS

Published by

DSP Publications

5032 Capital Circle SW, Suite 2, PMB# 279, Tallahassee, FL 32305-7886 USA
www.dsppublications.com

A Deadly Kind of Love
© 2018 Victor J. Banis.

Cover Art
© 2018 Adrian Nicholas.
adrian.nicholas177@gmail.com
Cover content is for illustrative purposes only and any person depicted on the cover is a model.

ISBN: 978-1-64080-251-3
Digital ISBN: 978-1-64080-252-0
Library of Congress Control Number: 2017953660
Published March 2018
v. 2.0
First Edition published by Dreamspinner Press, June 2011.

Printed in the United States of America
∞

This paper meets the requirements of
ANSI/NISO Z39.48-1992 (Permanence of Paper).

Thanks to my readers, Murphy Cutler and Nowell Briscoe,
and to Martha Edgmon, executive assistant to the mayor
and council of the City of Palm Springs,
for much valuable information.
And a special thanks to Laura Baumbach—she will understand why.

A DEADLY KIND OF LOVE

VICTOR J. BANIS

CHAPTER ONE

"Whew. That was quite a party!" Chris Rafferty breathed a weary sigh and leaned back against the car's headrest, letting his eyelids drift closed. "I'm just past the next bend."

"Sweet." The car leaned gently around a final curve. "Whoa, you're staying here?" the driver, Eddie, exclaimed. "At the Winter?"

"Umm-hmm." Chris's reply was heavy with threatening sleep. He was having trouble staying awake. "Is that special?"

"Special?" Eddie whistled faintly under his breath. "Gosh, the Winter Beach Inn is like the top place to stay in Palm Springs these days. The top gay place, for sure. I don't know, maybe the top place period." He turned his head to look at Chris in the pale greenish glow from the dashboard. "So are you some kind of millionaire or what?"

"Me?" Chris laughed. "Hardly. I'm a nurse. I told you earlier. Did you ever hear of a millionaire nurse?"

"No, but I don't know many nurses who could afford to stay here either. It's mostly rich, older queens. Let me guess, you've got a sugar daddy, right?"

Another laugh. "Not me. My best friend, Stanley Korski, he works sometimes for this big-name decorator in San Francisco, Wayne Cotter, and Wayne drops enormous bucks here whenever he comes to town. He might even own a piece of the pie. I don't know. Anyway, when I said I was coming to Palm Springs, Stanley called Wayne, and Wayne called the Inn, and voilà. I got a room on the house."

"Talk about lucky." The car slowed. "So what suite are you in? They're all named for movie stars, right?"

"Right. I got the Jeanette McDonald. Oh, no, wait, they switched my room. Just as I was coming out tonight, as a matter of fact. I was headed for the door and stopped to powder my nose, and I realized my toilet had backed up, and as quick as you please, they moved me lock, stock, and barrel to the Alice Faye. I didn't even have to lift a pinkie. You can drop me here."

They pulled up by the massive gates—locked at this late hour. Eddie switched off the headlights. "You sure you don't want to, uh… you know?" he said. He glanced upward. The sky was still dark but with the opalescence that foretold the morning. "We could greet the dawn, so to speak."

"Ah, thanks, um," Chris mumbled the name, afraid he wouldn't get it right. "I would, but I'm beat. I'm not as young as I used to be. Next time, okay?"

"Sure." Eddie sounded disappointed, but not too. "I'm kind of ragged myself, to tell the truth. You wanna have lunch tomorrow?"

"Too early. I'm going to sleep in. Let's say dinner. Why don't you call me? Only, not before noon, okay?"

"Sounds good. Hey, you know what, can we eat here? I've always wanted to see inside this place. This is probably the only chance I'll ever get."

"Absolutely. The food's good too." Chris leaned across the seat to give his companion a quick peck, which turned into something a bit more prolonged. They rubbed together for a long moment, lips locked.

"Sure you don't want to change your mind?" Eddie asked when they came up for air.

"Trust me, it would be a futile gesture," Chris said. He opened his door to slide out. "Tomorrow, okay? Not too early."

He used his key card to let himself through the gates and took the yellow brick path about the main building. During the day the swimming pool was sometimes so crowded with bodies that you could hardly see the water, but now it was empty, a huge turquoise kidney, smelling of chlorine. The fronds of the palm trees overhead rattled like ghostly castanets. A white napkin, missed by the cleaners, blew past his feet in the desert breeze, caught on the leg of a chair, a linen tumbleweed.

He got to the door of the Jeanette McDonald suite before he remembered he had been moved, and half staggered to the next door over. He'd had way too much to drink tonight, plus smoking a couple of joints, and what was that pill he'd taken, anyway? Not to mention he had danced until his legs actually felt shaky.

"Getting old, Christopher," he mumbled, letting himself into the Alice Faye suite.

The room was dark. From his earlier brief inspection, he remembered blue ruffles and lots of frills and a parasol for a lampshade. More frills, maybe, than he wanted to face just at the moment. He didn't bother turning on the lights. The faint glow through the curtains was enough to show his way to the bathroom door, a first stop his bladder was absolutely demanding. Always listen when your bladder demands, was his motto.

In the harsh glare from the bathroom's overhead light, he blinked and glowered at his disheveled appearance in the mirrors that covered all the walls—eyes bleary, hair in disarray, a big stain of some sort on the front of his shirt. Multiple appearances, he corrected himself. You could watch several of you, or maybe several of somebody else, take a leak.

He smiled sleepily, thinking of a friend or two who would find that pleasantly kinky—but at the moment, business was more urgent than admiring, or not admiring, himself. His little playmate popped out of his trousers just in time for a noisy pee that went on and on and on. It was definitely blessed relief. He sighed and rolled his eyes heavenward. There were times he honestly believed it was better than an orgasm.

Flushing, he avoided looking at the mirrors again. One glimpse was enough to remind him he was no longer a kid and that late-night carousing took its toll in ways it hadn't ten years earlier. His wool-coated teeth really needed a good brushing, but he was too tired. He flipped the light off before he opened the door and went out.

After the brightness in the bathroom, the bedroom was dark as pitch, nothing to be seen but the pale rectangle of the window across the room, the blue-green light from the swimming pool leaking through. He felt his way in what he thought was the right direction for the bed and, bumping into it, dropped down on it with a noisy *oof.*

In a minute or two, he told himself, he would get up and strip off his clothes and get under the covers like a civilized man. For the moment, though, he just wanted to lie there, catching his breath, savoring the memory of a great night on the town.

His breathing slowed. He did not, after all, exactly feel like going to all the trouble of getting up and undressing. He thought instead he'd just snooze for a little bit. There was always time to take your pants off, wasn't there? It wasn't like there was somebody with him to take them off for.

Which reminded him briefly of the young man who had dropped him off at the gate. Eddie—was that his name? Cute. Japanese, with almond skin and soft dark eyes and lips of velvet, sweet to the kiss. And horny, certainly, despite the late hour and all the entertainment. Maybe he should have…?

Too late for that, he told himself sternly. And he didn't think he had the energy to masturbate either. He really was getting old. He turned onto his side, let one arm flop limply across the bed—and discovered there was something in the bed with him.

One hand went tentatively up and down. Yes, it was just what he'd thought at first, a body. As if his horny thoughts had conjured it up—a male body, lying on its back; it took only seconds of exploration to confirm the gender. A naked male body, which made the confirmation much easier than it otherwise might have been.

Even drunk and tired as he was, he thought there was something to be said for having a warm naked body in bed with you. Pleasant to contemplate, certainly. There was just one slight problem with that scenario, however.

This body was not warm.

CHAPTER TWO

STANLEY KORSKI woke conscious of the warm body next to him in the bed. Or sort of woke, rather. He was really more asleep than awake when he answered the phone. It was nearly four in the morning, after all. He fumbled the receiver from the cradle, got it upside down at first, and reversed it.

"Stanley?" the phone asked his ear.

"Chris… uh, hi." He waited for his friend Chris to say something more, explain why he was calling in the middle of the night. Beside Stanley, warm-bodied Tom Danzel stirred slightly.

"Who is it?" Tom asked in a grumpy mumble.

"It's Chris," he said in a whispered aside to Tom, then into the phone asked in a groggy voice, "So, uh, how is Palm Springs?"

"It's nice. Hot, though, really hot. In the daytime, anyway, but it cools down in the evening. I spent most of the day in the pool here at the hotel, very festive, and then I danced the night away. The boys down here really know how to party."

"That's nice." Another long pause.

"What's he want?" Tom grunted. "What time is it?"

"Umm, Chris, honey, it's, like—" Stanley squinted at the clock with its oversized numerals, easy to read with his contact lenses out. "—it's like four o'clock in the morning."

"Three forty-eight."

"Is something wrong?" Tom asked, rolling onto his back and running his fingers through already tousled curls.

"Is something wrong?" Stanley asked into the phone.

"Yes. Stanley, there's… there's this guy in my room."

"You're calling me at four in the morning—"

"Three forty-nine…."

"Three forty-nine in the morning to tell me you got lucky? Let me guess, he's hot and he's hard—"

"Stiff."

"That's just semantics. I don't do semantics in the middle of the night. Sweetie—"

"No, I mean, he's stiff. As in, he's dead."

"Dead?"

Beside him, Tom sat up. "Huh? Who?"

"Stanley, there's a dead guy in my room. In my bed, to be specific."

"Naked?"

A loud sigh. "Of course he's naked, silly. Why would a man be in my bed with his clothes on?"

"I don't think I understand what he's doing there naked."

"I don't either." Chris sounded as if he was about to cry.

"But he's there? In your bed?"

"Yes. He's in my bed. He's naked."

"And he's dead?"

"As a doornail."

"And the police…?"

"Are on their way. Oh, Stanley, I need you guys. Please."

Stanley flipped the bedside lamp on, kicked the covers aside, and sat up on the edge of the bed, the phone still to his ear.

"What's going on?" Tom asked. "Who's dead? Where are you going?"

"Get up, Tin Man, and get dressed," Stanley said, already shimmying into his trousers. "We're off to see the wizard."

Chapter Three

On his own, Stanley would most likely have flown from San Francisco to Palm Springs. The flight only took about an hour and twenty minutes on Alaska—but that, of course, was not counting all the hassle one went through at airports these days.

And the hassle was particularly vexing for Tom. He had been caught in an explosion and a fire some time before, and the incident had left him with burn scars and, more tellingly, a metal plate in one hip—and Stanley's nickname for him, Tin Man. Inevitably the steel set off alarms and created confusion at airports. Sometimes it took longer to get through security than it did for the flight.

Tom preferred driving down the I-5 in his big Dodge Ram truck, supercharged, and considering that his attitude toward speed limits was pretty cavalier, and with those airport delays factored in, the travel time generally wasn't all that much longer.

Plus, as Stanley liked to put it, it gave them quality space together. They talked, or alternatively, since Tom wasn't a chatty type, drove in comfortable silence. When the silence grew a bit lengthy, one or the other of them turned on the radio. Tom liked old jazz, and Stanley's tastes ran to musicals, but heading through the middle of the state, both of those were the proverbial hen's teeth. Stanley had better luck finding country music on a Bakersfield station. Hank Williams cried lonesome blues while the big wheels ate up the highway, Kitty Welles sang of faithless men in a twang you could have sliced with a butter knife, and Dolly Parton's sweet soprano provided the leavening to all that rural angst.

Hank and friends began to fade in and out as they left the Bakersfield station behind, climbing the Grapevine up and down again, and got closer to Los Angeles. Stanley fiddled with the dial some more, found some jazz for Tom on a Hollywood station: Miles Davis, Nina Simone, Bix Beiderbecke. The music somehow evoked an older Hollywood— dark smoky clubs, dry martinis, Bogart and Bacall sparring wittily and swapping great lines.

They skirted the big city on the 210, which took them east through air already smeared with smog even in this early season. In summer's heat it would be brown and poisonous, blown inland by the ocean breezes. Had always been so. The Chumash Indians, long before the city had sprung up, had called the Los Angeles basin "the valley of the smokes." The coming of civilization had only aggravated the problem. Aggravated it greatly.

Past San Bernardino—and back to the country music—the air got better, but the urban sprawl did not. Strip malls, casinos, and truck plazas had taken over here too, stood in for the old desert, but at least the sky was arrogantly blue, and between the malls and the commercial buildings you could still catch glimpses of spidery tumbleweeds nestled against bleached-out fences, brown sugar canyons in the distance, and sand that glittered so brightly in the afternoon sun it hurt the eyes to look at it for more than a second or two. The occasional scrub brush or mesquite broke the vast expanse, and in the far distance, mountains loomed purple-gray, their tops still capped with winter's snow. It was the fifth of March, early spring.

They made a brief pit stop at a rest area, a grassy stretch enjoying the welcome shade of cottonwoods and willows. Families ate lunch at picnic tables, and children played in that hyper way they did when finally freed from the confines of a car on a long road trip.

Back on the highway, Stanley turned off the air-conditioning and put down the windows. The air blowing into the cab was warm, not too hot, and dry, with what Stanley could only think of as "that desert smell, pungent and sweet all at the same time."

He had read once that what distinguished the "primitive" painters, like Grandma Moses, was that they painted snow as white, when in reality it almost never was white but a reflection of its surroundings, or the sky above, a hundred different shades of gray or blue or green.

In the same way, it seemed to him, amateur painters always painted the desert sand beige, but he saw a myriad of subtle shades that only the first-rate artists—Georgia O'Keeffe sprang instantly to mind—managed to capture.

They passed the wind farms, acre after acre of whirligigs arranged on a hilltop in rows, turning lackadaisically in the faint breeze, looking like giant aliens from some other world.

"I wonder what the archeologists will think when they discover these wind machines a few centuries from now," Stanley pondered.

"Probably think we worshipped them."

"I guess some people do." Stanley reached across the seat and put his hand on Tom's muscular thigh. Tom smiled briefly sideways at him—a smile that never failed to pierce Stanley's heart—and put his hand over Stanley's.

It felt good to Tom, holding Stanley's hand in his. Things hadn't always gone well for them. Tom was straight, or had been when they had been thrown together on their first case. Now he was, he admitted to himself, he didn't know exactly what.

The rubbing of a couple of bits of flesh together didn't explain love any more than the string a guitarist picks explains music. He loved Stanley. That was as much as he knew and as gay as he got. Otherwise, he had no interest in men. If it weren't for Stanley, he'd be doing what he'd done all his previous life, and with impressive success—chasing women.

But Stanley was there, trumping all the other cards in the deck. Tom didn't know what exactly it was they had, or ever would have, but he knew if he wanted it, he had to work at it. That meant no more chasing women. At least men weren't a problem for him in that respect. He had never lusted after men, and had been mostly unaware of them lusting after him.

The ropes of love were impossible to break, but they had both learned through bitter experience that they were easily raveled.

AFTER THE wind farms, the desert really did open up, but the increasing presence of billboards touting restaurants, hotels, and gas stations announced that they were nearing Palm Springs. A grandiose RV park proclaimed itself "a retirement community for active adults."

"Better check in with the locals first thing," Tom said. At one time, they had both been homicide inspectors with the San Francisco Police Department, where Tom had been something of a legend and Stanley, no way around it, a misfit. Stanley was thirty years old, Tom a tad older—though not enough older to qualify as a "daddy," a term used fondly in gay circles.

Now they were licensed private detectives. Some police departments were welcoming of private operatives, some were not. Since it was never a good idea to get on the wrong side of a department, checking with the local police was always the first item on Tom's agenda whenever he came to a strange town. Just in case. They had come because Chris wanted them, and Chris was a friend, but they would have no jurisdiction here, no authority other than what the Palm Springs cops were willing to allow them.

Best-case scenario, they got leave to snoop around, sometimes pretty freely. Worst-case, the cops would shut them down. If it turned out that way, they'd have a couple days' vacation in the high desert, go back to San Francisco, and leave things up to the locals.

Stanley had gone to the computer and printed out maps for them before they left San Francisco. They exited the freeway on the Gene Autry Trail, skirted the airport, and drove directly to the Palm Springs Police Department—a modern structure, one-story, poured concrete with vertical grooves cascading down its front, and a flat roof. In the parking lot, two pigeons were squabbling over a leftover scrap of doughnut and blinked resentfully at them when Tom drove over their dessert. A couple of fan palms tried hard to give the building some charm, and a sculpture out front showed a policeman helping a fallen comrade.

"Nice touch," Tom said of the sculpture. "Comrades in arms. I like it."

Stanley noted that the sculptor had made both the officers hot. Gay artist, he'd bet money. And probably Tom hadn't even noticed that part of it. Much of Tom was still a mysterious and unexplored continent to him. Stanley loved him, but he totally did not understand him.

Who ever understood anybody, though, beyond the surface stuff? What he knew, knew for certain, was that Tom was there for him. Anybody who wanted to hurt him—and there had been a few of those— would have to come at him through Tom, and Tom made a hell of an effective barrier.

It didn't hurt either, that Tom was dynamite in the sack. Really dynamite. Stanley didn't love in quite the same way Tom did, he knew that, but he loved the way Tom's big stick went boom.

INSIDE THE station, a small blonde woman in a black uniform waited at the front desk behind bulletproof glass. She would have been pretty were it not for a long-ago bout with severe acne that had left her well-modeled face pitted beyond what makeup could disguise.

Trying not to stare at her pockmarked skin, Tom felt a brief pang of sympathy. His once handsome face had been scarred in that crime-related fire, the same fire that had left him with a metal hip.

Much improvement had been made to his face, but he was ever conscious of its damaged state. Oddly, some other people—women, and a lot of gay men—felt it made him more attractive, not less. That wasn't how he saw himself in the mirror, though. He would have given a lot to have his old face back, but that wasn't going to happen. Instead, he'd had to make peace with what the mirror showed him.

He saw the acne blonde register his glance and read it correctly. Feeling guilty, he asked her if they could see whichever detective was working the murder at the Winter Beach Inn. She slanted a measuring look up at him and just behind him at Stanley, a little surprised by the request and obviously trying to decide if she should ask them any questions.

"Have a seat," she told them, apparently deciding someone else could ask the questions, and disappeared through a door behind her desk.

Since they had been sitting for most of the last few hours, they remained standing instead. In any case, the wait was brief. A short, pudgy man in rumpled trousers and red suspenders appeared within minutes, an unlit cigar in one hand. He looked them over with small eyes that came close to matching the color of his suspenders, sizing them with a professional's speed and certainty.

"You're the fellows from San Francisco," he greeted them.

It was Tom's turn to be surprised. "As a matter of fact, we are from San Francisco, but…."

"I'm Detective Hammond. Dick Hammond." He nodded for them to follow him and led them to a small two-desk office at one end of the building. Through the window, Tom could see the parking lot and the Ram. Probably, Detective Hammond had watched them arrive.

The second desk in the room was unmanned at the moment but looked as if it were usually well occupied, its surface strewn with paperwork that was all too familiar to Tom from his time in the San Francisco bureau. Casework detail. Sometimes it felt as if you were drowning in paperwork, like a miracle that anybody ever found time to actually solve murders.

"Sit," Hammond said, indicating a pair of hard wooden chairs in front of his desk. "Either of you want coffee?" They both shook their heads. "Wise choice," he said. "It's like road tar."

It wasn't coffee, however, that Stanley smelled on the detective's breath. Apparently Detective Hammond was partial to Eau de Bourbon. Probably that explained to some degree the red-rimmed eyes—which, nevertheless, managed to look plenty shrewd as he looked over his visitors.

"So, I'm curious, how did you know we were from San Francisco?" Tom asked, taking one of the chairs. Stanley sat beside him.

"These days, just about everybody in town is, seems like. Ah, shit, it's no big mystery, though. We got a call from San Francisco PD, from homicide. An Inspector…." He paused to open a folder atop his desk and take a quick peek inside. "Inspector Bryce. He called to tell us you'd be stopping by."

"He did?" Another surprise for Tom. He had worked with Bryce not so long ago in the past when he'd been in homicide detail there. But how had Bryce gotten onto this, he wondered? He hadn't called him, though if he had thought of it, he'd have considered it a good idea. He and Stanley had no official police connection now, but Bryce could open doors for them. Cops responded to cops.

Stanley answered that question for him. "I called Bryce," he said, looking a little embarrassed about it. "I asked him to call and put in a good word for us. I thought it might help."

"Really?" Stanley and Bryce had never been the best of friends. It was no secret that the deeply closeted Bryce had the hots for Tom, a fact that Stanley resented. Which to Tom's way of thinking made it doubly surprising that Stanley should have called him to ask for assistance and that Bryce should have agreed. Not for the first time, he marveled at Stanley's ability to get things done.

Ignoring their exchange, Hammond went on. "Anyway, this Bryce, he said you were on your way, and he asked us to, well, to cut you some slack, sort of. You're not with SFPD, as I understand it."

"Not anymore," Stanley said, and quickly added, "We used to be." Hammond gave him a not-quite-convinced look.

Stanley was used to that. When people, especially police people, looked at him, homicide detective was not generally what they saw. Tom was masculine and burly, with a massive chest and long, heavily muscled arms, and shoulders as wide as a football field. He looked the part of a detective out of some fifties pulp novel. Made most of the fictional tough guys, in fact, look like sissies.

Stanley, by contrast, was little and just shy of effeminate, and even in the often macho world of gay San Francisco—bears and bikers and serious leather drag—he was frequently marginalized. When gay conversations turned to uniforms, as they often did, he liked to say he had an old WAAC outfit from World War II he could don in a pinch. Serious uniform people, and uniform queens could be serious indeed, did not laugh when he said it.

Or, put it another way, Tom was body shirts and denims or camo, with boots. Stanley was cashmere and designer jeans and sneakers. They were mismatched, except according to the law of opposite attraction.

"We have a detective agency now," Tom said.

Hammond looked a bit unhappy with that. "That's what your Bryce told me. Private dicks."

"Yes," Stanley said, still a bit miffed at that look Hammond had given him, "definitely private."

Tom leaned forward in a kind of man-to-man gesture. Hammond responded by leaning forward slightly as well. Stanley looked from one to the other and suppressed a titter. Bad boys bonding. Next thing they'd be arm wrestling.

"Look," Tom said, "here's the thing. We don't plan on getting in your way. The gentleman who has the room where this body was found—"

Hammond took another peek at the file folder. "Christopher Rafferty."

"Right. Chris," Stanley said. He leaned forward into the conversation. Hammond settled back in his chair. "He's a friend of ours. He called us about the body and asked us to come down. I guess as much to hold his hand as anything."

"But to be honest, we would like to poke around a little while we're here," Tom said. "Enough to make our friend feel better, anyway. You know, like we're doing something. If that's not a problem for you."

Hammond sighed and put the folder aside on his desk. "No," he said, a shade reluctantly. "Not a problem, exactly, as long as we all understand this is a police matter. Palm Springs PD is doing the investigation. Anything you learn with your poking around, as you put it, I'll expect you to turn over to PSPD first thing."

"Agreed." Tom gave a shake of his head and added diplomatically, "And most likely, we aren't going to learn anything your boys don't already know anyway. I've worked both sides of the street. It's a bunch of bull that private dicks are better at figuring things out than the police. That's just in the books and movies."

"Glad to hear you say it," Hammond said.

"Still, it can't hurt to have a couple extra pairs of eyes looking things over, can it?"

"Probably not. Are you carrying?"

"I'm not," Stanley said. He wasn't fond of firearms. Some while back he'd had to shoot someone—dead. His own brother, as it happened, though for most of his life he hadn't been aware that he had a brother. Even when he had been with the San Francisco Police Department, he hadn't liked firearms. Since then, since shooting his brother, he'd had a serious aversion to them.

Tom opened his sport jacket to reveal a shoulder holster.

"Sig Sauer?" Hammond asked. Tom nodded. "You're licensed?"

Tom dug out his PI license and the permit for the gun and handed them across the desk. Hammond gave them a cursory read and handed them back.

"For the record, Stanley's licensed too," Tom said. "And he has a Beretta, but it's back in San Francisco."

"Just bear in mind," Hammond said, "you're here on private business. The laws apply to you the same as to all other citizens. Act accordingly." He thought a moment. "And understand, a lot of wealthy people live here. Wealthy, powerful people. They can be funny about their privacy. Be careful whose toes you step on."

"Got it," Tom said. Stanley started to say something, but Tom bumped his shoe unobtrusively against Stanley's, and Stanley bit off his words. When dealing with other police officers, it was generally wiser to let Tom do the talking.

Hammond saw the hesitation and lifted an eyebrow in Stanley's direction. "You okay with that?"

"Absolutely." Stanley bobbed his head appropriately. "Not stepping on toes is a specialty of mine."

"Uh-huh," Hammond said, in a not-very-convinced tone.

"Can I ask," Tom said, "have you got any leads on the murder?"

"Well, now, to tell you the absolute truth, we're not even one hundred percent sure it was a murder."

Another surprise. "A dead guy dumped in a stranger's room…?"

"If he was a stranger. Right now, we're not sure about a lot of things, to be perfectly frank."

"We know Chris Rafferty. If he says the victim was a stranger, you can take that as a given," Tom said emphatically. "How did this guy die anyway, if you don't mind telling us?"

"I don't mind." Still, Hammond hesitated as if he might in fact mind. "Snake bite, it seems like," he said finally.

"Snake bite? Inside a hotel room?"

"Might not have happened there, of course. Somebody gets bitten, they don't always just keel over on the spot. Generally they don't. That's just in the books and movies too. But that was the initial report. You'd be surprised how often snakes show up inside. Scorpions too, or black widows. It goes with the territory. Responding officers said there was evidence of a snake bite, though. Which means, being where we are, it was probably a green Mojave. Ever heard of them?" Tom shook his head. "Meanest rattlesnake there is. Aggressive bastards. Get 'em riled up, they'll come after you."

"So you think—" Tom started to say.

Hammond interrupted him. "I expect we'll know more in a bit." Hammond's face was blank, but the pause this time seemed oddly significant. "The body's over at the county morgue. I doubt they've started cutting on it yet."

Tom thought about that, about the pause. It felt like Hammond was giving him a hint. Something Hammond wanted him to pick up on but couldn't actually say. "Can we see it?" Tom asked. "The body?"

Hammond nodded, as if Tom had correctly answered some unasked question. "I don't see why not. Like you said, some extra eyes can't hurt. The morgue's in Riverside. I expect if you're going over there, though, you probably should go pretty quick. That's if you're wanting to see anything before they start cutting."

"Gotcha," Tom said, standing.

"Sandy out at the desk can draw you a map. Ask for Doc Murphy when you get there, he's the chief forensic. I'll call and tell him you're coming."

"Thanks." They started toward the door.

"Oh, Danzel…," Hammond called after him. Tom paused at the door and looked back. "You got a car phone?"

"I drive a Ram pickup," Tom said. "That big red one you can see out your window there. They don't usually come with car phones. Why?"

"Cell?"

"Sure. Both of us." He waited for Hammond to take it further.

"Just wondered," Hammond said instead and turned his attention back to his desk. He opened a bottom drawer, looked down into it, and glanced up again at Tom and Stanley—obviously waiting for them to go.

So he could have a nip at the bottle stashed in the desk drawer, Stanley rather supposed.

They were half out the door when Hammond thought of something else. "Just so you know, the doc, Murphy—he's not the coolest guy in the desert." He looked significantly from one of them to the other and settled his gaze on Stanley.

Meaning, Stanley thought but did not say, the forensic expert was homophobic.

Well, he'd run into that kind before. And he could dish it out as well as take it, if he had to. But he did wish the straight world could just get over it.

Chapter Four

"What exactly was that all about?" Stanley asked when they were back in Tom's truck and on the road again.

"About the doctor?"

"No, that part I understood well enough. He was telling us this Doctor Murphy doesn't like gays. What I'm wondering about is, first, the part about not stepping on toes. That's kind of obvious, isn't it? I mean, sure you've got a lot of funny money here, and people who have lots of that don't like to be bugged. But I meant, why is he being so agreeable to our looking around, for starters, if he's worrying about us stepping on the wrong toes? I half expected him to warn us off, but he practically invited us to stick around for the party."

Tom steered his way around a slow-moving RV. "Um—the way I read it, he's saying they don't have much to go on, and there's something holding him back, somebody in the way, maybe. Those toes he doesn't want us to step on, only he really does, he just wants to cover his butt. You were with SF long enough to know how the politics work. Everybody wants the detectives to solve the crime, but not if it points fingers in the wrong direction."

"You wouldn't think, this being a small town…."

"Same crap everywhere, babe. All of which means, from his point of view, it's possible that as outsiders, we'll have better luck at finding stuff out than he will, if only because our hands aren't tied. It sounds like his are."

"He smelled like a bourbon distillery, if you didn't notice."

"I noticed. I have a notion he's feeling frustrated, which is good for us, in a way. It means he's okay with our helping, so long as he gets any credit."

"And we take any crap. From the toe people."

"Exactly."

Stanley thought for a moment. "Okay, why did he ask about a car phone? And cell phones?"

"I'm thinking he's telling us someone might be monitoring. Us or him. Or both. Car phones, cell phones, they're radios. Anybody can be listening. My guess is the department is restricted to land phones only for this investigation to avoid leaks, and he wants us to do the same."

"Meaning?"

"Meaning somebody big and important and good at snooping is maybe involved, and we should be careful what we say and where we say it."

"Well, you know me, I always am."

Tom started to make a reply. Stanley had a genuine talent for getting into trouble. But he thought better of mentioning it, and focused instead on following the directions Sandy had given them.

THE COUNTY morgue was in the City of Riverside, west of Palm Springs, which meant backtracking for about an hour, down the same interstate they had driven in on. Sandy's directions were precise. They found the building easily enough, and the forensic examiner, Doctor Murphy.

The doctor was waiting for them when they arrived at the morgue. He turned out to be a tall, spare man with thick glasses and a funny tic that pulled the corner of his mouth awry every few seconds, as if he were about to spit something out of it. Stanley kept waiting for a stream of tobacco juice to erupt, or Ma Kettle to appear around a corner.

"You're the pair from San Francisco," he said, and when Tom nodded, he glanced at Stanley and said, "I figured." Neither his tone nor the look he gave them could be regarded as friendly. "Well, I was asked to let you have a look-see, and I was just getting ready to start the autopsy. Either of you likely to upchuck or faint, anything of that nature? It makes things awkward when people do that."

"We've seen it before," Tom said.

Murphy looked at Stanley, who only nodded.

"Well, then." The doctor led them along a corridor to a white-walled room, cooler than the rest of the building and with the sharp odor of disinfectant. He gave them both masks and gowns as they came in. A sheet-covered body lay on a stainless steel table, and when Tom and Stanley had donned the necessary gear, Murphy tugged the sheet off and threw it into a large hamper nearby.

The naked body of a young blond man lay exposed on the metal surface. His eyes were closed, his mouth open, as if he were gasping for air. Except for the coloration, already graying, he might have been asleep.

"Hell, he's just a kid," Tom said.

"Eighteen, I'd say, or nineteen," Murphy agreed.

"Pretty," Stanley said.

"If you're the sort to call boys pretty," Murphy said in a frosty voice. He looked like he was about to spit.

"What do you estimate for time of death?" Tom asked before the two of them could start sparring. "The body was discovered about four in the morning, as I understand it. In a room at the Winter Beach Inn."

Murphy nodded. "Yes, and the corpse was already cold at the time it was found. So I'd say he died between midnight and three. I'll know more exactly when I've finished my exam."

"Detective Hammond said the victim had been bitten by a snake."

Doctor Murphy hesitated slightly. "That appears to be the case," he said in a cautious tone. "He's got puncture wounds, and the initial blood work shows Mojave toxin. That would suggest he was bitten by a green Mojave. Rattlesnake. Crotalus Scutulatus, to be precise."

"And that's pretty lethal stuff, right?"

"Mojave toxin?" Murphy nodded emphatically. "About thirty times more deadly than other rattlesnake venom, as a matter of fact."

"Hammond told us it's an aggressive snake," Tom said.

"Very aggressive. Most rattlers, you come along the trail where they're sunning themselves, they're as anxious to avoid you as you are to avoid them. If you don't, say, step on one, they'll try to leave, get out of your way. But the Green will stay and defend his turf. Come right at you, even. They're pretty ornery."

"How fast does the venom act?"

"Now, that's an odd thing, not as fast as other snake venoms. It's a neurotoxin. There's little pain with the initial bite, and the serious effects don't kick in for a while. It starts with difficulty breathing, and after that, it gets progressively worse. Then worse still, and at that stage things deteriorate fast."

"But if it doesn't happen right off the bat," Tom said, "and if someone gets bitten, they would have time to get help?"

"Yes, most likely. It varies, depends on the snake and where you get bitten. But most likely you would have enough time, anyway. There's a good antivenin for it too—CroFab—if the victim gets it in time, generally within an hour even, though as I say, that can vary. Most of the hospitals around here keep it on hand or can get it quickly, for obvious reasons."

"On the other hand, let's say the victim didn't know he had this venom in him, getting ready to take him down…?"

The doctor thought, shook his head. "But you would know, wouldn't you? If a snake bit you? It's not a painful bite, as I said, not at first, but, well, these aren't little snakes. The Mojave is big and mean and ugly. If one of them came at you, you couldn't not see him. You'd know what was happening. If it was me, I'd be doing my damnedest to get out of his way. So, sure, you'd know, I'd think."

"Maybe. Maybe not. Anything else show up in the toxicology?"

The coroner gave him a reluctant smile. "You're pretty sharp, aren't you?"

"I worked a lot of homicides in the past. One thing I learned, there's always surprises waiting for you, especially at this stage of the game. So, what else did you find?"

"He had a trace of flunitrazepam in him," Murphy said, then qualified that. "At least it looks like he did."

"Roofies," Stanley said. "What do you mean, looks like?"

"If you're familiar with the drug, you know that the usual screening for flunitrazepam is in the urine. Obviously we didn't get to do that. And it's volatile. It degrades quickly. So, all I can tell you at this stage is that a trace of it showed up in the initial toxicology report. But if we retested the blood, it likely wouldn't show at all now. That's why we try to do an initial toxicology screen as quick as we can."

"So maybe a date rape thing," Tom said.

"If you accept that boys get raped."

"They do," Stanley said.

"Maybe." The doctor sounded unconvinced. "It's hard to say what it means in this case anyway. It's not unusual for folks to take it for recreational purposes, from what I hear. And this kid looks a little loosey-goosey to me. There's no way to know if he ingested it voluntarily or someone slipped it to him in a drink, trying to get into his pants. At this point, that's all just conjecture. What I am prepared to say, and I expect my autopsy will confirm it, is that it was the snake venom that killed him, not the so-called roofies."

Tom looked down at the body on the table, his eyes going slowly up and down, studying carefully. "So where did the snake bite him?" he asked. "I heard the original officers saw the wound."

The coroner pointed wordlessly to the left hand. There were two puncture marks visible on the upper surface, close to the wrist. He looked blank-faced at Tom. Tom felt as if he were being tested. He leaned closer and peered intently at the marks on the hand.

"Funny snake," he said, straightening.

"What makes you say that?"

"All the venom, or most of it anyway, came from one fang. This one"—Tom pointed at one of the wounds—"is all red and swollen, typical of snake bite, but the other one is hardly swollen at all. And looking up close at them, they don't really look like fang marks, seems to me."

"Which leads you to think…?"

"It looks more to me as if he was injected with a syringe. He got the venom, or most of it, in the first wound, the one on the left."

"And how do you imagine this happening?"

"Well, let's say the victim ingested roofies—of his own volition or someone else's doing. Either way, he's semiconscious, maybe out cold. Easy enough for someone to inject him with a syringe. And when the venom starts to take hold, say half an hour later or something like that, the perp gives him a second stab with the needle, spaces it just so, for cosmetic purposes, to make it look like a snake got him. At a glance, that's what you'd think you saw. Or maybe he even did both wounds at the same time, but either way he didn't reload the syringe. This one is just a hole. Maybe a little venom still in the syringe, but way less than what he got the first time. Right place for the puncture, but I never heard of a snake loading up one fang more than the other."

The doctor smiled and nodded in reluctant approval. "I hadn't either. I had the same idea."

"So we're talking murder."

"It's one way of looking at it. I'm not entirely convinced the punctures are from a syringe and not a snake, but the autopsy should tell us. You're right, though, the venom pattern isn't right. It would be a very peculiar reptile." He paused and drew his shoulders back, did that about-to-spit thing with the corner of his mouth. "Bear in mind, though, this happened in Palm Springs. Lot of hinky stuff there. A lot of queer folks. A queer snake wouldn't surprise me." He gave Stanley a meaningful glance.

"And I take it that would make you uncomfortable?" Stanley asked in a cool voice. "A queer snake."

"Let's say I'm more comfortable with things following their rightful natures. As it says in the good book, 'Who knowing the judgment of God, that they which commit such things, are worthy of death.' That's Romans, 1.32."

Stanley replied, "'The soul of Jonathon was bound to the soul of David, and Jonathon loved him as his own soul.' 1 Samuel, 18.1."

"That doesn't mean they were queer," the doctor said, his eyes frosty.

"No, it means they loved one another," Tom said. "Come on, Stanley, let's get some fresh air."

"I'm about to start cutting," Murphy said. "You want to stay and watch the show?"

"No," Tom said, shedding the gown and the mask. "We've seen enough."

Chapter Five

"Turn here," Stanley said, consulting his map. They were back in Palm Springs and looking for the Winter Beach Inn. The growing evening traffic had added half an hour to the drive time back from Riverside. It was daytime still, but the sunlight was fading, shadows spilling down the distant mountains, the air cooling noticeably.

A wide boulevard wound graciously past what looked like some very expensive real estate, turned in a wide arc, and brought them to oversized wrought-iron gates. The gates were closed. Tom gave an intercom their names, and the gates swung inward. He drove in, past a small structure the size of a woodshed. They had a glimpse of a uniformed guard inside it, watching their progress. Stanley waggled his fingers, with no response.

"Lots of security," Tom said, following the drive up to a pale pink villa that sat on a slight knoll. Considering its reputation for swank, the Winter Beach Inn looked almost spartan from outside. They came to another set of gates before they got there, but these swung open for them as they approached, probably controlled from the same security office.

If the hotel itself was plain, however, the grounds they now passed gave it the look of a mega resort and not just another Palm Springs gay motel. Pink walls high enough to guarantee privacy surrounded what appeared to be several acres of perfectly groomed, even fanciful, landscaping. Jacaranda and bougainvillea provided splashes of red and magenta, and what looked to be an authentic stream, but surely was not, cascaded over a shallow waterfall and meandered among the flowers until it formed a small lake. The sand surrounding it might well have been an oceanfront beach, as the hotel's name implied—at least a lakefront beach, if you accepted the concept of a small lake. Of course, artificial beach or no beach, this was still the desert, as it might have been designed for Disneyland.

The parking area in front of the hotel was mostly filled with an array of high-end automobiles. Lots of Mercedes and Jaguars, no fewer than two Rolls Royces, a Bentley, and a lone Cadillac, sitting embarrassed off by itself at a far end.

Tom parked his Dodge truck in the welcome shade of a portico, and they got out. Wide steps led up to etched glass doors that gave crystalline glimpses of a lobby beyond, but on an impulse, Stanley led the way instead along a curving walkway—yellow brick, he noted with a smile; Judy would have approved—around to the side of the building, following the sounds of splashing water and a babble of laughing, masculine voices.

Still another metal gate blocked the view of the pool area, but it was unlocked and swung open when Stanley pushed at it, revealing a large patio area with a turquoise-watered swimming pool.

"Jesus," Tom said, "that pool is larger than our entire apartment."

"Yes, but not by much," Stanley said.

A crowd of men—not a woman in sight—lounged about on the patio where dinky tables shaded by lavender umbrellas held cocktail glasses, many of them gaily decorated with their own umbrellas in a rainbow of colors. More scarlet bougainvillea cascaded down one wall, and cacti bloomed suspiciously in enormous earthen pots scattered here and there.

One naked young man swam the length of the pool energetically, a butterfly stroke, his water-polished buttocks rising and falling from the water with each stroke. A dozen other young men, most of them splendid to behold, stood in the shallow end or sat on the tiled edge, watching his progress with keen interest, one or two of them cheering him on. Stately palm trees behind the pink wall craned their necks to ogle the well-muscled bodies about the pool.

The bodies at the tables, many of them, were considerably less well muscled, however. The men crowding the patio seemed to divide into two distinct ranks—young and admired, or older and admiring.

"Looks pretty posh," Tom said.

"The poshest, I hear," Stanley agreed.

One or two men turned their heads, appraising them frankly. As usual, Tom lit fires in several eyes. Stanley let the gate swing shut with a faint clang, and they started back toward the front of the building.

"A thousand a night to start, I'm told. And up. A lot of up, apparently."

"A thousand a night?" Tom was astonished. "Uh, Stanley, are we going to be staying here?"

"Of course. This is where Chris is. This is where the body was found. Where else would we want to be? Plus, I've heard nothing but wonderful things about this place. Why? Are you uncomfortable because it's a gay resort?"

"No," Tom said, drawing it out in such a way that it was clear he was. "But a thou a night? The last number I remember from our checking account, we can afford to stay until"—he glanced at his wristwatch—"six fifteen, which is about an hour from now."

"Well, silly, of course we couldn't afford it if we were paying," Stanley said with a deprecating laugh.

"Aren't we?"

Stanley paused and looked at him. "Let us sincerely hope not. Wayne said he'd arrange it."

"Wayne? Your…?"

"Decorator friend, yes. This is his kind of place. He's the one who got Chris reservations. You don't imagine Chris could afford it either, do you?"

Tom frowned. He wasn't real keen on Stanley's decorator friend. With rare exceptions—Chris was one of them—he really wasn't keen on Stanley's gay friends, period. "I don't like the idea of somebody else paying our way."

"Don't worry, neither would Wayne. He's not that generous, and that's not how things are done in this social set. Vulgar money is rarely mentioned."

"Well, then?"

"What I'm expecting is that our stay will be comped by the management."

They had come back to the steps that led to the etched glass doors. They went up them, and Tom opened a door for Stanley.

"Okay, why would they, though?" Tom asked. "The management, I mean. Why give us free rooms? It's not like we're movie stars or something."

"Take a look at this lobby," Stanley said. Tom did.

If the building's exterior, at least as seen from the street, was a bit on the Spartan side, the interior was not. The floors were a desert of inlaid marble in varied sand hues, with deep-piled red carpeting like crimson streams washing up at the reception desk, the attached bar and restaurant, the elevators. The ceiling was glass and high above, the air-conditioning silent but effective, the lighting soft and discreet. More palms stood in huge planters shaped and colored to look like outcroppings of rock. Art, expensive art, not so much imitating nature as disdaining it.

"This is not the kind of place that likes to have any unpleasantness lingering on," Stanley said. "But unfortunately for them, a body was found here. The owners will want that little incident resolved as quickly and as cleanly as possible, and these are the kind of people who will not altogether trust the local police force to do it with minimal damage to the establishment's reputation. All that talk about stepping on toes—somebody has sunk a lot of money into this place. I suspect if one were to dig deep enough, there are other bodies to be found, and a careless policeman might uncover one that's inconvenient."

"Which explains Hammond's warmhearted greeting."

"Yes, I think so. Although the bourbon probably had something to do with that too. But we, my handsome darling, are ace detectives, come down from Baghdad by the Bay. We're going to provide them—everybody, local police, hotel management, victims—with all the answers they need. More importantly, the kind of answers they want, and we are going to do it in record time and with a minimum of embarrassment for all concerned. And that's worth a few nights of free sleeping accommodations, as I see it."

Apparently he was right in his assessment. The clerk at the desk—quite fetching, Stanley could not help noticing—greeted them with a warm smile. "You're in the Joan Crawford suite," he told them when he heard their names, handing over a pair of key cards. "You can go by the pool, it's at the far end of the patio and just to the left, or you can follow that corridor over there, down the red carpet."

Stanley looked at the little plastic room card. "There's no number," he said.

The clerk gave him another warm smile. "Oh, you can't miss it. Think Mildred Pierce."

No mention was made of payment, no credit card requested, no register to sign. Just smiles and nods, as if they had all agreed on something. Smiling back at the welcoming clerk, Stanley wondered what all might be included in the agreement, but he thought he'd better keep that question to himself. Tom was a sweetheart, but he could be stuffy about some things.

They went by way of the interior corridor, following the red carpet. As the young man at the desk had promised, it was easy to recognize their room when they found it. A life-size decal took up much of the door's surface—the actress in full Mildred Pierce regalia, flouncy dress and apron—and you could almost smell the pies baking and hear Eve Arden's snappy remarks.

"The Joan Crawford," Stanley said, beaming with pleasure. "Isn't it wonderful? They've given us the Joan Crawford suite."

"Is that good?"

"Are you crazy? Joan was practically a goddess." He opened the door and stood on the threshold, surveying the room. "Oh, look at the bedposts."

"Are those high-heeled shoes?" Tom asked, a bit bewildered. The enormous bed's four posts ended at the carpet in carved replicas of sling-back pumps.

"Fuck-me pumps. Just like Joan used to wear."

Tom scratched his head. "Why would a bed wear high-heeled shoes?"

Stanley swatted Tom's shapely rear. "For ambience, dummy. And look at these bathrobes." Stanley held up one of the white terry robes that had been draped gracefully across the bedspread. "Shoulder pads."

"In a bathrobe?"

"Joan always wore shoulder pads. It was like a trademark."

"Stanley, in case you haven't noticed, my shoulders are plenty wide. I don't need shoulder pads."

"You do if you're going to pretend to be Joan Crawford."

"I wasn't planning on—"

"This crystal is Lalique," Stanley said, lifting a cocktail glass from a tray. "And look, the rug is definitely handwoven. I've heard Joan's house had Aubusson on the floors. This is so classy."

Tom scowled and went to the closet with his hanging bag. "Huh," he said. "Not too classy, if you ask me."

"What?" Stanley came to peek around him.

"Nothing but wire coat hangers here. You'd think they'd provide the nice padded ones, wouldn't you? Even that Holiday Inn we stayed at last year had those."

Which struck Stanley too, as a little peculiar. He was about to reply when the door to the suite burst open behind them. Tom whirled around, one hand automatically reaching for the Sig Sauer in his shoulder holster, but it was Chris standing in the open doorway.

"Thank God you're here," he said. He started to run in Tom's direction, but before he reached him, he changed his mind, veered, and flung himself instead into Stanley's arms.

Chapter Six

THE GREETINGS they exchanged were quick and excited, Chris and Stanley both chattering away at the same time, but Tom's mind was on business.

"We need to talk," he said.

"Yes, and I think serious conversation is easier with refreshments," Stanley said. "We all need a drink."

"The room service is fast," Chris said.

Stanley placed a call to the bar, and as promised, a tray of margaritas and a cold Dos Equis for Tom arrived within minutes—delivered, Stanley took note, by a drop-dead good-looking waiter. All of the help, it seemed, was gorgeous and friendly. He was beginning to understand how the Winter Beach Inn could get away with charging the steep prices they did.

Tom sat in one of the plush upholstered chairs, and Stanley and Chris sat on the edge of the oversized bed. "Okay," Tom said, taking a sip of his beer and smacking his lips approvingly. "So tell us your story. You come in late, and you find a body in bed with you, and then you…?"

"Well, once I saw that he was dead—which was pretty obvious, he was cold to the touch—I called down to the desk and said I needed to talk to Frederick, emergency fast."

"Who's Frederick?" Tom asked. "And why not call the police?"

Chris shrugged. "It's the kind of place you sort of suspect they'd want to handle things their own way, isn't it? Everything is very… well, you know, *very*. Anyway, Frederick was here in a couple of minutes, but he must have called the police immediately himself, because they were just a few minutes behind him. In the meantime, I had called you."

Tom was thoughtful for a moment. Stanley and Chris sipped quietly and waited for him to think things through. "And before you found this dead man, you were out on the town?"

"Right. Making the rounds. Dancing, you know, making out here and there, the usual. I had just gotten in."

"Okay, then, somebody brought the body in here while you were out dancing—but why here? Why your room?"

"Maybe they meant to frame Chris for the murder," Stanley said.

"That's a possibility," Tom agreed. "Which poses the question, why you? Who did you piss off?"

"You know," Chris said thoughtfully, "I've been stewing over this ever since I found him, and I don't think it was actually about me. I think I got in the way accidentally. I mean, this was in the Alice Faye suite, but that wasn't my original room. I was in a different one to start, the Jeanette McDonald, which is right next door."

"Oh, the Jeanette McDonald, I'll bet that was something," Stanley said, rolling his eyes.

"It was." Chris's face lit up. "You can't believe it. This garden swing made of paper flowers, hanging from the ceiling—you expected Charles Pierce to go sailing over your head singing 'San Francisco.'"

This had been a favorite routine of the popular female impersonator from the sixties. Stanley and Chris were too young to have seen him perform in person, but luckily his routines had been preserved on tape, and they had nearly worn their tape out watching and rewatching him as he swung gaily over the heads of his audience, lip-synching Jeanette McDonald.

"Uh, I hate to spoil the chitchat," Tom said, "but how did you get from one room to the other?"

"Oh, there was a plumbing problem. The toilet in the Jeanette MacDonald backed up. Maybe some of the paper flowers got into it. And apparently they'd had a last-minute cancellation—"

"Sounds awfully convenient," Tom said.

"So they gave me the keys to the room next door, the Alice Faye."

"And when you moved to the new room, you didn't notice a body on the bed?" Tom asked.

"I don't think it was there then. But I admit I didn't take more than a quick peek. I was just about to go out to one of the clubs for some dancing, and the cab was already waiting, so I only glanced in and headed out. Then, when I got back, it was late, and I seriously had to use the loo, so I let myself in and headed straight there, tout de suite, as the French like to say, and when I was finished in there, I came out and just kind of fell onto the bed."

"Which by this time had a body on it."

"Yes, but I didn't see it. Not right off. It's a big bed, bigger than king-sized. Like this one. All the beds here are huge."

Stanley looked at their bed. "You could do a Busby Berkeley routine on top of this one and not kick somebody at the far side. Not anybody you'd care about, at least."

"Exactly. Anyway, I didn't turn on the room light when I came in. There was enough light to see my way to the bathroom, which was very much on my mind. And I turned on the light there, of course, and I took a pee, and then I turned that light off, so when I came back out into the bedroom, it was extra dark, if you know what I mean, and I bumped into the bed and half fell onto it, and I thought, what the hell…. Okay, to tell the truth, I was wasted. I just laid back and closed my eyes for a minute or so, and I was almost asleep, until I turned over and realized I wasn't alone. That's when I turned on the light and… well, I could see right off the bat he was dead. Actually, I knew that before I turned on the light. He was stone cold."

"So it sounds to me like probably you weren't even intended to find the body," Tom said. "Someone just stored it there temporarily, not knowing you had switched rooms, thinking that room was empty."

Chris sipped and nodded. "That's what it seemed like to me too."

"Which suggests," Stanley said, "someone with the hotel management, doesn't it? Someone who knew there had been a cancellation."

"Only, if it was somebody with the hotel, wouldn't they have known the rooms had been switched too?" Tom said. "Which kind of eliminates the hotel people, it seems to me."

"Well, it had to be someone with a key," Stanley said. "Maybe it was a cleaning lady?"

"They use boys," Chris said. "And none of them are ladies. Trust me."

"So, a cleaning boy, then."

"Not necessarily," Chris said. "Listen, this place, it's like an endless game of musical beds. I don't know how they could keep really close tabs on the keys. I mean, anyone could keep one or have it copied. These guys, the older ones, they're high-powered types. Not the type you'd question too stringently if they said they'd lost a key. The management here plays everything by the golden rule, which is, he who has the gold, rules."

"So we're back to square one," Stanley said.

"Maybe not all the way back," Tom said. "We know this kid—does he have a name?"

"Barry," Chris said. "When Frederick saw him, that's the first thing he said, 'Oh God, it's Barry.'"

"Just Barry?"

"That's all he said. But since I've been here, I've learned this isn't a last-name kind of place. Not for the younger guys. They mostly just go by first names. The older guys use last names. A lot of them are Misters. Mr. Smith is very common, if you get my drift."

"Okay, Barry, then. And you didn't know him?"

"Well…." Chris scrunched up his face.

"You did know him?" Tom was surprised. "That changes things."

"No, I didn't *know* him… but I'd seen him. Around. He was a regular here. So I knew him to recognize him is all. He was awfully good-looking. It would be hard not to notice him."

Tom took a moment to digest that. "Okay," he said. "We know this Barry was a regular here, and we know he was murdered, and not by a rattlesnake as we were meant to believe. And we can suppose someone put him in your room by mistake—meaning, they didn't know you would be coming in there during the night. Hmm—raises the question, if it wasn't someone with the hotel, how did they come to think the room would be empty?"

"Anybody could see the previous occupant check out," Chris said. "Especially if he left by way of the pool."

"Whatever. One thing is clear, this all ties in to this hotel. I think the first thing we need to do is talk to this what's-his-name, the manager," Tom said.

"Frederick," Chris said. "He's expecting you. I told him you were on the way. I told him you were friends of mine and you are private detectives and you always solve your cases fast."

"And he was cool with that?" Tom asked. "With our being private detectives?"

"I don't think he's real enthusiastic about the local police."

"You think they're homophobic?"

Chris thought about that. "In Palm Springs? No, not really. Not most of them, at least. I am sure of that. Gosh, this town is practically a gay resort—but there's always one or two lemons in the basket."

"We met one of the lemons, up in Riverside," Stanley said. Chris looked a question at him, but Stanley only said, "I'll tell you later. But you don't think there's a problem with this place and the local constabulary?"

"Maybe not the constabulary. But this place, the Inn I mean, it's a little out of the ordinary. Way out of the ordinary, as a matter of fact. It's just not your typical gay club, and I think the locals don't quite know what to make of it. It gets a lot of the power crowd, and that makes people nervous. And Frederick, he can be a little… well, you'll see for yourself."

He picked up the phone and said, "Is Frederick available? My friends would like to chat with him." He replaced the receiver and said, "He'll meet us by the pool."

Chapter Seven

THE CROWD by the pool seemed to have multiplied since they'd glanced at it coming in. Several heads turned their way when they came out onto the patio. Tom, as usual, got lots of admiring glances. Something about him was like catnip to gay boys. Stanley had ever to be vigilant.

A thin man of middle height stood up from a table in one corner—a power table, Stanley would have called it, and he guessed this was their host, Frederick.

He took in Frederick in quick snapshots as they came toward him—expensively layered salt-and-pepper hair, pale watery eyes, a mouth with almost no lips, and those undistorted by smiles. He wore a white Hermes shirt with a butter yellow ascot at his throat and white linen trousers that had obviously not come from Wal-Mart.

He watched them without expression as Chris led the way across the patio, weaving in and out among crowded tables, saying hi to a few of those they passed. It was typical of Chris, Stanley thought, that it had taken him no more than a day or two to get to know many of the regulars.

"Frederick," Chris said, "these are the friends I told you about, Tom Danzel and Stanley Korski. This is Frederick, the manager."

They shook hands all around. "Frederick Ralston," Frederick said. "But you can call me Frederick. Everybody does."

"Not Freddy?" Stanley asked.

Frederick gave him a chilly look. "Frederick," he repeated firmly. "Please, won't you sit down?"

Frederick asked if they wanted drinks, and when they did, summoned a waiter with the slightest flutter of his fingers. They made small talk while they waited for the drinks.

"Did you fly in?" Frederick asked.

"Drove down," Tom said. "I've got some metal in my hip. Gets them all excited at the airports."

"I had a friend who forgot about his Prince Albert," Chris said.

"What's a Prince Albert?" Tom asked.

"It's a ring through the foreskin," Stanley said. Tom winced.

"Talk about embarrassing," Chris said. "Apparently the security help had never heard of one, so he had to show them. I'll bet that made for a lot of excited conversation afterward."

The drinks came—another Dos Equis for Tom, a pitcher of margaritas for the others, a Perrier for Frederick, however. "I'm working," he said, toasting them with his glass.

"So, this guy, this Barry…." Tom came to the point. "Did he have a last name, incidentally?"

"Palmer. His name was Barry Palmer," Frederick said.

"Okay, Barry Palmer. We hear he was here a lot of the time. Did he work for the motel?" Tom asked.

Frederick drew himself up with a haughty air. "Inn. We prefer to call ourselves an inn. You may have noticed our sign when you arrived. It's about a block high, and it says in bright red letters, The Winter Beach Inn?"

"Okay, inn, then." Tom was unimpressed by the show of grandeur. "And this Barry Palmer worked for your inn?"

Frederick frowned. "Well, not exactly," he said in a somewhat hesitant voice.

"He was a guest, then," Stanley suggested.

"Umm, not exactly a guest, no." Frederick and Chris exchanged glances.

"So, what is not exactly a guest and not exactly an employee?" Stanley asked Chris. "You mean he just hung out at the bar?"

"Don't look at me," Chris said. "I'm not in that league."

"What league is that?" Tom asked. Chris gave Frederick another look.

"He was… if you must know, we call them icing," Frederick said. "Just among ourselves, you understand."

"Icing?" Tom gave him a puzzled look.

"Yes. As in, the icing on the cake."

"The cake being…?"

"This, obviously." Frederick made an expansive gesture with his hands that took in the patio and the palm trees—and the swimming pool, with naked and mostly naked men clustered here and there, in the water and out, on beach towels and chaise lounges, and seated at the glass-topped tables with their lavender umbrellas shading them from the desert sun. "The Winter Beach Inn. The ambience. The over-the-top rooms, the enormous pool, the bar, the restaurant—it is one of the best restaurants in Palm Springs, if you'll pardon my saying so."

"One of the best I've eaten in anywhere," Chris said with enthusiasm.

"Thank you. We try to be. It's what our clients expect of us." Frederick gave him a watery smile and turned his attention back to Stanley. "But when I refer to the ambience, I mean more than anything else, a matter of style. We're not like other resorts. Even our rooms are created especially to charm our visitors."

"We're in the Joan Crawford suite," Stanley said. "Those robes with the padded shoulders, the whole setup. It's wonderful."

"Of course it is." Frederick took the compliment in stride, as if it were expected. "It's meant to be wonderful. We know our clientele. We cater to their tastes. This is *the place* to stay now in Palm Springs, for gay men certainly. We have more requests for bookings than we could possibly accommodate. We turn people away every day. The Joan Crawford, by the way, is one of the most requested suites."

"The closet is full of wire coat hangers," Tom said.

The movement of Frederick's lips might have been a rare smile, but carefully smothered. "Our little joke. By the time you return to your room, you'll find that they have been replaced. I assure you, we want our guests to be happy. When we asked your friend here, he said he thought you'd be very pleased with the Joan Crawford suite. As a matter of fact, we moved someone else to accommodate you."

"We are pleased. And we're very appreciative too," Stanley said. "I do know you're fully booked."

"Yes. But your friend recommended you highly. And I would like to see this whole unpleasant business dealt with as expeditiously as possible."

"You're not confident in Detective Hammond?" Tom asked. "Or the Palm Springs Police Department?"

Frederick gave him an oh-please look and pursed his lips as if he'd bitten into a particularly sour lemon.

"What exactly is it you're expecting of us?" Tom asked.

"I should think that would be evident. We want you to resolve this unpleasantness. Find out who murdered this boy—if he was murdered. My impression was that he died from a snake bite."

"He was murdered," Tom said in a no-argument voice. "The snake bite was faked."

"Well… that is doubly unpleasant," Frederick said. "That being the case, then, I want you to find out who murdered him and bring this whole business to a close. Preferably keeping the Inn out of it."

"I don't see how that would be possible," Tom said. "You are involved, like it or not. The body was found here, the victim was a regular. We can't make the facts go away."

"Perhaps not, but you can certainly minimize the damage to our reputation. And no, I don't think the local police department would concern themselves on that score."

"You have my word, we'll get everything straightened out for you," Stanley promised. "Have no fears."

"I still want to know more about this icing business," Tom said. "I'm not clear on that yet."

Frederick gave him a scornful glance. "It's surely not that mysterious a concept. Look, apart from being the best, we're also one of the most expensive resorts in town. We charge more because we're worth more. Which means we mostly get a pretty wealthy clientele. Which in our case means mostly older gay men. And older gay men appreciate the cake, everything we offer here, but they want the icing on it too."

"Pretty boys," Stanley said, glancing about the patio. There were lots of pretty boys to be seen.

"Bingo. Yes. As you can readily see, the prettiest. And young. They are the icing on our cake."

"So, what you're saying is, you hire B-girls," Tom said. "Or B-boys, in this case. To keep the johns happy."

"No, we don't employ them—this isn't a bordello. As I said of Barry, he was not on the payroll. Neither the Inn nor I make a penny off of any of their interactions. We just let nature take its course."

"But you give nature a little nudge here and there."

"Have you ever been to a Hooters?" Tom's expression answered the question for him. "I suspected as much. Do you think those women are hired for their intellects and moral characters? We don't hire these young men. We simply encourage them to come here instead of some other place."

"And to hang around," Stanley said.

"Exactly."

"Encourage them, as in…?" Tom lifted an eyebrow.

"We make it as—" Frederick hesitated. "—as pleasant for them as we can. They get free drinks at the bar, if someone isn't buying their drinks for them, which usually happens after the first one. If one of the older gentlemen isn't buying a young man's drinks by the second round, the young man is probably not going to become a regular. The same with their meals. The first is on the house, the others are generally paid for by their new gentleman friends. Occasionally one or the other of the young men spends a night, again free."

"In return for what, exactly?" Tom asked.

"Mostly in return for being here, for being young and handsome, for being decorative. Which boils down to keeping the older clientele interested. And coming back again and again. They come here, the older men, they stay here because there are always good-looking young men hanging around, dozens of them, scores even, at the bar, at the pool, dancing in the cabana. A veritable feast for gay eyes. Older gay eyes especially."

"And these young guys are available," Tom said.

"I should think some of them are," Frederick agreed. "Most of them, perhaps. We leave that up to the individuals involved."

Stanley nodded. It was standard practice in gay bars everywhere. A smart bartender bought the occasional free drink for a handsome young stud because it sold lots more drinks to the guys at the bar drooling over him. He had just never heard of it on such a grand scale before.

"And I'm supposing that sometimes it turns into a feast for more than just the eyes?" Stanley said.

Frederick sniffed. "As I have said, that is entirely up to the individuals involved. We neither encourage nor discourage that kind of liaison. Of course, the young men know perfectly well that it's to their advantage to be friendly to the older gentlemen. And yes, certainly, sometimes a pair of them retire to a room together. Or, as I've said, there are sometimes sleepovers."

"Like rather grand pajama parties," Stanley said. Again, Frederick's lips moved just enough to suggest a smile without actually displaying one.

"Does money trade hands?" Tom asked. "Say, at these pajama parties?"

Another sniff. "I wouldn't know. That's their private business and none of mine. As I said, we aren't operating a bordello. Whatever these people do on their own is strictly up to them."

"But aren't you being just a trifle naïve?" Stanley asked. "You must know—"

"Oh, look, we're not fools here," Frederick snapped impatiently. "And neither are they, the young or the old. I have no doubt that sometimes the gentlemen involved reward their new friends for pleasures received, though it probably is not as crass as just shelling out dollars for doughnuts. All kinds of things happen. Drinks get bought, as I've already said, dinners paid for, couples go out on the town, gifts are given."

"And sometimes cash?" Tom insisted.

"I'm sure that happens too. For a young man struggling along on minimum wages as a busboy or a hamburger slinger, it can all be very welcome. But there's also a lot more to it than that. This isn't like standing on a street corner hustling for dollars. I think that most of the young men who come here are hoping something special in the way of a friendship will develop, something a bit more permanent than a free dinner or a few hundred dollars slipped into a pocket."

"A few hundred?" Tom looked amazed. "They get that kind of money for getting their flutes tootled?"

Frederick, though shorter than Tom, nevertheless managed to look down his nose at him. "This is not a tawdry setting, and the moneyed gentlemen are, most of them, very moneyed. They are used to the best, and they can afford to indulge their tastes. It's entirely up to the individuals involved, let me remind you, but if any of these young men you see around the pool there are pleasuring the older gentlemen they're seated with, and there's anything less than five hundred involved, I should say they're undervaluing themselves. That's just my opinion, of course."

"And the other stuff?" Stanley said. "The sugar daddies, the long-term relationships. Do the young icings find them?"

"Sometimes. Often enough to keep the dream alive, I should say. I do know that one of our young men, a regular by the pool there only a short time ago, lives now in Hollywood with a name producer—and no, I'm not going to mention the producer's name, but you would recognize it if I did so."

"And no doubt the young man is soon to be starring in movies," Stanley said.

"Perhaps. That's not my concern. But I rather suppose it's what all of the young men, or the majority in any case, are hoping for. If not movie stardom, a comfortable billet somewhere certainly. And it does happen from time to time. It's why they're here, the naked ones and the ones showing off big baskets and laughing maybe just a little too loudly at jokes they have surely heard scores of times before. None of this is new, you know. It's been going on since the young Greeks did their exercises in the raw, and the older

Athenians came to ogle them and shop for a new boyfriend. Everybody trades what they've got for what they want. Simple barter, regardless of what the moralists would like to make of it."

"Not so simple," Tom said, "when a young man ends up dead."

Frederick gave him a chilling look.

"And young Palmer was one of the icing crowd," Stanley said.

"Yes, I've already said so."

"He got his drinks free, his meals… a room?"

"Drinks, yes, I think that's a given, and probably some meals. As to a free room, no, not from us, but that's not to say he didn't spend an occasional night here without having to pay for a room. He was an attractive young man."

"Had he found himself a special friendship?"

Frederick shook his head. "That I couldn't say."

"Couldn't? Or wouldn't?" Tom asked.

"Either. That's another part of what we offer our guests, discretion. These men, many of them, are not the sort who want rumors circulating in gossip columns. We keep reporters away, and if we find out that anyone is leaking tidbits—it has been known to happen—they are permanently barred from the premises."

"A wall of silence," Stanley said.

"A wall of discretion," Frederick corrected him firmly. "It's to everyone's benefit, young and old alike."

"I'm a little curious. I can see that the older gents would like it that way, but in what way would this wall of discretion, as you call it, benefit the young men?" Stanley asked.

Frederick raised an eyebrow. "Some of those you see by the pool are almost certainly in the military, for starters. The Marine Corps has a major presence just over the mountain, at Twentynine Palms, and the naval stations are not so far away."

"And they come here for rest and recreation," Stanley said.

"Exactly. And it isn't only the military either. I know of one young man who is married, to a woman, I mean, and I can see him across the patio just now, flirting blatantly with a wealthy, older industrialist. These are not just your typical young gay boys, don't you see? They wouldn't suit our older gentlemen if they were. Those gentlemen are looking for an ideal, perhaps a dream from their own youth, the perfect male, handsome, hung, straight.…"

"But they're not straight, are they?" Stanley said. "Not if they're looking for sugar daddies."

"Oh, but people can be very good at fooling themselves, wouldn't you agree? Take a look at the young men around you. They look straight, don't they? They act straight. There's not a limp wrist to be seen. They could be the boy next door, the college jock, the schoolmate you had a crush on years ago who didn't know you existed. They are fantasies, but fantasies come to life."

"Like *Westworld*," Chris said, brightening. "You know, Stanley, that old movie with Yul Brynner."

"People went there to experience their adventure fantasies," Stanley said.

"Yes, it's much the same thing." Frederick nodded. "Only the fantasies here are different. How often in life do you get a second chance. How often can you make your sexual dreams come true? Men do here, I tell you. And if it isn't the whole truth, it's as close as these men are ever going to get, and they are old enough, and wise enough, to know that. They may be looking for love, but they know the limits to what they're going to find."

"In this case, it was a deadly kind of love, wasn't it?" Tom said.

"Those who are not sensitive to love are ignorant of its power."

"You said you've got more bookings than you can handle, but when he had a plumbing problem, you moved Chris from one room into another one, an empty one. How was that possible if you're booked solid?" Tom asked.

"A last-minute cancellation. Even we have them. Our guests are, many of them, extremely busy people. Things come up. We don't charge cancellation fees for that reason, though most hotels do. We try in every way to accommodate these gentlemen, and they reward us with their patronage. Some of them come to us every weekend. And some, the locals, spend part of nearly every day here. You can see for yourself, we are quite popular."

"We're supposing that the killer stashed the body in Chris's room by mistake," Tom said. "Somebody knew the room was empty…."

"Anyone could have seen the previous occupant check out. They would assume the suite was empty."

"But whoever it was apparently didn't know that the room had been immediately re-rented."

"Exactly. Which eliminates hotel staff, I should think."

"But not the guests."

Frederick glanced around the patio as if one of the men in the crowd there might raise a hand to identify himself. "No," he said, his voice cautious, "not the guests."

"You keep saying *we*," Tom said. "Who else…?"

"I represent the owners," Frederick said in his haughtiest voice. "For all intents and purposes, I am *we*."

Meaning, Tom thought, he wasn't going to give them any names. That wall of discretion again.

A young Latino man in tight black trousers and a formfitting white shirt approached and handed Frederick a note on a silver tray. Frederick glanced at it and then up at Chris. "You have a guest, Mr. Rafferty," he said. "For dinner, he says."

"Oh, Jesus," Chris said, rolling his eyes. "Eddie. My date from last night. In all the excitement, I forgot I had invited him for dinner."

"Not a problem," Frederick said. "We encourage our guests to have guests. Of the appropriate sort, of course." Meaning, Stanley supposed, no toads welcome.

"Oh, he's definitely appropriate," Chris said with a grin. "Cute as a bug."

"In that case, bring the young man in," Frederick told the waiter.

The Latino left and was back in a moment, leading a very handsome young man of Japanese descent to the table.

"Eddie, Eddie Ishiguro," Chris introduced him around.

"Will you all be having dinner as well?" Frederick asked Tom and Stanley.

"Oh, please do," Chris said.

"Yeah, sure, I could eat something," Stanley said. "It's been a long while since breakfast."

"I could eat a horse," Tom said.

"We don't serve horse, I'm afraid, but I believe they have seafood on the menu for today. Pepe," Frederick addressed the waiting Latino, "show Mr. Rafferty and his guests to table number seven in the dining room. Number seven," he explained, "is the house table. You may be assured of the best service."

On the way inside, Stanley gave Chris a nudge. "You were out with *that* last night, and you came home to a dead body?"

"You know my batting average with tricks," Chris said. "I never end up with the live ones."

Chapter Eight

PEPE SEATED them at a large table in the corner, from which they could see everyone else in the dining room and everybody could see them. Another power table, Stanley thought. A waiter—also handsome and young, an Italian type—introduced himself as Pauli and took their orders for drinks. He was back in a moment to pass the drinks around.

"May I suggest your dinner?" he said.

"I'd like to look at a menu," Tom said.

"I'm afraid we don't have a written one," Pauli said. "Our offerings vary each day, sometimes from hour to hour, depending on what's freshest and best. It's simpler for us to tell you what we have. Just now we're serving—"

"I'll have a rib eye," Tom said. "The biggest one they can find. Rare. Just slap the cow on the butt and send her in."

"We don't serve steaks, sir."

Tom gave him an astonished look. "I never heard of a restaurant that didn't serve steaks."

"Our chef's special tonight is abalone with pan-seared vegetables topped with squid and a sea salad on the side. As an alternative, we have—"

"I've been having the chef's specials," Chris said quickly. "So far everything has been really good. That's what I'll have," he told their waiter.

"Me too," Eddie said, and Stanley said, "Sounds good to me."

"And for you, sir?" Pauli raised a pencil-thin eyebrow at Tom.

"Well, fuck it," he said, "I'll go along with the crowd. You better bring me another beer, though. I think I'm going to need it."

The waiter went. Stanley sipped his margarita, and Tom took a long draught of beer. "I don't care what that Frederick guy says. He's running a whorehouse," he said to the table at large. "Which suggests some possibilities. Any of the studs hanging around underage? We could be talking statutory, all kinds of charges. Which could mean blackmail."

Eddie blinked and looked from Tom to Chris.

"Tom and Stanley are detectives," Chris explained to Eddie. "They're here to investigate a murder."

"A murder? Here, at the Inn? I heard someone died, but I thought he'd been bitten by a snake."

"It was made to look that way," Tom said.

"And no," Chris said, "I doubt anybody's underage. The ones I saw drinking, the bartender was pretty careful to check IDs. I don't think the management here wants that kind of trouble."

"Blackmail sounds like a possibility, though," Stanley said, thinking. "There are a lot of wealthy men in Palm Springs, and a lot of them apparently hang out here. That could be something."

Chris shook his head. "Today? In Palm Springs? It's just not that big a deal anymore, is it? I mean, even movie stars are coming out of the closet. Rock stars, athletes, you name it. It might make somebody a little unhappy, but enough to murder over it? I can't see it."

"So how long are you here for?" Eddie asked Tom, looking at him from under lowered lashes.

"Till we find our murderer," Tom said.

"That sounds exciting."

"Nah. Detective work is pretty boring. Most of it's just thinking things out. That's Stanley's department, the thinking stuff. Every once in a while you get some action. That's where I fit in."

"I'd like to see you in action," Eddie said in a low voice, his long dark lashes fluttering.

"Like he said." Stanley scooted his chair an inch or so closer to Tom's. "It's mostly pretty boring."

Chris cleared his throat.

Tom seemed oblivious to any hidden meanings. "You know what we need? We need to talk to one of these rent boys."

Chris gave Eddie a look. "Well, if you want to get in on the action, there's something you could do. They're having a dance tonight. How about if we do a little fishing, and you're the bait?"

Eddie blushed—rather becomingly, Stanley had to admit. "You think these guys would find me that interesting?"

"Everybody gets tired of eating the same thing over and over," Stanley said. "Even rich old men."

The waiter returned with a cart, took their dinners from it, and set them on the table. Tom glowered at the plate filled with rice—but not white rice, this was a funny black color—and some cut up green stuff he couldn't put a name to, with what looked like large white bugs atop everything.

"Is this an octopus?' he asked, holding one of the white bugs up on his fork.

"It's squid," Chris said.

"This is called Pacific Rim cuisine," Stanley said.

"Huh. Not the best rim I've ever had." Tom pushed his plate aside, finished the beer, and signaled for another one.

Pauli was back in a few minutes. He whisked away Tom's plate and sat another in front of him, this one with an oversized hamburger, oozing bloody grease, on a toasted bun.

"This is the best I could do on short notice," Pauli said. "Unfortunately the cow was busy elsewhere."

Tom took a bite, wiped some juice from his chin, and grinned up at the waiter. "Delicious," he said. "I owe you one."

"I'll remember that." Pauli smiled back. He caught the look Stanley gave him, and his face went blank. "Is everybody else fine?"

"Peachy," Stanley said in his driest voice. He was used to it, though. Tom had some scent that drove gay boys crazy. Women too. And Pauli was Italian. Italian men, he had decided long ago, learned to flirt while they were in the cradle and only stopped when they were on the wrong side of the grass.

Still, he liked to keep any potential poachers at bay. Tom wasn't into guys, but you never knew when somebody might change his mind. After all, he had. Someone else might get lucky too. It was best to maintain vigilance.

Chapter Nine

After dinner, they went dancing—as it turned out, not very far to go. The Inn had its own club too: a large space for dancing, a raised stage, empty for now, where a band could perform, two bars down either side, and above it all a kind of balcony. Though it was still early in terms of club hours, the dance floor and the areas in front of the bars were already crowded with many of the same people who had crowded around the pool a short while before, some of them still in swimwear.

"You know," Stanley said, "whoever killed Barry Palmer could be here right this minute."

"Probably is," Chris agreed. Both of them looked at the crowd of men as if they might recognize the guilty party when they saw him.

"But how do you pick the deadly needle out of the innocent haystack?" Tom asked.

Stanley took a long look around. "I don't think this particular haystack is all that innocent."

"Lots of hotties here tonight," Eddie said.

"You said it," Chris agreed.

"Look at that cowboy over by the exit sign," Stanley said, pointing. "Like the old saying, he looks like he was poured into those jeans and forgot to say when."

"The VIP room is up there." Chris indicated the balcony overhead. "I'm sure Frederick would okay our going up if anyone's so inclined."

The others looked as if they thought that was a good idea, but Tom said, "Better if we stay down here. I want you guys to move around, to mingle, see who you can fasten on that knew this Palmer kid. Maybe we can dig up some information."

"And you will be…?" Eddie asked. He glanced in the direction of the dancers gyrating nearby. "You don't dance?"

"He's got some moves," Stanley said in a cool voice.

Eddie grinned. "I can see that."

"We were talking about dancing," Stanley said. "Besides, Tom's not much of a mingler. Not in gay bars. Come on, let's look around."

"I'm surprised he's here at all," Chris said when they moved off a few feet. "Tom's not into the gay scene," he explained to Eddie.

"He's working on it," Stanley said. Eddie gave him a curious look. "It's called love," Stanley told him, and didn't miss the flash of disappointment on Eddie's face.

Get over it, Stanley advised him silently.

TOM REMAINED by the bar, trying not to look uncomfortable and feeling completely out of place. He hated gay bars. He went to them only as an appeasement to Stanley, who had begun to feel cut off from his gay friends. Something Tom had thought a good idea, but Stanley had not been happy. If he wanted to keep Stanley happy, he had to make some adjustments in his thinking. If you wanted a relationship, you had to work at it. This was him working on it.

Stanley, Chris, and Eddie had drifted toward the dance floor, talking and laughing together. Tom watched them for a moment, glad anyway to see Stanley enjoying himself, and turned back again to face the bar.

"You must spend a lot of time in the gym," somebody said beside him.

"Some." Tom glanced in the direction of the voice, and saw a tall, lanky cowboy. The one, in fact, that Stanley had commented on a few minutes earlier, poured into his jeans. His hair was dark and straight, his skin desert-weathered, his eyes so dark they looked black. Tom wasn't interested, but he was glad for someone to talk to. Apart from the too-tight jeans, the guy looked okay. He didn't, in fact, look gay at all.

"Those are some massive biceps," the cowboy said.

Tom glanced at his arm as if he'd never seen it before, and shrugged. "It's just my arm," he said.

"What do you do? No, don't tell me, let me guess—construction work. Or, alligator wrestling. Or...."

"I'm a detective."

"Oh." For a few seconds, the man looked uneasy. People often did when they found themselves chatting with a detective—which, for most people, meant police detective. "Like, with the police, you mean? Here in Palm Springs?"

"No, San Francisco. Private detective."

"Wait." The cowboy snapped his fingers. "The detectives from San Francisco. Now I remember. Only I hadn't heard you were so hot."

"You've heard about us?" Tom was surprised. He had rather supposed their arrival here had gone unnoticed.

"Are you kidding? The town's buzzing. First the murder, and then two big-time detectives swoop in from San Francisco to clear things up. Have you figured out who killed Barry?"

"Not yet. It's a little early. We're working on it, though. You knew him?"

"Everybody knew Barry," he said with a wink. "He was… hmm, popular, I guess is the word. He hung out by the pool pretty much every day."

"Only I hear he wasn't always by the pool. Like, he disappeared inside from time to time."

"To be expected." This delivered in a cautious voice. "Barry was, um, desirable."

"Are you one of the guys he disappeared with?"

The cowboy laughed drily. "I wish. No, he was beyond my pay grade. Way beyond. Which isn't to say I didn't sometimes fantasize about it. Barry was the kind of kid who inspired you to think of stuff like that."

"Well, as it turns out, he inspired someone to kill him. You got any thoughts who or why?"

"He was a hot tamale," the cowboy said evasively. "I expect there were plenty of guys who'd kill to get a piece of that."

Tom looked at him directly. "You, for instance?"

The cowboy laughed again at the suggestion, but there was a hard edge to his laughter. "No, no, I like 'em alive when I fuck 'em, preferably alive and moving, but in a pinch I'll settle for alive. Say, pardon my manners," he said, pointedly changing the subject, "I'm Randy Patterson, by the way."

"Tom Danzel." They shook hands. Patterson's grip was firm, manly. And held maybe just a shade too long.

"So tell me, Tom Danzel, when you're not solving crime in Palm Springs, what does a private detective with big biceps do in San Francisco?"

"Ah, you know, the usual." Tom freed his hand, resisted an urge to wipe it on the leg of his trousers. *Smarmy* was the word that popped into his mind. "Wrestle alligators. Beat up people. Overturn cars. Can I ask you a question? Where were you last night? Say between midnight and maybe three in the morning?"

"Here," he said, unconcerned. "Like most nights. When the bar closed, I hung around by the pool for a while, then I split. Why, you think I offed Barry?"

"Somebody did. Just like to keep things sorted out."

Another laugh, this one more genuinely amused. "Can I buy you a drink?" Tom hesitated. "Just to be neighborly," Randy added, projecting total innocence.

"Uh, sure, I guess so." Tom was definitely out of his comfort zone now. *Was that a pass?* He couldn't tell if the guy was just being friendly or hitting on him. Where was Stanley, anyway? Tom glanced toward the dance floor, but Stanley and friends had disappeared. "Ah, a beer, I guess."

"Oh, we can do better than that for a famous visitor." Randy gave the man behind the bar a smile and a wink. "Paco, how about a race horse for my friend here?"

The bartender gave Tom a measuring look and shrugged. He poured some vodka into a tall glass and turned his back on them. Tom glanced past Randy, looking for Stanley again, and saw him engaged in animated conversation with Chris and Eddie. A fourth young man had joined them and looked to be very interested in Eddie. Someone had taken the bait. Well, sure, why not? Eddie was a cute little thing. He could see why Chris had hooked up with him.

When Tom turned back to the bar, the bartender was just setting a tall glass on the counter in front of him. No ice in the glass, but it was steaming slightly. Tom picked it up, looked at it curiously for a few seconds. What kind of drink steamed? Randy and the bartender watched him closely.

Stanley had finally noticed the transaction and walked quickly over. "What's that?" he asked, indicating the glass with the steam lifting off it.

"This guy bought me a drink," Tom said. "It's a… what did you call it?" he asked the cowboy.

"A race horse," the cowboy said, biting back a grin.

"For crap's sake," Stanley said, and behind him, Chris laughed aloud. "Put that down. Don't you know anything?"

"Not about this shit. Why, what's in it?"

"Vodka and piss," Stanley said.

"Oh."

"Didn't you see the bartender filling it up?"

"He had his back turned." Tom set the glass down on the bar gingerly, as if it might explode.

"I'll take it," an effeminate older man a few stools down said.

"Hey, you," Tom said to the cowboy.

Randy put his hands up in a defensive gesture. "Sorry. I thought you knew what I was talking about. No harm done." He turned, laughing, and walked away, disappearing into the crowd around the dance floor.

CHAPTER TEN

STANLEY SLAPPED Tom's arm. "I turn my back on you for five seconds, and you're already in trouble."

"Well, how was I to know? You know I don't know anything about this scene, and you weren't here."

"Fine. Just do me a favor. The next time somebody hits on you, refer them to me, okay? As in, I'm your boyfriend, remember?"

Tom looked in the direction in which the cowboy had disappeared. "He was hitting on me? By ordering me a glass of piss? You gay guys are really weird, you know that?"

Stanley slapped his arm again. "And don't say 'you gay guys,' okay? You've got a boyfriend. Like it or not, you sing in the choir."

Tom signaled the bartender. "Dos Equis," he said. "Make this one straight, okay?"

"Sure." The bartender gave him an apologetic grin. "I thought you knew...."

"'S okay, just a plain beer this time, is all."

Eddie and the newcomer had joined them. "This is Larson," Eddie introduced the young man with him. Larson was little and dark-skinned, his chin beard-stubbled, and he looked a bit uncomfortable about talking to them. "He knew Barry," Eddie added.

"The dead kid?" Tom was glad for a change of subject.

"Barry, Barry Palmer," Larson said, glancing around as if to see who might be listening. "Well, sure, I knew him, but that's all. I mean, not in any Biblical sense, just to see him around. But the thing is, I was just telling Eddie...." He hesitated.

"What?" Tom asked.

Larson looked Tom up and down, seemed to like what he saw. "The thing is, Barry had a boyfriend."

"As in a significant other?" Stanley asked.

"Hmm, I don't know how significant. I mean, they both played around. Here, with the daddies, at least. But I think they were maybe lovers. For sure they were fallback for each other."

"Is he here?" Tom asked. "The fallback? What's his name, anyway?"

"Jeff. And no, he's not here. I haven't seen him for a couple of days. Which is kind of unusual, really. These guys, Barry and Jeff, they were regulars, hardly ever missed a day. And they were really popular. They disappeared regularly."

"Inside," Tom said.

"Yes. If you know what I mean. Two or three times a day, sometimes more often than that."

"With the rich guys?" Stanley said.

"Pretty much. But I saw the security guard giving Barry a blow job a couple of days ago, though, and for sure he's not rich."

"Where was this?"

Larson jerked his head in the general direction of the gates. "In that little security room, you know, by the entrance. Anyway, Mario, that's the security guard, he couldn't afford Barry's rates, so it had to be a freebie. Or, well, some guys turn on to uniforms, I guess."

"Yes, sure, I know a lot of uniform queens," Stanley said. "But… a security guard?"

Larson shrugged. "Maybe he was doing the guy a favor. Or maybe it was love. All I know is, I happened to glance in there as I went past, and the lucky joker was down on his knees and seriously sucking. But that's all I know. Like, I didn't stop to ask them what it was all about. I couldn't help being a little envious, though. I made a pass at Barry myself not very long ago, and he turned me down flat. He just about laughed in my face." He shook his head, clearly still perturbed by the memory. "I mean, if you'd seen that pole. It must have been ten inches. And here this dude was chowing on it for free. Doesn't seem fair, does it?"

"Still, it sounds like this Barry could afford to pass around the occasional freebie. Him and his friend, Jeff, they must have been making a lot of bucks from their other playmates," Tom said.

Larson shrugged cautiously and lowered his voice, looking over his shoulder again. "I don't know about that."

"Or you don't talk about it?" Tom suggested.

"That's right. It's a good way to get eighty-sixed."

"Tell me something," Tom said. "Do you ever disappear inside with one of the guests?"

"Maybe. From time to time. I wasn't in Barry's class, though. But, say, listen, I'd rather not get into that. If the management finds out you're talking about that stuff, you're out of here. No one wants that."

"The goose that lays the golden egg," Stanley said.

"Well, we know what happened to Barry's golden eggs," Tom said, "but what do you think happened to his friend, Jeff? Do you think he got scared and ran?"

Larson shrugged again. "It's hard to say. If he knew that his boyfriend had been whacked...."

"Only, he disappeared before then, right?"

"I guess. If he disappeared. He might have just gone off with a daddy. But there's something else. Jeff was, well, it's sort of an open secret, but he was kind of kinky. He was the go-to for the edgy stuff. You know, if somebody wanted to play a little rough, or a little dirty. Bondage. Water sports. Stuff like that. A lot of the daddies knew about that. You'd be surprised. People can be weird."

"Huh," Tom said, staring at where the cowboy had disappeared, thinking. Water sports meant piss, didn't it? He still had to learn a lot about the gay scene, but that much he already knew. He wondered if there was a connection between this Jeff and the cowboy who ordered drinks with piss in them. Seemed an odd coincidence.

"Where did this Barry live, if you know?" Tom asked. "When he wasn't hanging out here?"

"He had a place in Cathedral City. I think Jeff lived there, too, or he was there a lot, anyway. I got that impression. I was only there once. I… well, I was trying to get something going, you know. With the two of them. But, like, nothing happened. With them, it was cash on the line. Or one another, I guess. Except for that security guard." He said it in a way that indicated it still rankled.

A Japanese man in a dark suit strolled by just then and paused to say, "Why, Eddie, is it not? Hello. I have not seen you here before, have I?"

"No, it's my first time, Nakamura-san," Eddie said.

"And you are enjoying yourself?"

"Very much." Eddie beamed, apparently flattered to have been noticed.

"You are here with friends?" The newcomer gave the group a quizzical but friendly glance.

"Yes. Mr. Nakamura, may I present my friends Chris Rafferty, Tom Danzel, and Stanley Korski. They are from San Francisco. And this is Larson."

"Yes, Mr. Larson and I are acquainted."

"Mr. Nakamura is head of operations for Mikosa Industries in Los Angeles," Chris said.

"And, increasingly, in Palm Springs," Mr. Nakamura said.

Stanley looked impressed, but Tom's face was blank. "Movies," Stanley said. "Rising Sun Studios."

"Among other things. We are only part of a *keiretsu*, a, how would you say it, a consortium of businesses." Nakamura gave a slight bow. "But please, call me Johnnie. We like things on a first-name basis here." He put out his hand, and everybody shook. "So, what brings you boys to Palm Springs? You are looking for a little fun in the sun?"

Eddie slanted a look at Tom, waiting for a cue. "We're detectives," Tom said. "Private detectives."

"Ah." Nakamura shook his head knowingly. "Now I understand. You are the San Francisco duo."

"Jesus," Tom said, "everybody in town knows we're here. Did someone send out Indian runners?"

Nakamura laughed softly. "It is a small town. And a murder…." He turned his hands palms up. "It may surprise you to know this is a quiet town. Most of what happens here is discreet. And you are very big news. Not Indian runners, no, but the telephones have been very busy."

Tom was staring hard at Nakamura. He was a man of medium height and stocky build. Jet-black hair framed a craggy, intense face with dark, flinty eyes that seemed to see everything at once.

"Funny," Tom said. "I have this feeling I know you from somewhere. Ever been to San Francisco?"

"Many times." Nakamura grinned. "But that is perhaps not why I look familiar to you. Maybe if you saw me with a ponytail?" He put his hands up, tugged his neatly styled hair back from his temples, and scowled fiercely.

Tom looked hard at him for a moment and snapped his fingers, recognition dawning. "You're the samurai. The movie guy."

Nakamura laughed, looking pleased. "I was. You watch samurai movies, Mr. Danzel?"

"Tom has every samurai movie ever made," Stanley said.

"Well, probably not all of them," Tom said, "but a lot. You did, let me think… *Samurai Times Seven* and…." He paused, thinking.

"And *Samurai Fourteen* and *Samurai Endless…* which is a sort of good description of my career." He looked apologetically around the circle. "What Mr. Danzel is trying to say, politely, is that I was a hack."

"No, no, I thought you were terrific," Tom said. Nakamura gave him a doubtful look. "Okay, some of the movies weren't, well, they weren't the best. But you were kick-ass, it looked like to me. You looked authentic. Authentic samurai, I mean. Course, I'm no expert, but it looked real to me."

"Thank you. I took my part in them seriously, but the movies were mostly mediocre, though. Which is why I moved on into the business end of things. Still, a part of me will always be samurai, I suppose."

"I wouldn't apologize for that. The samurai way is pretty impressive, even in a B-movie."

Nakamura smiled faintly and nodded. "If you appreciate things samurai, Mr. Danzel, perhaps you would do me the honor of stopping by my house while you are in the area. If I may say so myself, I have a quite good collection of swords and other memorabilia."

"I'd like that a lot," Tom said with evident enthusiasm.

"Excellent. Can we say tomorrow for lunch? I will give you directions." He signaled the bartender for pen and paper.

"Uh, lunch…." Tom hesitated. "This isn't going to be more of that, what'd you call it, Stanley, Pacific Rim food, is it?"

Nakamura laughed. "Not if it is not to your taste. Let me say, in your honor, I will tell my chef to prepare macaroni and cheese. Is that American enough for you? And I have some excellent ham. That goes with macaroni, does it not? I have been waiting for someone to share it with." He looked around the group, and his face lit up as if inspired. "But perhaps you would all honor me and come as well? Eddie? Mr. Korski? Larson? Mister… uh…."

"Rafferty," Chris supplied.

"Mr. Rafferty, of course, how boorish of me not to remember. Yes, we will make a party of it. My chef will be pleased. I fear I have rather neglected his talents of late."

"I'll have to take a rain check," Larson said with genuine regret in his voice. "I've got plans for tomorrow."

"Ah, so," Nakamura said. "We shall miss your presence."

After he'd written the directions down for Tom, Nakamura gave each of them a slight bow and moved on. Eddie looked over Tom's shoulder at the slip of paper.

"Gosh," Eddie said. "Big-time. That address is in Palm Desert. Where the really serious money lives."

"He is really serious money," Larson said, staring after the departing businessman. "And a very private man. I've never known anyone to be invited to his house before."

"Do you know this guy well?" Tom asked Eddie.

"Well? No, hardly at all, but everybody in Palm Springs knows who he is. He's very wealthy. And that samurai business—did you notice that tattoo on the back of his hand?"

"A peony, wasn't it?" Stanley said. "Somehow I've always associated the peony with the Chinese culture."

"Yes, but it's big with the Japanese too," Eddie said. "*Hanakotoba*, the flower language, is an important part of Japanese culture. The old princes and lords embroidered flowers on their kimonos to show their status. The *kigiku*, for instance, the yellow chrysanthemum, was the symbol of royalty, but every flower says something. Sometimes the meaning changes with the color. Giving someone a white lily, for instance, means you think they are pure or chaste, but flinging an orange lily at him signifies hatred and anger."

"And the peony means…?" Tom asked.

"In general it symbolizes daring and risk-taking, but it is very common among the samurai, for whom it represents the samurai mindset, that each day may be his last. The samurai live by that tenet. But you must know that."

"I guess I never put it in so many words. Interesting," Tom said in a voice that suggested he didn't really think so. He stuffed the note into his pocket and said to Larson, "Right now, though, I'm more interested in seeing where this Palmer kid lived. Think you can find the place?"

"I'm pretty sure," Larson said.

Tom finished his beer and set the bottle down on the bar with a loud *thunk*. "Let's do it," he said.

"Uh, should we talk to Hammond about this?" Stanley asked.

"Better not. Don't want to step on any toes."

Chapter Eleven

Larson, Chris, and Eddie led the way in Eddie's Toyota, Tom and Stanley following in Tom's truck. The street Larson brought them to was on the fringe of the desert in one of the plainer sections of town—not a slum, exactly, but more than merely a few blocks distant from the palatial homes of the rich.

Eddie slowed and turned into the driveway of a small bungalow, then stopped in the visitor's parking area. Tom turned off his lights and parked at the sidewalk just before the drive, then looked around with care. Palm trees provided deep shadows here on the street and in front of the bungalow, and the nearest house was thirty feet away and dark. The sidewalks were deserted, nobody out walking, no dogs on leashes.

They were off the main street, so there were no passing cars either, and only a faint rumble of traffic from the nearby interstate. The only other vehicle to be seen was a pickup with faded green paint, smaller than Tom's, sitting at the curb across the street, facing in the opposite direction—but it was empty, its lights off.

Tom got out and walked over to Eddie's Toyota, signaling for him to lower his window.

"Are we going in?" Chris asked, eyes excited.

"We are. You guys are going back to the club."

"But we—" Chris started to object.

"No buts. That's crime scene tape, the yellow stuff. If you go under it, you're breaking the law. You could get into all sorts of hot water."

"So could you and Stanley," Eddie said.

Tom smiled. "We're ace detectives. No one's going to spot us. We're going to sneak in unnoticed, but it's hard to sneak inside with a whole crowd of people in tow. Go."

The three in the Toyota looked decidedly disappointed, but Eddie put up his window and backed out of the driveway. Tom waited until his taillights had disappeared around a corner. Stanley, watching them go, was thinking he'd rather be with them. He hated doing stuff like this.

"Do you really think…?" he started to object.

"Piece of cake," Tom said. "No outside lighting to speak of, except what that streetlight back there casts, and that only reaches part of the parking lot. Nobody's going to see us. I just didn't want all the guys trooping around. If there's anything to be seen inside, they were more likely to mess it up than pin it down. Crowds are never a good idea for a crime scene, especially crowds of amateurs."

He approached the bungalow's front door and lifted the tape for a reluctant Stanley to scoot under it. Tom followed him through.

Tom was an old hand at picking locks, and he had his picks with him—but in this case, it wasn't necessary. As a matter of routine, he tried the door first, and to his surprise, it opened. He stood motionless in the doorway for a minute, listening to the darkness within.

"What?" Stanley asked in a whisper.

Tom stepped inside. "Someone just went out the back way, trying to be very quiet." He moved quickly to the front window, pulled aside the wispy curtain, and looked out in time to see a shadowy figure dash around the corner of the building and across the shadows of the driveway. He disappeared into the night, and a few seconds later a car door slammed. An engine roared to life, and the green pickup that had been parked at the curb took off down the street, headlights still off.

Tom had brought the big Maglite from the truck, but the ambient light was enough to let them walk through the house without using the flashlight. In the kitchen at the rear, the back door stood open, swinging faintly in the evening breeze. Tom went to it, glanced out just to be safe, and closed the door, latching it.

"You think it was a burglar?" Stanley asked.

"Of sorts. Somebody looking for something, that's for sure," Tom said.

"We must have scared him off. I wonder who it was?"

Tom grunted. "I know who it was. What I'm wondering is what Randy Patterson thought he would find here at the dead kid's house."

"Randy who?" Stanley asked.

"Patterson. The cowboy from the bar. The one who tried to buy me a glass of piss."

He turned on his flashlight and played the beam around the kitchen. Not much to be seen. The cupboard doors were open, revealing a few chipped dishes, a box of cereal, a tin of coffee. The refrigerator held some milk, gone sour, and a half-empty carton of orange juice.

"Didn't do a lot of eating in," Tom said.

"It sounded like most of his meals were bought for him."

"Probably."

The living room was sparsely furnished—a futon, a television with a DVD player, a big bowl used as an ashtray with a couple of roaches in it. The bedroom beyond wasn't any more luxurious, box spring and mattress on the floor, rumpled sheets, a battered dresser—again, with the drawers open. A box of neon-colored condoms had been spilled on the floor. The air smelled stale, like windows too long unopened.

"Patterson was looking for something, that's for sure," Tom said, flashing the light at the gaping drawers. He looked in them, shifting their contents around carefully. Socks, bikini briefs, a selection of tees and pullovers—one or two sweaters, a yellow-stained jockstrap, stretched large. Stanley lifted that out of the drawer and gave it a tentative sniff.

"Boy, I know some guys would pay big-time for this," he said.

"Stanley," Tom said in a disapproving voice.

"Hey, I'm just looking for clues." He put the jockstrap back, fingered a robin's egg sweater. "Cashmere," he said. "Good cashmere too."

"There's bad?"

"No, there isn't any bad, but there's cheap and expensive. That yellow number I have that you like me to wear when we, you know...."

"Yeah, it feels sexy. Makes me horny." Stanley gave him a look. "Especially horny," Tom amended.

"Well, that sweater's the cheap stuff. Ninety-nine dollars at Macy's. This is the expensive stuff. Six hundred or so, at Neiman's. Big difference."

Tom fingered the sweater as well. "Huh," he said. "Might be worth the investment. You know, for, well, for whatever. Maybe your birthday."

"My birthday's not until summer."

"Oh, sure, your real birthday. I meant... you know. For a celebration." Tom pushed the drawer closed. "I'll bet these were presents from the johns."

"Most likely."

"Still...." Tom paused, shined the light around the room, stepped to the door of the bathroom, and glanced in there. Not much to be seen but a hamper overflowing with dirty clothes, a balled-up towel on the floor. The door to the medicine chest stood open, revealing glass shelves, mostly empty. And dirty. "For a hustler as popular as he was supposed to be—and as expensive—it doesn't look like much, does it?"

"Maybe he was saving the money up for… well, for something. Maybe even to get out of here. I know if I lived here, I'd be looking for an escape hatch."

"Maybe. But where is it? The money, I mean? We can ask Hammond, but he didn't say anything about finding a stash of cash. I think he'd have mentioned it if he had."

"Maybe the cowboy found it."

"Instead of the cops? They're pros when it comes to doing a search. Cops can screw up same as anybody, but I'd guess they gave the place a good once-over."

"Maybe the cowboy knew where to look."

"Maybe. But it sounded like he was still searching when we came in. I heard a drawer scrape just before he ran. And I'm curious how he got in. Did he pick the lock? Or did he have a key? And if he had a key, what does that tell us?"

"That he and Palmer were involved?"

"He said not."

"If you believe him."

"Oddly enough, I do. About that, at least. He sounded downright resentful of the fact." Tom flashed the light around the room again and sighed. "I'd say there's not much to see here. Let's go."

"To the club? The cowboy might head back there."

"I doubt it. He must have seen us arrive. If he did, he saw who we were. Most likely he won't want to bump into us again tonight."

Tom looked around the room one last time. It was not much shy of squalid. But if the information they had gotten was to be believed, Palmer must have been making a thousand, two thousand dollars a day. Two or three—or more—johns a day, five hundred bucks a pop—had to add up.

What had happened to the money?

Chapter Twelve

THE MORNING newspaper gave minimal attention to the death at the Winter Beach Inn—only a brief mention on the second page that a young man had been found dead, the apparent victim of a rattlesnake bite earlier.

"Someone's got a lot of influence," Tom said. "Even in San Francisco, this would have gotten front-page headlines."

"Those toes Hammond doesn't want us to step on must be very important," Stanley said.

"Seems so. Might make things more difficult."

THE DRIVE to lunch later that day was the same arrangement as before, but without Larson, Tom and Stanley bringing up the rear in Tom's truck, Chris and Eddie leading in Eddie's Toyota.

Eddie took them through the shopping district on El Paseo, which Stanley suspected was merely a show-off detour, past high-end jewelry stores, shops with famous names on them, coffeehouses where espresso sold for four dollars a cup. A Rodeo Drive look-alike. Palm Desert at its most pretentious.

After their look at the town's expensive retail scene, Johnnie Nakamura's house was something of a disappointment. The neighborhood was grand, certainly, with big expensive-looking houses sitting in elegant isolation from one another.

Nakamura's house was large enough, but the exterior was decidedly plain, nothing more than a stone-slab box set back from the street beyond a giant cactus and a jacaranda tree.

"It's the Japanese way," Eddie explained as they went up the walk together. "Everything important is saved for the inside. The Japanese meet the world in the same way, the face carefully masked, no clue to what's going on inside. It's all about appearances."

Nakamura himself greeted them at the front door and invited them in. "*Hajimemashite*," he said, bowing low. "How do you do? Welcome to my humble home, please."

Eddie had warned them in advance of one thing they should expect.

"The Japanese do not like outside shoes worn inside the house. They believe it brings in too many germs."

"Probably they're right," Stanley said. "I remember reading somewhere that shoes are the biggest source of germ contamination in the typical house."

"Yes. Anyway, we'll almost certainly be expected to leave our shoes at the door," Eddie said.

"And spend our time barefoot?" Tom asked.

"Usually the host provides some sort of slippers. But yes, if need be, barefoot, or in our stocking feet."

In this instance, a row of paper slippers were lined up by the wall just inside the door. Heedful of Eddie's advice, everyone had worn slip-on shoes. Their host watched, pleased, as they discarded shoes, lining them in a row along the wall, and donned paper slippers.

It was obvious at a glance that Eddie had been right about the house too. The interior of the house was as lavish as the outside was plain, expensively furnished but without ostentation, spare, really. A single red peony—the symbol of the samurai—stood in a black glass vase atop a carved teak table in the foyer. Hidden speakers played a Mozart string quartet in the background. The living room into which Nakamura led them from the foyer was white—white walls, white carpeting on tiled floors, white furniture. For contrast, a terra-cotta fireplace, conically shaped, stood on an umber hearth of Mexican tile in one corner.

"Let me guess, that's in case the temperature drops below ninety," Tom said, indicating the fireplace.

"Exactly," Nakamura said with a laugh. "How is your case progressing, if I may ask?"

"It's coming," Tom said. "At this stage, it's a matter of collecting details, sorting things out."

"We like to consider what each soil will bear and what each refuses," Stanley said.

Nakamura raised an admiring eyebrow. "I must say, I have never heard a detective quote Virgil before."

"You watch too many old movies," Stanley said—which even he knew was ironic, since he was an avid fan of old movies.

"Touché," Nakamura said. He hesitated briefly and made a gesture in the direction of the sunlit patio visible beyond sliding glass doors. "Please, I thought we might have drinks by the pool, if that is agreeable."

He ushered them through the living room to the patio outside, only slightly smaller and less grand than the one at the Winter Beach Inn. A handsome young Japanese man in a white jacket stood behind a glass and chrome bar. He flashed a bright smile at them—at Chris in particular, it seemed to Stanley—and waited to take their drink orders.

"Please, have whatever you would like," Nakamura said. "Yoki is an excellent bartender, and I think we are well stocked."

The boys debated and settled on vodka gimlets. Yoki nodded his approval at the suggestion and made them with fresh-squeezed limes, which in turn met with Stanley's approval.

"I'll just have a beer," Tom said.

"Very good, sir," Yoki said and reached into the miniature refrigerator under the bar. The bottle he handed across to Tom was like a work of art, sheathed in copper and looking like a miniature brewery vat. It made the usual glass bottle look shoddy in comparison.

Tom admired the bottle and read the label aloud. "Samuel Adams Utopia."

"It is an excellent beer, in my humble opinion. Are you familiar with it?" Nakamura asked.

"I've heard of it," Tom said. He did not add that, at a hundred dollars a bottle, he had never felt inclined to treat himself to any. He took a cautious swig—it was also the world's strongest beer—and decided it was probably worth the price—if you liked to throw that kind of money around. Still, he felt like he could very easily get used to the stuff, so long as someone else was buying.

Stanley and the boys took seats at the glass and granite patio table next to the sparkling pool.

"Danzel-san," Nakamura addressed him.

"Tom, please."

"Very well then, Tom," Nakamura said, "perhaps you would like to see my samurai collection?"

"I'd like that very much. Stanley, want to come with us?"

But Stanley was in the middle of sharing a funny story with the others, and he waved his hand dismissively. "You two go ahead. Not to be rude, but *Rashomon* is as far into that subject as I get."

"An excellent film," Nakamura said, but he took no apparent offense at Stanley's lack of interest. Stanley did not look to be the samurai sort.

Tom left his beer on the patio table and went with Nakamura back into the house, to a room off the large front room—a room, Tom noted, kept locked. Nakamura took a key from his pocket and fitted it into the lock with an apologetic look.

"Some of these items are very valuable," he said. "More than just monetarily valuable, I should add. To a serious collector, especially to another Japanese, some of them can be precious far beyond what they could command in a marketplace. So, they must be protected."

He stepped aside for Tom to precede him into the room. Tom went through the doorway and paused, taking in a deep breath. At a first impression, it was like entering a room of glass. Glass cases rested on tables, more of them stood on the floor, and the walls were covered with still more glass cases, holding a deadly array of blades.

What really caught Tom's eye, though, were two suits of samurai armor mounted on clothes dummies in the far corners of the room. At a quick glance, a pair of samurai warriors might have been waiting to greet them.

"Wow," Tom said, impressed more than he had expected to be. He'd seen armor like this in his movies, but never the real thing—and here were two complete outfits. Authentic, he'd have bet money.

"You like my friends?" Nakamura said. He indicated the armor to the left. "This one is from the *Sengoku jidai*, the period of the warring states, when different princes sought to achieve supremacy. The helmet, or *kabuto*, is of iron, and the *menpō*, the face mask, of leather. The horizontal steel plates across the chest and the back are typical, but the variegated lacing is a bit unusual."

"You said they are of special value to collectors," Tom said, "but this baby has to have monetary value too. If you don't mind my asking…?"

"Yes, yes, it does. I paid fifty thousand for it, American dollars." Tom whistled. "But that is nothing. This one—" Nakamura led the way to the armor in the opposite corner. "—would command twice as much, at least. It is a rare treasure indeed. Edo, seventeenth century, *gomai-do yukinoshita*. This might have been, probably *was*, worn by one of the ronin, the roving samurai of the time. Even the *kabuto*, the helmet, is special—*suji bachi*, black lacquered. You do not see that often."

Tom leaned closer to look at a small imperfection in the chest armor. "Is that what I think it is?"

Nakamura nodded. "Yes, it is a bullet hole. The matchlock gun, the arquebus, was introduced into Japan in the sixteenth century, and by this time, the Edo period, its use among the samurai was widespread. But the sword remained the symbol of the true samurai. Perhaps too much so."

"What do you mean, too much so?"

"In the movies the emphasis is on the swords to the exclusion of every other weapon, but the samurai armed himself with more than just his sword. He carried clubs, too, *kanabō*. Like this one, for an example."

He opened a glass case and handed a wooden club to Tom. It was perfectly balanced, fitting into Tom's hand as if made for it. "There were clubs made of iron, too, many strips of iron welded together, some of them with iron spikes. They are not often documented in art and literature, and you almost never see them in the movies, but they were commonplace—and very effective weapons."

"I'll bet," Tom said, handing the club back.

Nakamura returned the club to its case, locking it again carefully, while Tom looked around the room.

Despite the occasional club, and what he took to be one of those matchlock rifles Nakamura had mentioned, what he saw was mostly swords. It was a room of blades, dozens of them in the glass cases mounted on the walls, glittering wickedly in the sunlight from the patio, looking almost like living things.

Nakamura opened another case and took a short sword from it. "This is the *wakizashi*," he said, "the samurai's weapon of honor. It never left his side. He slept with it under his pillow and even when he entered a house and left his main weapons outside as protocol demanded, he took the *wakizashi* with him, for personal defense, if need be. Being shorter, you see, it would not catch on ceilings or doorjambs when it was swung, so it was ideal for use in a fight as an indoor sword, but in the hands of a samurai, it could be as deadly as the long sword, the *katana*."

He took a still smaller blade from the same case. "And this is the *tantō*, the little friend, as it was known to the samurai. It can slash and cut, of course, but it was not made primarily for cutting like the others, rather for thrusting at close range. If a samurai put his weight and strength behind it"—he demonstrated, holding the knife out straight in front of him and lunging forward on one foot—"he could drive it right into the heart."

"Lethal, for sure."

"Yes, certainly. But the special importance of both the *tantō* and the *wakizashi* was that they were the means by which a disgraced warrior could avoid dying in shame."

"Suicide," Tom said.

"*Seppuku*, yes, disembowelment of a highly ritualized sort. The samurai rams the blade into the left side of his stomach, here"—he indicated the spot on his abdomen—"and he draws it across just below the navel."

"And pulls out his guts, right?"

"Only if that is necessary. If the samurai does it right, and cuts deeply enough, the intestines slip right out of their own accord, which is, of course, to be hoped for. But yes, if they do not fall out, then he must help them. Either way, death is very nearly instantaneous. Eight seconds, it is said."

"But a hell of a tough eight seconds, I'd guess."

"As it was intended. The samurai must suffer this pain to offset whatever disgrace has befallen him."

"The samurai were really as tough as that?" Tom asked. "As tough as the legends and the movies have them?"

"Tougher, really. But understand, please, for them it was not only a matter of toughness in battle. In that regard, the legends have become distorted. They were not just battle-hardened mercenaries, as they can seem to be in the movies. Samurai were expected to be cultured men, too, and literate. You must remember that they served lords and princes. The great warrior Tadanori was as famous for his skill with the pen as with the sword. They called it the '*bun bu ryo do*,' the harmony of learning and fighting. By the time of the Edo period, the era of that armor you looked at over there, Japan had a higher literacy rate than Europe, probably higher than anywhere else on earth. And that was thanks mainly to the samurai."

He put the two knives back into their case. "But of course it is the swords that you want to see, the *katana*, as the long sword was called. Here, this is what you Americans might call a real beaut."

Nakamura opened one of the tall cases on the wall and brought out a sword in its wooden scabbard. "This one dates from the seventeenth century, the year sixteen fifty-one. The Edo warrior who wore that armor over there might have carried this very sword, or one much like it."

He handed Tom the sheathed sword. Tom looked at it reverently. "It's beautiful," he said.

"Yes. The *katana* was considered the soul of the samurai. Go ahead, please," Nakamura said, "remove it from the bed where it sleeps. But be careful, it is very sharp. I keep all of them in pristine condition. And these swords like to cut. It is what they were born for."

Tom drew the weapon cautiously from the scabbard, or *saya*, of white wood. The sword looked delicate, like a work of art, but it was heavier than what he had expected. The blade was slightly curved. It seemed oddly alive in his hands, as if it did indeed want to cut something. Or somebody.

"The blade is made mostly of soft steel, for easier shaping," Nakamura said, "but the edge is harder, for cutting. This was the invention of the great swordsmith Masamune in the fourteenth century. See, there, that dappling along the blade is where the two steels meet. Each weds its greatness to the other. Together, they become invincible."

A groove went up each side of the blade, and the tip was not just a point, as one might expect, but a strange pattern of upturned ridges. The handle was big enough to hold in two hands, but the sword was so well balanced that it could be wielded one-handed as well. Tom lifted it into the air, swishing it cautiously back and forth. The blade thrummed faintly with speed, the grooves making it almost sing.

He very gently returned the sword to the *saya* and handed them to Nakamura, who bowed to him as he accepted them.

"Why don't you show me some of the old moves?" Tom suggested. "I would be honored."

Nakamura hesitated for a moment. "Very well, if you wish," he consented, bowing again. "I will demonstrate for you the *kasumi gamae.* The initial stance."

He closed his eyes for a moment, seeming to turn within himself. Then, abruptly, his eyes flew open, blazing with a fierce, dark light. He cried, "Ai," loudly, and unlike the careful manner in which Tom had unsheathed the sword, he snapped it from its *saya* in one lightning-fast movement and immediately struck a familiar pose, his knees slightly bent, the sword held two handed above and slightly to the right of his head. Tom had seen the same stance in a score of samurai movies—maybe even seen this same man in the pose.

He felt a faint shiver zigzag up his spine. To a casual observer, it could have looked as if Nakamura meant to cleave Tom in two, and Tom had no doubt he could do so if he chose. The blade of the *katana* seemed to blink at him. Tom found he could not take his eyes from its glistening surface. *Like being hypnotized by a swaying cobra*, he thought, and wondered if the samurai's victims felt like that before the sword descended upon them, hypnotized into surrender.

Nakamura gave a little self-deprecating laugh instead and sheathed the sword once again, then returned it to its glass case and carefully locked that. "No," he said, "it is like trying to capture curls of smoke, or recall to your tongue the bubbles of some old glass of champagne. Shall we rejoin your friends?"

The only non-samurai item in the room was a large framed portrait that hung on the wall next to the door, hidden from view when they came in, but which now caught the eye as they went out. Tom paused to glance at it—a portrait of a beautiful woman in what looked to his untrained eye like full Geisha regalia.

"My late wife," Nakamura said, following his glance. "She left the earth three years ago. Cancer of the, what do you call it, the esophagus."

Tom was surprised to hear about a wife. Nakamura, watching his face, said, "You are thinking about those pretty boys at the Inn. Yes, it is true, I, too, avail myself of their charms."

"Not my business," Tom said. He was hoping Nakamura would think it was, though. It did seem curious.

"It is quite simple, really. Your Freud never made it to Japan, you know. Neither did Christianity. Japanese men do not have all those hang-ups about sex—kinky sex, homosexual sex, whatever, it is just a bodily function to us. Some people do it one way, some people do it another. We think Americans are crazy the way you get your, how do the boys say it, your panties in a knot over sex."

"Makes sense, probably," Tom said.

"Take you, for instance, if I may be so bold. I sense you are not altogether comfortable in the world of the homosexual. When I saw you at the bar last night, you looked to me like a man out of place."

"I guess I was, sort of. Am."

Tom glanced in the direction of the patio, at Stanley, laughing, his head tilted back. He looked like a little boy. Something tightened in Tom's chest. It always did when he looked at Stanley.

Nakamura followed his glance. "Ah," he said, nodding sagely. "But, you know, that is very samurai."

"Is it?" Tom was surprised.

"Yes. Again, that is not as well-known, but to the samurai, *shudō*, the love between an older and a younger warrior, was thought to be the very flower of the samurai spirit. It was an honored practice in the higher-class samurai, the main way in which the ethos and the skills were passed down through the generations."

"I didn't know that."

"No, unfortunately it is usually left out of the movies. It was called *bido*, too, the beautiful way, but *bido* sometimes referred to a close friendship that was not necessarily sexual in nature. Those partners were not always physical lovers, but *senpai* and *kōhai*. Perhaps Stanley is your *kōhai*?"

Tom gave him a blank look. "I don't know that expression."

"The *senpai* is the older of the pair, and the younger man is his *kōhai*. That, too, is a traditional samurai relationship."

"Stanley talks a lot about the ancient Greeks. They had that sort of thing, too, didn't they?"

"Yes, similar, but not quite the same. The *senpai* is the *kōhai*'s...." He paused, seeking for the correct word.

"His tutor?" Tom suggested.

"Ah, more like a loving parent, I think you would describe it. The *senpai* is expected to indulge his *kōhai*, to put up with his youthful excesses."

"Well, Stanley has his youthful excesses, but I don't think either of us thinks of me as his parent."

Nakamura laughed. "No, I suppose not, not even his daddy, as gay men like to put it. I suppose one would say he is your fair torment."

Tom looked back at him without laughing, not willing to discuss that relationship with someone who was, really, no more than a stranger.

"He can be a fair torment," he said aloud. "But we all can, can't we? Relationships are never easy."

Nakamura's gaze seemed to turn briefly inward. "No, they never are," he agreed in something very near a whisper.

And who, Tom wondered, was his fair torment? But he thought it was time to change the subject.

"Can I ask a personal question?"

"You may ask," Nakamura said, with no assurance of an answer.

"When you gave all that up—the samurai business—"

"I gave up the movies."

"Okay, you gave up the movies, and you went into the business world. Has that worked for you?"

"Let me say that the business world is only a part of my life. I like to read the poetry—the haiku—of the ancient masters. Sometimes I write my own. When I read the old scrolls, I think I hear the breath of men who have vanished, and when I write, I like to think that eyes centuries from now will caress the words I pen."

"Is that enough to keep you happy?"

"Few men find true fulfillment in life. Ultimately, one has to choose between the struggle and acceptance—between the Titans and Olympians, as those Greeks you mentioned might have expressed it."

Which maybe, Tom thought, was an answer, or maybe it wasn't.

Chapter Thirteen

The macaroni and cheese Nakamura's chef prepared for lunch was a far cry from the Pacific Rim food at the Winter Beach Inn—an authentic and delicious Southern style macaroni and cheese, but topped, as Nakamura pointed out, with Japanese panko bread crumbs.

"So my chef can maintain his honor," he said. "Otherwise, he might commit *seppuku*. Suicide," he added for the benefit of the others.

"Like Madame Butterfly," Stanley said. "To die with honor is better than to live with dishonor."

"Exactly. The Japanese are obsessed with death. The samurai especially were so obsessed. Death and honor."

Yoki, the bartender from the patio, was now their server, gliding softly back and forth between kitchen and table. He poured wine from a bottle, carefully wrapped to conceal its label, into a glass for the host. Nakamura sniffed at his, sipped noisily, and nodded, and the waiter poured for the others into glasses that Stanley recognized at a glance as Baccarat.

"Do you like the wine, Mr. Danzel?" Nakamura asked.

Tom sipped and nodded. "Tastes okay to me, but Stanley's the expert. He's the one to ask."

Nakamura smiled at Stanley and raised an eyebrow, as if he were issuing a challenge. *Uh-oh*, Stanley thought, *better get this right.* He lifted the glass to the light to better make note of the wine's color. It was opaque purple, regal, clearly a well-aged wine.

He sniffed at the rim of the glass and sipped noisily, taking in air with the wine. The flavors seemed to jump out of the glass at him. He swirled the wine around in his mouth before swallowing it, tasted crushed blackberries, cranberries, and a hint of mint. It was a spectacular wine, and an uncommon one.

But he'd had this same wine before, hadn't he, or one very much like it? The memory teased him for a moment and, like a fog lifting, was suddenly clear in his mind. He remembered a sunny day in Barcelona, seated at a sidewalk café, the air perfumed by the flowers that cascaded down the wall behind him. In the distance, someone thrummed a guitar and sang of lost love in a deep, mournful voice. Across the table, a dark-eyed Spaniard flirted….

"Spanish, I'd say," Stanley smiled back at their host. "Ribeira del Duero, isn't it? And well aged. I'd guess a 2000."

"Very good," Nakamura smiled openly now, flashing white-crowned teeth. "And quite close. It is a Tinto Pesquera. And yes, a 2000. You do know your wines."

"A lucky guess," Stanley said modestly, while Chris beamed at him. Tom seemed to take it for granted, however. He already knew Stanley was smart.

Stanley took another sip. "But I should have guessed a Pesquera. From Señor Fernández, yes? It's definitely his style."

"Just so," Nakamura said. "No one else is quite like him."

Yoki the waiter was back shortly with plates of thinly sliced ham, placing them in front of each of the diners. Since Nakamura waited without sampling his, the others did the same, aware that this was as much about ritual as lunch. In a moment Yoki returned with a cruet and carefully drizzled a few drops of pale yellow olive oil on each plate with the ham.

Stanley was aware that Nakamura was now watching him carefully. Taking their cue from their host, everybody else stared at him as well, awaiting his judgment. He felt like he was back in college, about to tackle a very difficult exam.

Okay, he thought, *in for a penny, in for a pound.* While everyone watched, he sliced off a morsel of ham and chewed it thoughtfully. It was beyond good. For whatever reasons, Nakamura had pulled out all the stops to impress his guests.

"Much easier," Stanley said. "There's nothing that tastes anything close to Iberico ham. To be exact, I'd say Jamon Iberico de bellota."

"Exact indeed," Nakamura said, and added, "*puro*, of course. But how did you know?"

"It's almost like cheating. I spent a summer in Spain," Stanley said, and to the others at the table, "They take ham very seriously there. There's even a string of *museos de jamon*, ham museums, if you can believe that. The Iberico is the Rolls Royce of Spanish hams, made from the Iberian pig—*puro* just means the line is pure on both sides of the sty. And *bellota* means the pig's diet toward the end is mostly acorns. Then it's cured for up to three years. Until 2007 you couldn't even get it in this country, unless it was somehow smuggled in. And it's still rare."

He didn't add, "and pricey," but he certainly could have. He knew the ham sold for up to one hundred dollars a pound. *And*, he thought, chewing another morsel, *worth every penny if you could afford it.* Which apparently their host could. But why exactly they were being treated to all this extravagance, he couldn't guess.

"And the olive oil?" Nakamura asked.

That, Stanley didn't know. Olive oil wasn't his forte, but the wine and the ham, both rare and expensive, gave him one certain clue, and he remembered Tom's surprised pleasure earlier when Yoki had handed him the copper-encased beer, meaning that, too, must have been something special. Tom might not know wines, but he knew his beer.

He took a breath, crossed his fingers mentally, and made a guess. "Manni," he said. "Per me."

Nakamura's expression, both pleased that a guest appreciated what he was being served, and frustrated at the same time that he hadn't been able to fool him, told Stanley he had guessed right. There was much Stanley did not know about olive oils, but he did know that the Manni from Tuscany was the world's most expensive olive oil. Stanley had felt sure Nakamura wouldn't have had anything less than the best and most expensive oil drizzled on his expensive ham. Not when he was trying to impress them, as he so obviously was.

"Wow," Eddie said, eyes wide. "How do you know all this stuff?"

"Stanley's smart," Tom said, digging into the macaroni and cheese, unimpressed by the fancy ham on the side. It was just ham to him. Tasted good, but it still came from a pig's backside. As for that olive oil, he'd have preferred some good old redneck redeye gravy, but he stopped short of asking for it. Probably the great chef had never heard of it anyway.

AFTER THE little battle of the palates with Stanley, Nakamura proved to be a gracious host, keeping the conversation around the table going smoothly, and occasionally asking questions of Tom, mostly regarding the investigation. All in all, it was a pleasant lunch.

Only one peculiar moment occurred. Stanley had been conversing softly with Chris and Eddie, while Tom and Nakamura discussed favorite samurai movies. Stanley glanced down the table to find Nakamura was staring at him with an expression impossible to read, while he pretended to listen to something Tom said.

When Tom paused, Nakamura, still gazing at Stanley, said, "I envy you what you share with your friend."

Tom blinked and looked at Stanley too. "We've had our challenges." He smiled, his grin lighting up his face as if from within. It was a smile that was known to make women and gay men melt in their drawers. Stanley smiled back at him. Notwithstanding the others at the table to witness, it was a strangely private moment between the two of them.

"Still, love, what treasure can equal it? Do you ever wonder about its nature?" Nakamura asked that of the table in general.

"Who doesn't?" Chris said. "How do two people share it, and not two others? Everyone wants it, but few find it."

"I think," Stanley said, "it's like a glass of wine. The lovers may sip it individually, but when they kiss a moment later, they share the taste that lingers in their mouths. It goes from tongue to tongue and back again, and you can't really separate it, say, this is my lingering taste and this is yours."

He would have added, but thought it was too personal, that he and Tom shared something that couldn't be separated into two parts, his love and my love. In a way, they were still two individuals, Tom and Stanley, but in another way, they had become TomStanley, a togetherness. But even if he'd felt inclined to share this with the others, he doubted anyone would really understand what he meant by it. He wasn't at all sure he understood it, but he knew it was so.

He had been looking mostly at Tom when he had spoken, but when he switched his glance back to their host, he found Nakamura staring at him in a rapt way. His gaze was so intimate, so intense, that Stanley looked away from it, embarrassed. It was as if Nakamura had made a pass at him in some subtle way that he'd never encountered before. Maybe, he thought, he had been just a bit too show-offy over the wine and food.

Nakamura said to Tom, "I say again, I envy you. I have never truly known that. I have resigned myself to the truth that I never will."

"I do not know that is so. You are not so very old, Nakamura-san," Eddie said. "Not too old to find love, surely."

Nakamura looked at him briefly as if he had not seen him before. He looked away and shook his head. "Time, the devouring dragon.... Even the most exquisite feast, once eaten, is gone from the table."

"YOU KNOW what puzzles me?" Stanley said when he and Tom were on their way back to the hotel. "All these people knowing who we are and why we're here. Hammond hinted at something like that, didn't he? That we might be observed. Someone might be listening."

"We've been careful about the cell phones."

"We have been since Hammond warned us. But Chris called us in the beginning, from the Inn, no less. And the Inn has got to be at the center of all this. Plus Bryce called Palm Springs homicide about us before we even got here. So, if someone had an ear to the ground right from the start—"

"Or a bugging device on the right phones."

"Right. They'd be waiting for us, wouldn't they? Expecting us?"

"It's an interesting thought. If you think about it, Nakamura approached us last night at the bar. It seemed casual at the time, accidental, but…."

"But maybe he didn't just happen to stroll by."

"Maybe. Same with that cowboy, too, Patterson. Either one of them could have been sniffing around, could have been looking for us. We caught Patterson at Barry Palmer's house. And Nakamura was certainly interested in how we were doing with our investigation. He asked a lot of questions over lunch."

Stanley shook his head. "But he would be interested, wouldn't he? We're probably the biggest gossip in town right now."

"What puzzles me," Tom said, glancing at the rearview mirror, "is why that cowboy's following us today?"

"Patterson?" Stanley started to turn in his seat, but Tom said, "No, don't look. Let's let him think we're stupid."

"How long has he been there?"

"Since shortly after we left Nakamura's house." They were on the 111, approaching Palm Springs.

"Maybe he's just smitten. He did try to pick you up—in his own crude way, of course."

Tom grunted disdainfully. "Tell you what," he said, "I was going to check with Hammond this afternoon anyway. Let's stop and pay him a visit instead. It'll give the cowboy something to think about, and we can talk to Hammond there without worrying about anybody eavesdropping."

"Unless," Stanley said, "the station is bugged."

Tom thought about that. "No, not bugged, probably. That wouldn't be easy to do. But somebody could be listening."

Sandy, the blonde with the acne, was working the front desk again. She actually managed to smile at them when they came through the door, and picked up a phone to inform the detective they were there.

Hammond looked surprised to see them, but not displeased. He led them once again back to his office. This time the other desk was occupied—which might have explained why the scent of whiskey was less pronounced than it had been the previous visit. A lanky detective, who looked to Tom like he ought to be in high school, glanced up from the neighboring desk at them as they came in, smiled vaguely, and with a show of disinterest, went back to the newspaper he was reading.

"So," Hammond said, "have you learned anything I ought to know?"

"Maybe," Tom said. "Or maybe it isn't news to you. The Palmer kid—did you know he had a boyfriend? Might even have been a roomie."

Hammond digested that. "Not a roomie. Not officially, anyway. That much I do know. Just the one name on the lease. I looked at it."

"These guys, the ones who hang out at the Winter Beach Inn, they like to keep things quiet." Tom hesitated, not wanting to get off on the wrong foot and not sure if Hammond was aware of the nature of the Inn. "Look, you know about that place, right? The kind of place it is?"

"The sugar daddies? The boy toys? That stuff?"

"Yeah. It's dressed up a lot, but at heart it's nothing more than an old-fashioned whorehouse."

Hammond leaned back in his chair, his expression noncommittal. "I think you're probably right."

"And you're okay with that? The department is, I mean?"

"I'm homicide. That's not my turf."

The other detective looked briefly at them, as if he might say something. He changed his mind, though, and went back to his reading. Stanley thought about what Tom had said when they were driving in, about someone listening.

"Still—it's pretty blatant," Tom said.

Hammond appeared uncomfortable with the direction of the conversation. His eyes drifted ever so slightly sideways, to the neighboring desk, but the man there was reading his newspaper with great concentration. He might have been alone in the room.

"Well, as you already know, there's a lot of big money in this town," Hammond said finally. He paused and added, "And some of it hangs out there, at the Winter Beach Inn. Some of those toes I mentioned stepping on. Or not stepping on."

"Ah" was all Tom said, nodding. Which meant that someone among the clients at the Inn had pull with the department. Hell, for all he knew, maybe the chief was one of those old queens out by that swimming pool. For sure, someone who knew the chief was. Someone who knew the chief well.

"So, who's this boyfriend you mentioned, and what brings him to mind?" Hammond asked.

"His name is Jeff, no last name. And he's gone missing."

"Is that so?" Now Hammond was interested. "Since when?"

"Since before the Palmer kid bought it. Leads me to think there might be a tie-in, apart from their being friends. Anyway, the way we hear it, Palmer and the missing Jeff were both regulars at the Inn. Like, pretty much every day. Then the boyfriend vanishes, and about the same time or not long thereafter, someone murders Palmer."

"It could be coincidence," Hammond said.

"Maybe," Tom agreed. "Or maybe not. If the boyfriend stays missing, I'd say probably not."

"Yeah," Hammond said. "I don't much like coincidences either."

He got up and went out of the office, then was back in a couple of minutes. "No missing person reports on Jeff anybody," he said.

"I don't know who'd file one," Tom said. "I doubt that he's got family here in town. The two kids sounded more like floaters. And if Palmer was his roommate, or even his boyfriend, we know why he didn't file a report."

"Get me a description," Hammond said. "We'll do some looking around. One dead kid, bad news. Two of them? Disaster for the city. People are going to want this wrapped up, quick and smooth, like in a Texas two-step."

"We're dancing as fast as we can," Stanley said.

"There is one person, though, who isn't in such a big hurry to see things wrapped up," Tom said.

"The murderer? Tough" was Hammond's reply.

"What if it turns out to be one of the big wheels?"

Hammond gave him a faint grin. "I'm hoping it is."

Tom glanced at the detective studiously reading his newspaper. "Walk us to our truck?" Tom suggested to Hammond.

Hammond shoved off from his desk, said to his fellow detective, "Back in a minute."

The detective raised his eyes from the paper and watched them go.

When they were outside, Tom asked, "How sure are you that our conversations here aren't listened to?"

"My partner? I trust him—mostly. Course you never really know, do you? What makes you ask?"

Tom told him about being approached the night before by Johnnie Nakamura and the young cowboy. "Someone could have heard our original call from Chris, and Bryce called you."

"And someone could know who you are and why you're here— but, hell, probably everybody in town knows that by now."

"The three fastest means of communication," Stanley said. "Telephone, telegraph, and tell a queen."

Hammond chuckled. "I know Johnnie Nakamura. Everybody does. He's big-time, big money. Mikosa Industries is mostly Los Angeles, but they're a presence here as well. A growing presence."

"Are his toes among those we don't want to step on?" Tom asked.

"Probably wouldn't be a good idea. He's powerful, and from everything I hear, ruthless. Let me put it this way, I'd rather have him as a friend than an enemy. As to your cowboy, what was his name?"

"He calls himself Randy Patterson."

"Doesn't ring any bells, but I can do some sniffing around. If he's got any kind of record, I can pull it. If his nose is clean…." He shrugged. "That's a little harder."

There was no sign of the cowboy's pickup truck when they left the police station. Maybe, Tom thought, he hadn't wanted to be seen hanging around here.

THEY WERE coming around the last curve before the Inn when Stanley suddenly said, "Wait, stop here."

Tom did so and gave him a quizzical glance. "What?"

Stanley stared for a moment at the exterior of the Inn. "It's the same," he said.

Tom followed his gaze. "What's the same?"

"The exterior. It's like Nakamura's house. The outside is downright plain. Everything special is inside. Remember, Eddie told us that was the Japanese way."

"So what do you think it means?"

"I'd be willing to bet Nakamura-san is one of the Inn's anonymous owners." Stanley pondered that for a moment. "But I don't know what that tells us."

Chapter Fourteen

THEY STOPPED by the club for a drink. Chris was at the bar, alone, nursing a cocktail.

"I've got to use the euphemism," Stanley said. "Be right back. Somebody order me a gin and tonic, please."

Tom ordered the drink and a beer for himself, and seeing that Chris's glass was nearly empty, another Bloody Mary for him.

"Nice lunch," Chris said.

"The macaroni and cheese was good," Tom agreed. "But that Nakamura is a funny kind of guy, isn't he? I think he's got his eye on Stanley."

"I don't think Stanley would…," Chris started to say, and stopped. He'd been about to say that Stanley wasn't likely to cheat on Tom, but Stanley had come very close to doing that not so very long ago, as they both knew.

"It's okay," Tom said. "We've talked about it. We're getting things worked out. It's a lot harder than I thought, this business of having a relationship. You know, in the past, I just came and went."

"You've got a heart of ice—except where Stanley is concerned."

"Not true. You and I are friends."

Chris looked him in the eye, started to say something, and again thought better of it. At one time, if fleetingly, he'd imagined them as something more than just friends. Luckily for everyone concerned, it had gone no further. Stanley was his oldest and best friend. It would have been a messy situation. He was glad after all that it hadn't happened.

"Okay," Tom said, "I guess I am a coldhearted bastard." He took a long chug of beer.

"No, I was out of line," Chris said. "Oh, don't pay any attention to me. I am glad to see you and Stanley working things out, really. Stanley is such a dizzy, but he needs someone. He needs you."

"I need him too. It's changed my life in ways I couldn't have imagined, having Stanley beside me. I still don't understand it, but I know that he is a big part of me."

Chris was looking past him, though. "Now that's interesting," he said.

Tom glanced over his shoulder. "What is?"

"That's our security guard, Mario, the one Larson said he saw giving Barry Palmer a blow job."

"Ah." Tom nodded and studied the Latino youth standing at the far edge of the dance floor. Mario was in a brown security uniform. He was small, round-faced, maybe five pounds over his ideal weight. Anywhere else, he'd have probably looked pretty good, but here he was outclassed.

"He must be on break," Chris said. "I've never seen him in here."

"Appears like he's looking for somebody." Mario's eyes were searching among the dancers on the floor.

"I wonder who?"

"Yeah, me too. Excuse me a minute."

Tom elbowed his way through the crowd and approached the young Latino. At the moment, Mario was standing alone.

"Got a minute?" Tom addressed him.

Mario turned large dark eyes on him and smiled expectantly when he saw Tom. "For you? Sure," he said.

"You're Mario, right?"

The smile faded a bit. "You know my name?"

"I've heard it, is all. I'm Tom Danzel." He extended a hand.

Mario stepped back as if he'd been stung by a hornet. "The detective," he said. "The guy looking into Barry's death."

"Well, Christ, yeah." Tom was getting tired of hearing that everybody in town already knew about them.

"Excuse me," Mario said.

"Wait," Tom said, but to no avail. Mario was gone, weaving his way hurriedly through the crowd.

Tom watched him, wondering if he should follow. Mario gave one last furtive look over his shoulder and disappeared through a door that led, Tom thought, to the kitchen.

"Now what was that all about?" he wondered aloud. For sure the kid had been spooked. And who had he been looking for?

He went back to Chris at the bar. Chris raised a questioning eyebrow. "Skittish," Tom said. "Doesn't like detectives, seems like."

Stanley came back then, smiling warmly at both of them, and took his drink from the bar. "If you were talking about me," he said, "I hope you said something nice."

"No, it was all vicious," Chris said.

"Well, what are friends for?" Stanley asked, taking a generous sip of his drink.

EDDIE AND Larson joined them shortly, both of them with a glow that suggested things might have progressed beyond casual acquaintance. The five of them drank and danced and made small talk until time to move to the dining room for dinner. This time, Pauli, the waiter, was ready for them, and he served Tom a burger without asking.

After dinner they went back to the bar. Some early arrivals were dancing already. The deejay was on a romantic music kick—at the moment, Dinah Washington, being unforgettable. Tom and Stanley danced together, a two-step, Tom holding Stanley close, Stanley resting his cheek against Tom's broad shoulder. People were invariably surprised to see what a good dancer Tom was. His hip with the steel plate in it sometimes gave him a slight limp when he walked, most of the time not conspicuous, but it disappeared altogether when he was dancing.

"They're sweet together, aren't they?" Larson said.

"Yes," Eddie and Chris agreed, neither with enthusiasm.

Stanley was surprised anew each time by what a smooth dancer Tom was. It was old-fashioned dancing, but very sexy. Stanley knew that others watched them with appreciation and envy, and he liked the feel of Tom's arms around him, Tom's hard body pressing close against his. Cheek to cheek, they used to call it, head to toe. Sarah followed Dinah. Tom nibbled his ear. Stanley giggled in response and pressed closer.

After a bit, Tom said, "You know what, Stanley? I think I'm ready to make an early night of it."

Stanley arched a glance up at him. Tom's eyes gleamed with a dark light. "Sounds like a plan to me," Stanley said, smiling, suddenly feeling shy in his lover's arms.

Both of them knew that this meant sex. And both of them were happy with the knowledge.

STANLEY HAD been in more than a few relationships. Despite the starting-out expectations, they had all turned out to be short-term, until this one. He and Tom were a year and counting now.

What surprised him as much as anything was how much their sex life varied, especially surprising because, until they had met, Tom had been straight—still was, maybe ninety-nine percent—but once he had accepted his relationship with Stanley, Tom had proven not only adaptable, but with astonishingly few inhibitions. There wasn't much he hadn't tried, and most of that he had quickly mastered.

Sometimes when they did it, Tom was incredibly romantic, even whispering sweet nothings in Stanley's ear while they made tender love. Other times, it was hard, pile-driving sex, grunts instead of words, just two sweaty bodies crashing together at a relentless and ever increasing pace.

Tonight was grunt night. Tom rode him like he was breaking a difficult pony. It was borderline painful and yet exciting too. Stanley had never known anyone who pursued his own pleasure with such single-minded determination.

Tom was in fuck mode, period. If, while he was at it, he felt any concern for the violence with which he was ravaging his lover, he gave no sign of it. Just, "Uh," and "uh," and "uh," with each long violent thrust, and the occasional low moan in answer from Stanley. Part agony, part delight. Stanley could never quite decide which part was paramount. Most likely that was because he didn't think too clearly while it was happening. He liked to just surrender himself to the assault.

Afterward, though, after Tom had sworn once aloud and slammed the considerable length of himself into Stanley's by-then-aching bottom, his juices spurting like a volcano erupting—why, then, he became gentleness itself, cradled Stanley in his arms, kissed him repeatedly and tenderly, nipped at his ear and, finally, slipping down on the bed, took Stanley into his mouth and gave him head with such skilled and delicate use of his lips and his tongue that it was all but impossible to believe that it was only a few short months before when he had done this for the first time.

When they had both come, Tom lasting out Stanley's orgasm until the last bead of juice had been drained from him, when their breath had returned to normal, Tom slipped up on the bed again, took Stanley in the curve of his arm, pulled him into a warm embrace and, with surprising suddenness, fell asleep.

Leaving Stanley to lie in the warmth of Tom's body, to drink in the odors from it—sweat and man-body scents and the sweet-sour reminders of the sex they had just shared. He drifted, half-asleep, half-awake, thinking about the whirlwind Tom that had just blown through their room, about their relationship, about all kinds of things, but mostly about the two of them.

He thought, not for the first time, that passionate sex, once satisfied, leaves in its wake a peculiar innocence. It seemed to Stanley they might have been two children lying abed together now for no purpose more needful than sharing their warmth. It was moments like this when he felt closest to Tom, when he most enjoyed, as Marguerite Yourcenar had so aptly put it, "the strange felicity of being loved."

But it was fragile, that innocence. All of it was fragile, he knew that now, their entire being together, fragile enough that it scared him. Tom's love shone on him like a star from above, but like the star, it made the surrounding night darker.

They, too, were mired in the commonplace, the same as others. Whenever Tom looked at him, he saw the love in Tom's eyes, but he could never quite shake the knowledge that the magic would one day inevitably wear off, and Tom would look at him with, if not quite indifference, certainly with no passion either. And he was just as certain that no one would ever look at him again the way Tom did now.

Like Tom's arm lying across him in the darkness, great love can grow heavy too.

THE FIRE was everywhere. He had been shot. There was a door in the distance, and Tom staggered toward it, knowing as he did so that he was never going to make it that far, not in his weakened condition. Had Stanley made it? The heat was so intense, it felt as if his entire body was on fire. His trousers were burning, his hip literally aflame.

Only one chance. His truck was inside the garage, ten, fifteen feet from the open door. He dropped to the floor, crawled under it, just as the world exploded.

Stanley? His eyes flew open. For a moment he was disoriented, the dark room alien and unfamiliar, the terror of the dream clinging to him like the sweat-dampened sheet.

He put a hand to his left, touched Stanley's back. In his sleep, Stanley murmured something and rolled over toward him, snuggling against him. Tom slipped his arm around him, breathed a sigh of relief. It was okay. Stanley was here with him. The fire hadn't gotten him.

His hip hurt like hell. That's what had brought the dream on. It always did. He remembered waking up in the hospital later, after the explosion, his hip burning as if the flames were still eating into it. Sometimes even now, after all this time, it still felt like that, a memory that came at him always in the dark of the night.

He lay for a long time, holding Stanley close, staring up at the ceiling, content just to feel him there. The pain kept him awake.

Sometime close to morning, he finally drifted off to sleep. The phone woke him. The clock by the bed said it was nearly noon. He groped for the telephone. Next to him, Stanley stirred, mumbled something. Stanley could sleep through the end of the world.

Tom recognized Hammond's voice immediately.

Chapter Fifteen

Carlo Tozzi ran every morning—just as the sun came up, when night was turning into day but everything was still cool. He and Gretel, a half-Shepherd half-anybody's-guess, usually ran the bike trail behind the Tahquitz Creek Country Club, and at that hour, they pretty much had it to themselves. Shadows were still deep but fading in the little wisps of ground fog that would themselves vanish soon in the heat of the sun. The yellow sage was in full bloom, the sand changing colors with the approach of day, but he could still see the red lights on the towers atop Mount San Jacinto. The nighttime breeze was dying down.

Carlo was an unenthusiastic runner. He did it purely to keep in shape, and at a pace that qualified as aerobic without really pushing himself. A mile and a quarter down, a mile and a quarter back, cool off, and home to the apartment for a hearty breakfast, pancakes and eggs, which he could then consume in clear conscience.

Gretel, who could have outdistanced him with no effort, mostly stayed with him, but she was wont to go exploring now and again, on the trail of a rabbit or a lizard, though she was careful about snakes. A desert-wise dog.

At some point in their run, she went off on her own. Carlo had continued along the path for maybe a quarter mile before he realized she wasn't with him. He stopped, running in place, and looked back and around.

"Gretel," he called. "Hey, girl. Where'd you go?"

No response. He looked down the path the way he'd been going. He was almost to his turnaround point anyway. He decided he might as well start back a little early and find her on the way. She never strayed far afield.

He went another quarter mile without seeing her and began to get just a trifle worried—usually, the desert rattlers did their searching in the cool of the night, and by this time, with the sun now definitely above the horizon, the air already warming rapidly, they were mostly looking for shelter from the sun. And Gretel definitely avoided them if she spotted one.

Still, if she carelessly crossed path with a green Mojave…. They were mean; they could be defensive of their territory.

He stopped dead, looking and listening, and heard her nearby, chuffing as if she were having a conversation with herself. He jogged up a slight rise to his left and found her, digging frantically at the sand with her front paws, tail swinging wildly. Something had excited her curiosity. Carlo wrinkled his nose. A faint breeze carried an odd rotting smell with it.

"Hey, girl, you're probably scaring the shit out of some harmless bunny rabbit. Why don't we head for home, and I'll get you a nice…?"

She was paying him no attention. He sighed and, coming closer, bent to take hold of her collar, meaning to pull her away from her task. As he did so, something flopped out of the crater Gretel had dug in the sand. Carlo stared at it. The sour smell got stronger. He took a step or two closer, not quite able to believe he was seeing what he was seeing.

Then, he bent over, away from the dog and the hole, and the coffee he'd downed before starting out came up in a violent heave.

"WE FOUND the missing boyfriend," Hammond said into the telephone.

"Jeff? He's dead, right?" Tom asked.

"Right. A runner found him in one of the canyons, buried, but not deep enough. Guy had his dog with him. The dog got all excited over a mound of dirt, started digging. Guy went to pull the dog off, and a hand popped out. Called us on his cell phone. At least he was smart enough to wait there till we arrived, or the coyotes would have been all over it."

"How did he die? Any idea yet? Not another of those phony snake bites, I hope?"

"No. At a glance, I'd say he was strangled. He's got bruises on his throat, look to me like finger marks. I'm on my way to Riverside now to meet with Doc Murphy. He may tell us otherwise, but I'd bet a wad on it. Want to ride along? I'll swing by and pick you up."

Tom glanced again at the clock, poked Stanley with his thumb. "Give us half an hour, okay?" He put the phone back on its cradle. Stanley blinked at him from the next pillow.

"Guess what," Tom said. "We get to take a shower together."

Stanley smiled back at him. This was his idea of water sports.

Tom correctly read the message in his eyes. "Not that much time," he said, but not in a discouraging way.

"I can be quick," Stanley said, throwing the covers aside. "If I have to be."

HAMMOND PICKED them up in a department car, the traditional Crown Victoria, plain gray. He drove, with Tom in front beside him, and Stanley sat in the rear. They had gotten coffees to go from the Inn's café and sipped them as they headed down the highway.

They rode for several miles in silence, nothing but disembodied voices coming at them from the police radio, when Hammond said abruptly, "Tell me something, do you miss it? Homicide detective?"

"Yes," Tom said.

"I don't," Stanley said, but the other two didn't seem even to hear him. Tom was like that, always quick to slip into cop mode with another officer, and Stanley knew Hammond didn't really take him seriously.

"The impossible mystery," Hammond said. "I always think of it like that."

"But most of them get solved," Stanley said, determined to wriggle his way into the conversation. He hated being shoved aside because he was, in anyone else's opinion, too gay. In his mind, he was just gay enough.

"By which you mean," Hammond said, meeting Stanley's eyes in the rearview mirror, acknowledging him, if reluctantly, "the murderer gets caught. But that's not what I meant. That's not the great mystery. What I mean is, there's always something that doesn't make any sense, some question impossible to answer."

"For instance?" Stanley asked.

Hammond considered for a moment. "For instance, why did the wife whose husband has been slapping her around for years decide to plug the guy now? What was it about this one night, this one beating, that changed everything for them? Or, this guy, he robs the corner liquor store, and then after he's gotten the money, for no apparent reason, he shoots the clerk who wasn't putting up any resistance. There's always a question left that you can never put an answer to."

"I hadn't thought of it like that," Stanley admitted, deciding maybe the policeman wasn't as dense as he had heretofore suspected.

"You know what I miss?" Tom asked. "I miss the buddy thing, the other guys. I never thought I would, but I do."

"Yes. I know what you mean. Only, it isn't them, exactly, it's the camaraderie."

"Sometimes you don't even like them as individuals," Tom said, thinking it out as he spoke. "Hell, some of the guys I worked with were real jerks, but there you are, all of you working together to solve something, focused on the same goal. There's a tension and an energy that you share, that you don't get any other way."

Hammond took a sip of his coffee and glanced briefly sideways at him. "Do you feel that same energy working as a private detective?" he asked.

Tom turned in the seat to look back at Stanley, who blinked owlishly at him. "Yes, and no," Tom said. "I like working with Stanley, we make a good team, seems like to me, but we're always on the outside of a case looking in, you know what I mean? Like this one. It's your case. All we can do is sniff around the edges. Hopefully we'll figure it out. Or more likely you will, but maybe, hopefully, we'll get to add something to the picture. But it's not the same thing either, not like working with a whole department."

Hammond thought about that for a mile or two. "Everything's changed, though, the last few years. At least it has here. Nowadays, it feels more like you're always working alone, in a sense. If you're seriously trying to be a detective, anyway. I expect you were. I get that feel from you, but there's not so many of them anymore, not real detectives. Take the Treasury boys, for instance, or the FBI, or, hell, most of the boys back at the station in the homicide division, when you come right down to it—they're just glorified clerks. Most of them are practically kids. Sure, they know how to do a wiretap or work a crime scene, they interview somebody and take a lot of notes, they've got technology we never used to have, but they don't know how to think things out. How to look at the clues and move them around until they come together to form a picture for you. You can't teach somebody that in school."

"I never thought of it like that, but you're right," Tom said. "That kind of thing, you either have it or you don't. That's the good part about working with Stanley. He has this, I don't know, this feel for things. Like pulling rabbits out of a hat. Sometimes it's damned amazing."

"Is that so," Hammond said, surprised, taking a quick look in the mirror. He drove in silence for a mile or so.

"Well, still," he said, "for an old-time kind of detective like me, in the end it always comes down to just you alone, trying to get into some killer's head. And the work cuts you off from everybody else. People are uncomfortable around cops. And that camaraderie you talked about, even that's not the same anymore."

"Maybe not," Tom said. He was thinking of the guys he had worked with in San Francisco. At one time he had felt close to all of them, but that had begun to fade in his last few months with the department. Or was that only because he'd linked up with Stanley? Once he'd been assigned to a case with Stanley, the others had begun to look funny at him, act differently. It had never been the same afterward.

At first, he had fought against that. He hadn't wanted to be paired with Stanley. But working with him, sharing the same dangers, covering each other's back, he had come to see Stanley in a different light. And, somehow, somewhere along the way, he had fallen in love. The kind of love he had never known before, or even imagined. It had necessitated his leaving the bureau. He couldn't pretend, he couldn't hide Stanley away somewhere, and he couldn't work with the other detectives knowing that he and Stanley had hooked up—hearing them snicker, seeing the funny looks they gave him.

It had come down to Stanley or them. He'd opted for Stanley.

"It's not just police work either," Hammond was saying. "It's the whole world, if you think about it. Take my oldest boy. He was the perfect son, did what he was told, played football—hell, he was the touchdown king—good-looking, smart. My youngest, the other one, he wears funny black clothes and his hair is braided. Goth, he calls it. Smokes too much weed, can't hardly stay in school. Just lays around his room, listening to some god-awful music. Rap, he says. Crap, I call it. Won't do anything I say. There's no parental authority anymore."

"In my opinion, most of us never really grow up," Stanley said. "We just learn how to behave in public."

Hammond might not have heard him. "Same with police authority, you ask me. That's gone too."

"What happened to the older boy?" Stanley asked.

Hammond glowered briefly over his shoulder. "What makes you think anything happened to him?"

"The way you talked about him, in the past tense."

Hammond drove for a moment or two in silence before he said, "He's gone."

"Gone? As in…?"

"Signed up for the Marines. Got himself shipped to the Middle East. Wasn't there any time at all before he got shipped back again. In a box this time."

Stanley didn't know what to say to that. He thought it best if he just said nothing. If Hammond noticed his silence, he didn't show it. After a bit, he began to talk again, more now as if he were talking to himself than to them.

"I tell you what, I think if I was to pick a job as the loneliest in the world, I'd say homicide detective."

"You think so?" Tom said, more to be polite than from any real interest. He was not much of a philosopher.

"Seems like it to me. Think about it. In time the friends of the victim, the families, everyone gets over it, at least they go on with their lives. I can't say they ever really forget, but they push it into a far corner, like the attic of their mind—but the investigating officer never really forgets an unsolved case. It haunts him forever. It always has me, anyway.

"Which is why," he said, looking sideways at Tom, "I want to get this one solved. I don't want those boys haunting me."

He was silent for a few more miles. Then he said, out of the blue, "They want me to retire."

Neither Tom nor Stanley responded. Tom was thinking that probably this was where the whole conversation had been headed. Stanley was thinking about that bottle of bourbon in Hammond's desk drawer. The result of them wanting him out? Or the cause of it?

Chapter Sixteen

Doctor Murphy looked no happier to see them this second time—but for the immediate moment, in any case, they were with a detective from the Palm Springs Police Department, which apparently somewhat negated his disapproval of matters homosexual. He was certainly more polite than he had been before.

"What have you learned so far?" Hammond asked when Murphy had escorted them to the autopsy room, seen them gowned and masked.

"We haven't opened him up yet," Murphy said, withdrawing the sheet that covered the naked body on the stainless steel table—to reveal, in Stanley's opinion, a young man who had been even more breathtakingly handsome than Barry Palmer, brunet where Barry had been blond, shorter, it looked, and a bit stockier. But his beautiful features were contorted in death, and accusations of sand clung to his nostrils, his hair, his lips.

"The cause of death appears to be pretty obvious—strangulation," Murphy said. "The finger marks at the throat indicate that quite clearly. The signs are that it was asphyxiaphilia. More commonly known as erotic asphyxiation."

It took Stanley a second or two to process that bit of information. "Are you saying he was a gasper?" he said.

"What's a gasper?" Tom asked.

"Erotic asphyxiation is the intentional blockage of oxygen to the brain," Murphy said. "Erotic, meaning, during sexual activity. Most commonly it is done at the time of orgasm, but it can be employed at any time during sexual congress."

"Wait—you're telling me these people get off on being strangled?" Tom looked astonished.

"Exactly. The carotid arteries, here and here"—Doctor Murphy pointed to either side of the throat—"carry the oxygen in the blood from the heart to the brain. When you compress the carotid arteries, say by strangulation or, alternatively, by hanging, the brain loses oxygen and carbon dioxide accumulates instead.

"The result is giddiness, light-headedness, and for some at least, pleasure, all of which can heighten sexual sensations. Mountain climbers sometimes experience something similar at high altitudes. The individual goes into a semi-hallucinogenic state called hypoxia. In that condition, orgasm is said to be a powerful rush. And like other sexual pleasures, it can become addictive."

"A habit?" Tom said.

"Same as any other. In time, for some, the asphyxia becomes necessary to achieve sexual release."

Tom looked down at the boy on the table, at the dark bruises on his throat. "And you think that's what happened with this kid?"

"The evidence suggests so. Here, you see." Murphy pointed with a scalpel. "These bruises, they're new, probably what killed him, but these, here, are old scars. They've faded, and there are traces of makeup, which makes me think he tried to cover them up. But this was clearly not the first experience of erotic strangulation for this young man. I would suspect a long history of such activity."

"You said he was one of the rent boys up at the Inn?" Hammond asked Tom.

"Yes. From what we've heard, he was the go-to for guys looking for kinky sex," Stanley said.

"Hmm. That fits for sure with what the doc is saying. Only this time, I guess things went a little too far."

"And I'm guessing his boyfriend, the Palmer kid, knew something," Tom said. "Saw it or heard about it. Maybe his buddy told him all about it. Which meant Palmer had to be eliminated, but in a way that looks like something other than murder. So the killer makes it look like a snake got him."

"Chances are," Hammond said, "it would have been accepted as an ordinary death from a snake bite, too, if he'd been found outside somewhere."

"If somebody hadn't got screwed up about that empty room and stashed the body there for Chris to find," Tom said.

"Right. If we'd found him, say, out in the sand, on a trail in one of the canyons, which was probably where he was meant to be moved to, nobody would've given it a second thought. Snakes kill people. Part of living in the desert. All kinds of snakes."

Tom looked back at the body on the table. "But, Jesus, I gotta say, I never heard of this way of doing it." He waved a hand in the direction of the corpse. "Getting strangled to get your rocks off? That's sick."

"Maybe, but it's not new," the doctor said. "It's been documented since the early seventeenth century. At one time it was used as a treatment for erectile dysfunction."

"Limp weenie?" Tom said, surprised anew. "You fix that by getting someone to choke you?"

Murphy winced, but he nodded. "Yes. It was noted that at public hangings, male victims often developed erections, which sometimes remained after death—in medical literature, the so-called death erection. Hanging victims even ejaculated from time to time."

"I have heard of this kind of sex play," Stanley said, "in the S and M crowd, though guys don't talk about it a lot. But I never thought of it as manual strangulation. I had a notion they put plastic bags over their heads."

"They do that too," the doctor said. "Or sometimes they do it by hanging themselves. There was an actor recently—"

"But was that definite?" Stanley asked, remembering the news stories. "I mean, that it was sexual hanging?"

"Probably it will never be declared one way or another. Homicide was ruled out, and suicide. Which leaves accident, but it's hard to imagine how you could hang yourself in a closet, which is where they found him, without some intent."

"He just misjudged?" Tom said.

"It's easy to do. Supposedly when they do this, people think they can control it, can get out of the situation, remove the rope or the plastic bag in time, before it's too late. The danger is that dizziness and even loss of consciousness can occur and lead to loss of control over the strangulation. In the case of this young man here, the intent may not have been murder at all, in the sense that you're meaning it. This could have been a voluntary cooperation between two partners, and the strangler simply went too far, didn't stop quite in time. Legally, it's a gray area."

"The guy's just as dead, though," Tom said.

All four of them looked down at the body on the table—that had not so long ago been a young man alive and in the prime of his life. Stanley felt a strange urge to brush those grains of sand from his lips, from his eyelids, but he kept his hands at his side.

"Yes," the doctor said. "He's just as dead."

Chapter Seventeen

"But who is our killer?" Stanley asked. Hammond had dropped them off, and they were in Tom's truck, headed for downtown Palm Springs.

"I don't know yet who he is, but I know what he is," Tom said.

"Which is?"

"He's one of those snakes we talked about. Not just any snake either; he's one of those green Mojave fuckers. You remember what Hammond told us about the Mojaves. Aggressive, he said. Most snakes will slide away when a man approaches, according to what Doc Murphy told us, but not the Mojave. He'll come right at you. He's the kind of creature who doesn't just kill to eat, the way most wild animals do, or to protect his turf. He kills because he can, for the joy of killing. There are animals like that. The lion, say. They love to close in on their prey, love the smell of fear and the pain, and that moment of absolute power when the eyes go blank and the blood runs. It's like being God for a moment. That's our killer. The Jeff kid may have been an accident, but Palmer wasn't. This guy enjoys the killing."

Stanley shuddered. Given his druthers, he'd just as soon have packed up and gone home to San Francisco. He didn't like looking at dead bodies, and he didn't like tangling with murderers. He would much prefer to have an ordinary queer-boy job as a decorator, at which he had sometimes worked and at which he was very talented.

Tom, though, loved all this. He loved matching wits with the killers, loved tracking them down, loved the action, the gore even. Tom would never leave Palm Springs now until he had nailed their murderer to the wall.

Stanley sighed. When you married a man, you married the whole package. Tom had quit a job he loved with the San Francisco Police Department to be with him. How could he have said no when Tom wanted to open a detective agency? But it was not the future Stanley had dreamed of when he was younger, playing with his paper dolls. What would Betty Grable do?

"It's Thursday night," he said aloud. "Chris tells me they have this street festival locally, Village Fest they call it, every Thursday on Palm Canyon Drive. Why don't we check that out?"

"Good call. I'll bet we can get some food there—real food."

"Tom…."

"I know, that Rim stuff is real food, just not my kind of eats. And I can't count on that little waiter taking care of my meat every night. Nice of him, though."

"That little waiter definitely has his mind on your meat."

Tom looked surprised. "You think so? Huh." He let that sit for a moment and decided maybe it would not be the wisest subject to pursue. "I'll bet I can get a burger at this fair."

Which, Stanley thought, was his not very subtle way of changing the subject.

As it turned out, almost every kind of food and drink imaginable was to be found at the Village Fest. The city closed the street to vehicular traffic for six blocks, and the people, locals and visitors alike, took it over, hordes of them. The result was sort of a carnival, a county fair, and Mardi Gras all rolled into one.

The sun had gone down, and like desert animals coming out of the dens in which they had hidden from the day's heat, the folks were out, savoring the night air, eating and drinking. And, Stanley noticed, a lot of them cruising. Which, as he saw it, always added a nice spice to an event. In his mind, cruising was de rigueur for a gay man, whether first degree, which was with intent, or second, without.

They passed a Moonwalk tent where preteen kids were jumping around and pretending to be weightless. Vendor stands ran down the middle of the street, offering arts and crafts, fruit, vegetables, and all manner of prepared foods. The aromas of sausages and falafels, Philly cheesesteaks, and fried onions perfumed the air. It was not yet seven o'clock and already dark, but the mercury streetlights overhead and the endless strings of Christmas lights made the street nearly as bright as day.

They stopped at a booth for shaved ices, mango for Stanley and pineapple for Tom, and ate them as they strolled, enjoying the street performers, the displays of art and flowers and produce.

The menu posted in the window of a small restaurant caught their attention. They paused to read it and decided it looked promising. Inside, a chatty host led them to a window table.

"The best table," he assured them, and Tom smiled at him and winked, which left the host so flustered that he forgot to leave their menus and had to come back with them. They ordered burgers and fries and drank ice-cold beers while they waited for their food, watching the passing parade on the sidewalk outside.

"It's funny to think about those two guys, isn't it?" Stanley said, licking the grease from the french fries off his fingers. "Barry and Jeff."

"In what way funny?" Tom asked.

"Oh, I don't know. They were lovers, it seems like. Some sort of lovers, anyway. And there were all those clients of theirs at the same time. You'd think one or the other of them would have gotten jealous."

Tom thought about that. "Maybe one of them did. Maybe Palmer got sore and offed his boyfriend."

"And killed himself?"

Tom thought some more. "He could have, maybe. The doc said the venom takes a while to kick in. So he could have injected himself." He took a big bite out of his burger and chewed thoughtfully. "They were awfully close, according to what Larson told us. If Palmer killed his boyfriend in a fit of jealousy—it's been known to happen."

"It might have been simmering for a long time."

"Where'd he get the venom?"

"They have the reptiles bite on parchment paper. The snake handlers, I mean. Palmer could have done the same."

They were silent for a minute or two. "Did you ever think about cheating?" Stanley asked hesitantly. "You know, getting it on with someone else. Someone else male, I mean."

This was a delicate subject. Not so long ago, Stanley had thought about cheating. Had seriously thought about it, had even gotten into the illicit bed, but had found at the last moment that he couldn't do the deed. It had been the worst crisis of their time together, and he had felt for a long time since as if he were walking on eggs. But Tom had never brought it up, seemed willing not only to forgive, but to forget—which to Stanley's way of thinking was the harder part.

Tom took a while to think about the question before he answered. "Not really," he said finally.

"What's that mean, *not really*?" Stanley gave him a suspicious look. "It took you long enough to come up with that."

Tom shrugged. "There was one time. Somebody wanted to. He didn't exactly say so, but we both knew that was where it was headed, and I thought about it for maybe a tenth of a second. But I knew it wouldn't work."

"Who was this somebody?"

Tom gave him a look that said he didn't like the question and didn't intend to answer it. "Nobody you'd know," he said, in a tone of finality.

"Well, maybe…."

"Drop it, Stanley," Tom said in a brook-no-argument voice.

So Stanley dropped it—but he couldn't help wondering.

BY THE time they got back to the Inn, the pool was lined with glistening, half-naked bodies, every table occupied.

The dancers were already out in force at the club. Chris was there, dancing with Eddie. Someone asked Tom to dance, and when he declined, asked Stanley, and they moved on to the floor, leaving Tom alone at the bar.

Tom ordered a Dos Equis, thought longingly about that special brew at Nakamura's. Probably they had it here too—but it was out of his class. Even if they comped it, what was the point of getting into the habit? He wasn't a hundred-bucks-a-bottle kind of guy. The only really rare, really precious thing in his life was Stanley.

Someone approached and clapped a hearty hand on his shoulder. To his surprise, when he looked, Tom found himself facing the cowboy, Randy Patterson.

"So, no hard feelings, right?" Randy said. "About the other night? The race horse?"

Tom considered the question. He'd been righteously sore at the time, but since then he had decided it was as much his fault. Stanley was right. He should have turned down the offer of a drink in the first place. What could it mean except someone was hitting on him?

"No. No harm done," he said. "But I'd have been seriously pissed if I'd taken a swig of that."

Randy laughed. "Seriously pissed. You making a joke?"

Tom had to laugh with him. He took their moment of shared laughter to look the guy over a bit more carefully than he had the other time. He was older than Tom had thought at first. Good-looking, in a desert-weathered way, his skin ochre-colored, lines around his oddly tilted eyes. Heinz 57, he thought. Typical Southern California.

"You grow up here?" Tom asked aloud.

"Palm Springs? Nah, in Los Angeles. Moved here ten years ago, something like that. Came to visit somebody, decided to stay on."

"Los Angeles. Let me guess—you were in the movies?"

Patterson looked surprised. "What makes you say that?"

"Oh, everybody in Los Angeles is in the industry, so they say. That's what they call it there, isn't it, the industry?"

"Exactly." Patterson's laugh this time had a bitter ring to it. "The fucking industry. You're right too, it seems like everybody is in it, even when they aren't. So, what, you think I'm an actor?"

"Just a hunch. Lots of good-looking people all the time flocking to LA, hoping to be the next star. You're as good-looking as most of them."

Patterson's eyes brightened. "You think so?" He looked around. "With all the beauties here?"

Tom shrugged. "Ah, hell, you can't go by me. I'm no judge. Not when it comes to guys."

Patterson sighed. "Well, thanks, it's nice of you to say it, but no, I never went that route. Never really had any desire to, to be honest. I guess you could say my mom was in the business, though. If you stretched the point a little. She worked at Fox, and yeah, now that you put it that way, she did refer to herself as 'in the industry.' Which sounded good, but the truth was, she worked in the mailroom. And from time to time, she got to date a few second-stringers."

"What about your dad?"

"My old man went missing in action," Randy said quietly. "Right from the get-go."

"Ah." Tom nodded.

Randy's look and his tone were defensive. "Look, it was the seventies. People didn't take getting married all that seriously. Women were feeling their independence. Nobody thought overmuch about a single mother raising a kid."

Tom put up his hands in a gesture of surrender. "Hey, I didn't mean to sound disapproving. I knew a lot of those single mothers, and most of them did a damn good job."

"She did. And I guess it's not really fair to say my old man was missing in action either. He was already married, but he was up front about it when they started dating, and when she found out I was comin' to town instead of Santa, he helped her. He didn't just walk away. He saw we were taken care of. A lot of guys didn't do that."

"You know who he was?"

Randy spread his hands out, palm up. "So, what, I'm a suspect now? I mean, the way you're throwing the questions at me."

"Sorry. No, I was just making conversation. It's a hazard of the job, I guess. You talk to people, you end up asking them questions."

"It's okay. Look, about the other night. I meant it when I said you were hot. In case you would like to…."

"Sorry, I'm spoken for."

Patterson glanced in Stanley's direction. "I wondered. He doesn't look like he'd be your type."

"He isn't, I guess, if you want to think of it that way. But he's what I've got. Or has got me, depending on how you want to look at it."

"Uh-huh," Patterson said, nodding. He looked Tom up and down. "You're really into women, right?"

"I was. But that was… well, before."

Patterson looked again in Stanley's direction. "Yeah, love changes things, doesn't it?"

"Are you in love?"

Patterson looked back at him, his eyes narrowed. "Who, me? No way. Things get too messy."

"They sure did for Barry Palmer."

"You think that was about love?"

"It was about something. And his boyfriend, Jeff—"

"Jeff Whiting?"

"That his name? All I had was Jeff."

"Well, if you're talking about Barry's boyfriend, that's who it was, Jeff Whiting. Good-looking dude—well, shit, he would be, wouldn't he—but a little weird, you ask me."

"We heard he was into the kinky stuff."

"Way kinky. My… well, a friend, said he liked to be choked?"

The tone of his voice made it more of a question than a statement. *Trying to pump me?* Tom wondered. "That's what the forensic said. Said it looked like he was in the habit."

Patterson's eyebrow went up. "Jeff's dead?" He didn't sound, to Tom, as surprised as he might have been.

Tom nodded. "You didn't know?"

Patterson ignored that question. "And you talked to forensic? I didn't think they let civilians in on stuff like that."

"We went with Hammond, from Palm Springs homicide. He's kind of given us his blessing to look around."

Patterson nodded knowingly. "And? What exactly do you see, with your looking around?"

Tom half smiled. "To be honest, at the moment I see a cowboy who's awful curious."

Patterson smiled back. "We all are," he said, totally unembarrassed.

Tom was wondering what Bryce could find out for him about Randy Patterson. Bryce was in San Francisco, but he almost certainly had contacts with the LAPD too. Cops thrived on contacts.

And Patterson was making him curious. Something more than just pecker itch going on with him.

Chapter Eighteen

Patterson glanced past Tom, and his eyes went wide. "Excuse me," he said. "I got to see a man about a horse." And with that, he was gone. The flickering lights and the thick crowd made it easy to disappear in a few seconds.

Tom looked over his shoulder to see what had spooked Patterson and saw Detective Hammond at the door, looking around. Hammond spotted him and came across the dance floor, dodging bodies in motion. Stanley caught sight of Hammond and, abandoning his dance partner, hurried after him.

"We've got another one," Hammond told them.

"Another body?"

"Yep. They're piling up. And I'm getting a lot of heat."

"Who was it this time?"

"We make him a Mario Alvarez. He's a security guard. Want to make a guess where he worked?"

"Here," Tom said.

And Stanley added, "At the Inn. We already knew that."

"You knew the guy?"

"No, but we heard the name," Stanley said. "There's a security room just inside the gates. They buzz you in. That's where this Mario worked."

"So, let me guess," Tom said, "is this another snake bite?"

"Not this time. Far from it. His throat was cut—really cut, like his head was all but severed, just hanging on by a bit of flesh and gristle. A clean cut, too, no hacking at it. Someone with a sharp knife who knew what he was doing."

"Interesting." Tom was thinking about all the blades at Nakamura's house. Was that a connection? But lots of people had knives. It didn't prove anything. "Where was he found? Here?"

"No, in an alley downtown, behind a bar—but it doesn't look like that's where he was killed."

"So maybe he *was* killed here," Tom said. "Maybe even out in that security shack."

"Maybe. We didn't look there before. No reason to. Nothing to connect it to the other murders."

"Barry Palmer," Stanley said. "We turned up a witness who saw the security guard giving Palmer head. In the security office."

"'Zat so?" Hammond thought about that information.

"And that in itself is odd, if you think about it," Stanley added. "Considering that the Palmer kid was high rent. More than a security guard could afford."

"Hey, what's a little lovin' between friends, right?"

"Only they weren't friends," Stanley said. "So far as we can determine."

Hammond sighed. "Well, it's probably too much to hope for now, that we'd find any kind of evidence out there, but for sure we need to check it out."

"Was there anybody there when you came in?" Tom asked.

"The gate was open. I guess they don't have a backup."

Hammond turned his head to look at the bottles behind the bar. He signaled the bartender and ordered a shot of Jack Daniels, but when it came, he let it sit atop the bar, studied it with an uncertain look. Finally, he picked it up, lifted it to his nose to sniff it—and dumped it on the floor, setting the empty glass back on the wooden counter.

Frederick hurried up to them just then, his sequined caftan a glittering cloud billowing behind him. His face was frozen into a stony mask, but his eyes looked worried. "Officer Hammond," he said, approaching. "What brings you to our little resort?"

"Your little resort is missing a security guard," Hammond said. "In case you weren't aware."

"You know about that? Yes, I am aware of it. Mario failed to show up for work this evening. We had to leave the gate open and untended, but I'm certain it will be just for a short while. Surely that's not a matter for the Palm Springs police, however? I'm expecting Mario any minute."

"I wouldn't expect him, if I were you. Mario's not going anywhere right now, except to the morgue."

Frederick's mouth formed an astonished O. He put a hand to his chest. "That's… that's dreadful," he said, taken aback. Then getting himself under control again, he said hotly, "This is outrageous. Three deaths now, and what are you doing about it?"

"What I'm doing right now is, I want to take a look at that security room."

Frederick drew himself up haughtily. "Do you have a warrant?"

"No, but I can get one pretty quick, if you want to play it that way. Meanwhile, we'll take care of your security problem for you. I'll have a couple of black-and-whites parked at the gate, nobody in, nobody out. If you'd prefer to handle it that way."

They engaged in a brief staring match. Frederick blinked first. He sighed in a long-suffering way. "No, that won't be necessary. But why do you think you need to search there? If you've already got a body, it means you found him somewhere else. What do you suppose you could find? It's just a room for the security guard to sit and watch the gates."

"I don't know what I'll find until I find it," Hammond said. "You might as well come along," he told Tom and Stanley. "Maybe you'll see something I don't."

"Well, I'm coming too," Frederick said.

Hammond gave him a cool look. "Sure. It's probably locked anyway. You can save us busting the door down."

THEY LEFT the club and started in the direction of the security office, Hammond leading the way. "So," he said to Stanley, "you said somebody mentioned this Mario to you earlier."

"A young man named Larson. He's the one who said he saw this Mario giving Barry head, but I've been thinking about that—it doesn't sound right, does it? I mean, Larson's pretty good-looking, and Barry turned him down…."

"So Larson says," Tom said.

Frederick was trailing behind them, but close enough to hear the exchange. "Larson? Our Larson? He's not the most reliable person," he said.

Stanley thought about Larson. "Maybe not. He did strike me as a little flaky. But let's suppose that he's telling the truth. In which case, why was Barry giving the gift to a lowly security guard who couldn't pay the kind of money Barry was used to getting? Larson suggested maybe it was a uniform fetish, but that doesn't work for me. I could see it if it were a uniformed cop…."

"Jeez, you're not suggesting that cops might play hide the salami, are you?" Hammond asked with exaggerated surprise.

"Oh, please. Are you forgetting I was a policeman?"

Hammond grunted. It might have been a smothered laugh, even. "I guess I was forgetting that."

"Or, say, not a cop. Maybe a Marine. There's a Marine base not far away, didn't you tell us that?" he asked Frederick.

"Twentynine Palms. Just over the mountain."

"Well, so there're Marines available here, I'm sure. Or even a biker in full leather drag, I could see that. Lots of gay men turn on to bikers. But come on, a security guard? That'd be about as much of a turn-on for a uniform queen as a plumber or the mailman."

"Personally I never got turned on by a mailman," Hammond said, "but there's a lady walks the beat downtown, fills out her uniform just fine."

"You know," Stanley said dryly, "I don't mind straight men if they're not too obvious."

Another grunt that might have been a smothered laugh.

The security room was locked. Reluctantly, Frederick produced a ring of keys and unlocked it, and made as if to precede them inside, but Hammond put up a beefy hand. "We'll take it from here, thanks," he said.

"I am the manager," Frederick started to say, but Hammond forestalled him in a no-nonsense tone.

"For all I know, this might be a crime scene. First rule of a crime scene, don't contaminate it. The more people moving around, the greater the chance of contamination."

"But you're going in?" Frederick asked of Tom.

"They're pros," Hammond answered for him. "Stay close, though. We'll whistle if we need you."

Frederick looked not at all pleased with this turn of events, but he stepped aside, only glowering at Tom and Stanley as they followed Hammond inside. As if to underscore his position, Hammond firmly closed the door after them, leaving an unhappy manager to wait outside.

The room was small, and at first glance, there wasn't much to see. A chair, a desk, a monitor that showed the front gate with an intercom beside it and a button that clearly opened the gate. A magazine lay facedown on the desk. Hammond picked it up with a pencil. Nude men. He dropped it quickly.

"Didn't really expect to see blood stains," Hammond said, though he sounded disappointed. "Not much chance really that he was killed here. Too likely to be witnesses. All those cars driving through."

"Maybe not," Stanley said. "I expect most of the people passing through the gate don't even look this way."

"Well, you said somebody saw him going to town on a tube steak," Hammond said.

"Yes, so we heard," Stanley said. He looked more carefully around the room. "What's this door, do you think?"

They all three stared at the door in the back wall. "Must be some kind of closet," Hammond said. "Not enough building for anything else." He tried the door and found it locked. "Go get that queenie manager?" he asked. "We need to take a look-see."

"Don't bother, I can handle it," Tom said. He took his lock picks out of his pocket. "Just happen to have these on me," he said in response to Hammond's raised eyebrows.

"Handy," Hammond said in a dry voice. Technically, Tom was breaking the law, but since the policeman was as eager to see what was behind the door as Tom was....

Tom had the door unlocked in a matter of seconds and pulled it open, stepping aside for Hammond to have the first look, but Stanley crowded close behind him to peer past his shoulder. His eyes went wide.

"They've got security cameras," he said, voicing what they all could see. "A whole array of them." A bank of monitors filled the back wall. "This entire place is wired for video."

"They must have cameras in every room," Hammond said. "I'll be damned. Smile, ladies, you're on *Candid Camera*."

"Huh. They're well concealed, that's for sure," Tom said. "I never spotted them, and it's one thing I generally look for. Something super up-to-date, apparently."

"Only," Stanley said, "it doesn't look like they're working right now. All the screens are blank."

Tom poked around the electronic equipment. "No, they've been turned off, is all." He found the switch and flipped it. The monitors came to life, glowing a dim gray-green, and the rooms came into view, six of them to a screen.

"There's our room," Stanley said, pointing, and added in an angry voice, "Those bastards have been spying on us. If I'd known that, I'd have given them a real Gypsy Rose Lee."

"I wonder," Tom said, "do they just watch, or do they tape what they see?" He opened drawers beneath the wall of screens. "Ah, here we are."

The drawer was filled with DVDs. "Jesus," Hammond said, his eyes growing wide, "you know what this means, don't you? If they're taping the rooms, we should be able to see who left that Barry guy in your friend's bed."

He dropped heavily onto one knee and began to thumb through the discs. The drawer was full of them, filed according to dates. "March 5," he said. "We're looking for one dated the fifth." He flipped through them hastily, muttering under his breath. "March the eighth, here's the seventh, sixth… the third…." He gave a weary sigh and sat back on his haunches.

"It's missing," he said. "We've got two days before and the day after, but not the fourth or the fifth. Someone beat us to it."

"Why two days?" Tom asked. "It didn't take two days to plant the body."

"No," Hammond agreed. "But there's something showing on that other disc. Something somebody doesn't want us to see."

"Who took them?" Stanley asked.

"I'm guessing it was Palmer took the one for the fourth," Tom said. "That's probably what got him killed. And Mario, too, because he knew too much. That's why Palmer let Mario play the magic flute for free. He worked out a deal to get that recording from Mario. The fifth? Well, somebody else had to take that."

"Or somebody else got it for him while this Mario guy was buried in the bush," Hammond said.

"These are pretty small quarters," Tom said, looking around. "It would be hard for someone to go past them unnoticed."

"Only they were all one big happy family at that point. I think the guard's mind was where his mouth was. Which still leaves the question of what was on the recording for the fourth. We need to talk to Missy Frederick," Hammond said.

CHAPTER NINETEEN

FREDERICK WAS waiting outside where they had left him. It was evident from his expression that he knew what they would find and was waiting to be confronted.

"We need to have some conversation," Hammond said in a major cop voice.

"In my office, please," Frederick replied. "We can talk more discreetly there."

He avoided the pool area and led them instead through the lobby, mostly empty at the moment except for a desk clerk who watched with unabashed curiosity as they crossed to Frederick's office.

Frederick ushered them in and took a chair behind the big mahogany desk. The other three remained standing. Tom leaned against the wall, his arms crossed over his chest.

"You found the monitors," Frederick opened the conversation, looking and sounding sheepish. "Of course. I knew you would. That's why I didn't want… well, never mind. It was inevitable, clearly."

"And the DVDs," Hammond said. "So, you record all your guests, everything that goes on in the rooms?"

"No, I knew you'd jump to that conclusion, which was why I didn't tell you about them before."

"What other conclusion could we jump to?" Hammond asked. "You've got video surveillance. Only one reason I can think of for that."

Frederick took a moment to sort out what he wanted to say. "We do record the rooms, yes, that's obvious. You've seen the evidence of it. Or we did, at least, until today. But the key thing is, not all of them, and not all of the time."

"You pick and choose?" Hammond asked.

"You might put it like that. We take the occasional peek, is what it came down to. The cameras were timed to go on and off at random, a minute or two here, a minute or two there. We record like that, intermittently, for thirty days, and then the discs are erased and used over. So the record we keep isn't permanent."

"But you've got it long enough for... for what? Blackmail?"

"No," Frederick said hotly, "nothing so crude as that, I assure you."

"What, then?"

Frederick hesitated, as if not quite sure how to explain. "The original idea... well, it was more a question of keeping tabs on our guests' interests. You know, most high-end hotels keep files on their important guests—what they eat and drink, special requests for bedding, that sort of thing. The next time that guest checks in, they know his preferences, that he likes these sheets, this brand of drinking water. We had reason to want to know our guests' preferences, too, just of a different nature. By studying their habits, getting glimpses of what they did, we had a better sense of how to be prepared for their wants and needs. That's really all it was meant to be."

"Like, which boys would interest the older guys the most?" Tom said. "Who was the most popular?"

Frederick was clearly embarrassed, but he nodded. "Yes. That was part of it. Some of the young men who come here, even though they are very good-looking, do not seem to appeal to our clients, for whatever reason. So of course there is no point in comping those individuals to free drinks and meals. It's just wasted money. Others... well, if we saw an individual was very popular, and sometimes we were surprised to see who that was, why, then we did what we could to encourage them to come around. They got the drinks, the meals, the special treatment."

"And while you were at it, you saw not just who your so-called clients were interested in, but what as well," Stanley said.

"As a for instance, knowing that Jeff Whiting was kinky," Tom said. "Keeping him around in case somebody was into that scene."

Frederick drew himself up a bit. "I'm not a judgmental person. There are men who like that sort of thing. People are how they are. And if someone is turned on by, say, the unusual, then it's as well if one of the young men hanging around shares his tastes."

"Or?"

"Or the older gentlemen would go elsewhere to find what they want. It's just good business methodology. We like to keep our clients here. Once they check in, there should be little reason for them to go elsewhere. In practical terms, that means seeing that their needs are met. Whatever those needs might be. And let me say, Jeff Whiting was very popular."

"And you say nothing so crude as blackmail was intended, but you *could* have blackmailed them," Hammond said. "Some of them, certainly."

"Yes, we could have. But we didn't. That's why we recorded to discs rather than directly to the computer's hard drive. People hack into computers. Anyone who did so would have had ample means for blackmail. But we were doing this for our own purposes, and the discs should have been safe enough. That room, the security room, is kept locked, and hardly anyone knows about the DVDs, but when Barry Palmer was murdered, I thought of the discs. That someone else might know the discs were there."

"Someone knew, that's for sure," Hammond said. "Who besides you?"

"Well, Mario did, of course. Oh… do you think that's why he was murdered?"

"It's a possibility. I'd say a very real possibility."

"How dreadful. I never imagined… anyway, when that occurred to me, that someone might use the recordings for that purpose, why, that's when I erased them, just today. I took care of that myself, and I stopped the cameras. I turned them all off. If you'd checked any of those discs, you'd have found them blank. I intended to have the monitors removed tonight when Mario came in." He hesitated, as if there was something more he wanted to say, but was reluctant to do so.

"There were two days missing from the drawer," Hammond said. "The fourth and the fifth. The fifth is when Palmer was murdered."

Frederick sighed and reached into a drawer and tossed a DVD onto the surface of the desk. "That's the one for the fifth." Hammond snatched it up. "Only," Frederick said, "there's nothing on it."

"You erased a critical piece of evidence?"

"No, somebody beat me to it on that one. It was already blank. I erased the others, though."

"Except you didn't erase all of them, did you?" Tom said.

Frederick gave him a pained look. "No, I…." Again he hesitated. "Here, you may as well see for yourself." He swiveled in his chair and turned on a computer atop the credenza behind his desk. The monitor flashed on, the picture on the screen in color, at first, and then, as the disc began to play, becoming a grainy black and white picture.

"This is the disc for the fourth?" Hammond said. "The day before the Palmer kid bought it?"

"Yes. I looked at it before I erased the discs and thought it should be saved."

"For what?" Hammond asked.

"You'll see." A room came into focus. "That's the Marilyn Monroe suite," Frederick said. "You can't appreciate it like this, but the décor is hot pink. Think of the dress she wore when she sang 'Diamonds are a Girl's Best Friend.' And of course, everything is trimmed in rhinestones."

Someone stepped into the picture. For a few seconds, his back was to the camera. Then he turned and, almost as if he knew he was being filmed, he smiled at them.

"That's Jeff," Stanley said.

"Yes," Frederick agreed. "Jeff Whiting."

It was eerie to see him alive and smiling. Only a short while before they had seen his body lying on a steel table at the morgue, dirtied with sand and stained with the marks of death.

Someone else stepped into camera range then, an older gentleman.

"Who—" Tom started to ask.

"Jesus. Hernando Vega," Hammond said, mouth gaping.

"Yes, Mr. Vega," Frederick said. "Young Mr. Whiting's last date."

Chapter Twenty

THE RECORDING ended at that point; the screen went blank.

"Has that been doctored?" Tom asked.

"No, I told you the taping was sporadic," Frederick said. "Off and on, briefly, rooms chosen at random. And if you think about it, trying to tape everything, full-time, would have been an extremely complex operation. What we wanted, what we got from the recordings when we ran through them, was a sampling, hints of what our guests were up to."

"I should have thought that would be obvious," Stanley said.

"Well, yes and no. Sometimes we got hints we weren't expecting. One of our gentlemen, as it turns out, rather enjoys being tied to the bed. I would never have guessed and would never have known otherwise. But knowing that, we were able to find a suitable partner for him. Introductions were made. All, as I say, done very discreetly. I think I can safely say he never suspected our involvement. But he was happy. He's been a regular visitor since. That's the kind of thing we got from the discs."

"But there's nothing here," Tom said, indicating the video, "except to show the two of them in the room together."

"Yes," Frederick said, clearly disappointed. "I wonder… perhaps if the cameras had been set to start taping when, well, whenever someone entered the room, would that have been…?"

"If you want my opinion," Hammond said, "I think you're already wide open for lawsuits."

"Do you really think that bondage queen I just told you about would want to go into court and have his dirty laundry aired?" Frederick scoffed, his smile catty. "He's well-known locally, though the name he uses here is not his real one. And, I might add, he's a married man, with an impeccable reputation. No, I don't think so. Anyway, as of now there's no evidence. I told you, the recordings have all been erased. Except this one."

"Who is this guy with Jeff?" Stanley asked.

"Hernando Vega. Mr. Palm Springs, some would say," Frederick answered him.

"He's a big real estate mogul," Hammond said. "Owns probably a third of the commercial real estate in town. And a big political backer. He likes to stay on the right side of the folks in office."

Which, Stanley thought, *explained why Hammond was cautious about stepping on toes. Still....* "Thanks to that disc, he's become the prime suspect in a murder. He can't have that much power."

Hammond looked as if he might disagree. "Is Vega around tonight?" he said instead.

"He was out by the pool when I went by there a little while ago," Frederick said.

"Why don't you invite him in here for a chat?"

AS IT turned out, Hernando Vega was still at the pool. Frederick sent him a note, and a few minutes later, Vega appeared at the office. He was a small man, dark-skinned, in a bright green shirt and cream-colored trousers. He wore a yellow diamond, too large really, for his small hand. It sent shards of light glancing about the room. He paused in the doorway, looking with suspicion at the men in the room.

"Hernando," Frederick said quickly, smoothly, "you must know Detective Dick Hammond, with the Palm Springs Police Department."

"Homicide," Hammond said.

Vega gave Hammond no more than a faint nod. He turned his attention to Tom and Stanley. "You're the dynamic duo," he said, "from San Francisco."

It wasn't a question, and neither Tom nor Stanley replied. "The gentlemen are giving me a hand with the Barry Palmer thing," Hammond said.

"Which concerns me in what way? I knew Barry, of course, everybody knew him, but frankly I thought he had rather an inflated opinion of himself."

"His prices were too steep?" Stanley asked.

"I don't—" Vega glowered at him.

"At the moment, Palmer isn't the topic of interest, except that he had a boyfriend," Hammond interrupted him. "Jeff Whiting. You did know him, didn't you?"

Vega's face shut down. "I want to talk to my attorney," he said curtly.

"Well, sir," Hammond said, "we can do that. But I'd have to Miranda you first, and take you down to the station and book you, which seems like it would be awkward for everyone, when we could just sit here and chat a bit like civilized people."

"If I am a suspect—"

"Not in the Barry Palmer business you're not. Not yet, anyway. Like I said, it's Jeff Whiting we want to talk about."

The look Hammond gave Vega was challenging, though. Vega couldn't yet be aware that they knew of his rendezvous with Jeff— unless, Tom added mentally, he already knew about the video. But that seemed unlikely.

Vega sighed and came the rest of the way into the room, closing the door after himself. "I'll talk," he said, "up to a point. But I reserve the right to decide when to call my attorney."

"That's fair enough," Hammond said. "Just for the moment, though, you might not want to share this with your attorney. You might prefer that no one else but us know about it."

"And this is informal? Off the record?"

"For the moment." Hammond nodded and signaled Frederick. Frederick turned to the computer and started the video. Vega's eyes opened wide when the room appeared on the screen.

"Why, that's the Marilyn…." He turned angry eyes on Frederick. "You son of a bitch, you've been all this time taping everybody? If I was to go out to the pool and tell—"

"Not everybody, no," Frederick said. "And not all the time, as you'll see. And I hope that you will keep all of this in confidence."

Vega watched the rest of the tape in angry silence, to the point where he could be seen in the hotel room with Jeff Whiting, and then the tape ended. He looked his surprise at the others in the room.

"That's it?" he said. "All that shows is the boy and me in a room together. Two men in a hotel room—it proves nothing. He might have asked to see me to ask for a loan, or… well, or anything."

"I'd say it was a safe bet some money changed hands," Tom said.

Vega looked about to make an angry reply. Then he exhaled noisily. "Okay, okay, so you know about that. So what? That goes on here all the time. I'd guess there's probably half a dozen meetings like that one going on in various suites at this very moment. Unless you're planning prostitution charges… and they'd be very difficult to prove. We're in a hotel. If two men decide to retire to a room for a little matinee action, that's their business. It's not illegal to have sex. And there's no harm in giving someone a gift."

"That's not what we're looking for here," Hammond said. "Frankly, I don't give a rat's ass who you fuck or how much you pay him for it. What I've got is bodies piling up, and you were with one of the dead kids the day he disappeared."

Vega sighed again. "Yes, of course, as you can see for yourself, I was with Jeff that day. I was really very fond of the boy. But he was a strange young man." He shook his head sadly.

"The strangulation stuff?" Hammond said.

Vega's eyes registered his surprise. "You're onto that too? Yes, it was frightening really, to be honest. I didn't like it at all. I tried to convince him I didn't want to do it. I thought it was dangerous, but he was insistent." His smile managed to look both pleased and guilty. "And he could be very persuasive."

"So, you put your hands on his throat," Hammond said. "You choked him while you fucked him."

Vega actually looked astonished by that. "No, no, that wasn't how it happened at all. Yes, I had sexual intercourse with him. I don't mind admitting that. While I was, well, while I was inside him, he put a plastic bag over his head, the sort of thing you get from the dry cleaners, and when we were both getting close to, uh, to finishing, he put his hands up and held the bag tight around his throat, to cut off the air. The plastic stuck to his mouth. I could see he wasn't getting any air. It scared me. I was afraid he really would choke."

"And he did," Hammond said.

"No, he didn't, I tell you. I swear it. Not then, at least, not when he was with me. He had his orgasm, an especially violent one, let me tell you, like to blew me off the bed, and when it happened, his hands let go of the plastic bag. As soon as they did, I snatched it off his head. But he wasn't dead, I assure you. He was happy, laughing. He was a sweet boy, really."

For a moment, Vega looked wistful, remembering. "Afterward, we took a shower together and I… I gave him some money, and I left him there and went back to the pool. That was, what, three days ago, four? I never saw him again. I was stunned when I heard he had been murdered. And heartbroken, to be honest."

Tom was unimpressed with the professed heartbreak. "How much did you pay him?" he asked.

"Well, I gave him two hundred dollars before I left him that day."

Stanley saw Frederick's eyebrows slide upward. Two hundred was well below what he'd suggested previously that the young men got from their clients.

"But we always treated the money as if it were a gift," Vega said in an offended voice. "He never put it so crassly as to suggest that I pay him for the pleasure of his company."

"That's putting a fine line on it."

"Look, I don't care what you think," Vega said, growing belligerent. "I've done nothing wrong."

"Just for the record," Tom said, "where were you on the night of the fifth? The night Barry Palmer was murdered?"

"Where I am most evenings. Right here. At the bar, I mean, or by the pool." He looked at Frederick. "You can vouch for that, surely?"

Frederick looked at him without expression. "Not really. I get so used to seeing certain faces, it's impossible for me to say whether it was this night or another."

"I think maybe we're going to have to take you down to the station after all," Hammond said. "This is too big a deal to just ignore."

Vega was indignant. "I can't imagine why. I told you everything. Jeff was alive when I parted company with him."

"He's dead now. And you were the last person to see him alive."

"But no, that isn't so. I wasn't the last to see him alive. Someone else saw him after I did."

"And who was that?"

"Why, whoever killed him, of course." Vega looked pleased with his rejoinder.

Hammond's cell phone rang. He barked into it, listened for a minute, and put it back in his pocket.

"The damnedest thing," he said to Tom. "We've tracked down a mother for Barry Palmer. She lives in Los Angeles, but she's on her way into town, driving, should be here in about twenty minutes. Let's go meet her." To Vega, he said, "Look, I'm not going to charge you with anything now…."

"That's a wise decision," Vega said coolly. "You haven't a single shred of evidence, and I would indeed have an attorney present before I said anything more to you. Do you hear what I'm saying?"

"Loud and clear. Now you hear me," Hammond said. "We have you tied to a murder victim. If you know anything more than you've told us…."

"Maybe I do." Vega had a coy smile on his face. "But that'll wait until I've talked to my attorney."

"Come on," Hammond said to Tom and Stanley. "I want to meet the grieving mother." And to Vega, as they were going out, he said, "Don't plan any out of town trips for a few days, Hernando. We'll talk some more."

"With my attorney present."

"You can invite the Pope to sit in if you want. I've got three murders to solve, and I—"

"Three?"

"A security guard here," Hammond said. "He—"

"Mario?" Vega's face had gone ashen. "You don't mean Mario, surely."

"I do," Hammond said quietly. "Why? Do you know him?"

"I… no, only casually. From coming in and out," Vega stammered. "I just… I was surprised is all. I hadn't heard…." His voice trailed off.

Watching him, Stanley wondered if his surprise on hearing about Mario had been genuine. It had looked it… but Vega struck him as a wily old bird.

"And, Hernando," Frederick said, "if I may just suggest, about the taping… if you were to share that information…."

"I'd spoil my own fun," Vega said. "I already thought of that. Don't worry, I'll keep my mouth shut." Frederick looked greatly relieved. "But," Vega added, shaking a finger at him, "I don't expect to pay for any more rooms either. For anything, far as that goes. Here on in, I'm on the house."

"So be it," Frederick said wearily.

Chapter Twenty-One

There were two women waiting for them when they arrived at the police station. Sandy at the desk said, "That's Detective Hammond there," as they came in the door. One of the women, a frumpy-looking blonde, hurried to meet them. She had been crying. Her eyes were red-rimmed, and she clenched the shreds of a tissue in one hand.

"I'm Dorothy Palmer," she said, "Barry's mother. And this"—she indicated the other woman, who had followed her across the lobby—"is my friend Elizabeth Whiting."

Tom and Stanley exchanged uh-oh glances.

"Detective," Elizabeth Whiting said, "we've heard about Barry, that he was bitten by a snake, but my son and Barry were the best of friends, and now my son is missing. I've been trying to call him for two days with no luck. Do you think there is any connection with what happened to Barry?"

"Let me guess," Hammond said. "Your son's name is Jeff?"

Elizabeth Whiting was a brunette, tall and chesty. Probably her complexion was dark, but just now it had an ashen quality. She looked like she hadn't slept in days. At Hammond's question, she lifted a multi-ringed hand to her bosom and choked back a sob.

"He's dead, too, isn't he?" she said in a small voice. Hammond nodded.

"Oh, Liz," Dorothy Palmer said, and the two women embraced, crying together. "It's so unreal," Dorothy said over Elizabeth's shoulder. "Those two boys, they've always done everything together. We used to say it was like they were joined at the hip. And now they've gone and died together. It's as if it was fated."

"Ladies," Hammond said, "your sons didn't just die. And it wasn't a snake bite. They were murdered." Both women gaped at him, startled out of their crying.

"But why on earth would anyone do that?" Elizabeth said in a choking voice. "They were such good boys. Perfect sons. And now…." She began to sob again.

Even with Hammond's detective partner out, the homicide office was crowded. He directed the two women to the wooden chairs, and Tom and Stanley took the ones from the other desk. By this time, the mothers had managed to regain their composure. Hammond pushed a box of tissues toward them.

"You couldn't ask for two better sons," Dorothy Palmer said, taking a tissue and honking her nose loudly into it. "I know mothers always say that about their boys, but in this case it's the truth. My husband walked out on me five years ago. He found himself some bimbo, twenty years old, and just left without a word. We haven't heard from him since."

"The bastard," Elizabeth Whiting muttered.

"You can say that again." Dorothy blew her nose louder than before and paused to think where she had been. "So, I got a job as a checkout clerk at a grocery store, but you know what that pays. Barry went to work to support us. From the time he was fifteen, he was the man of the house. And then, when Elizabeth's husband passed—"

"She's putting it politely," Elizabeth Whiting said in an angry voice. "He didn't just pass on. He killed himself."

"How?" Tom asked. "If you don't mind telling us."

She blinked back tears. "No, no I don't mind." She took a moment to compose herself. "He… he hung himself, in the garage. The worst of it is Jeff was the one who found him. I don't think he ever quite got over the shock of that."

She shook her head and stared down at the floor for a moment. "Well, anyway, because it was suicide, the insurance company wouldn't pay off. So, like Dorothy and Barry, we were strapped too. And Dorothy had the bright idea that we move in with them and pool our resources. It seemed the best solution, and the boys had always been good friends. Things were tough for a while, really tough, but we were surviving. And then Barry came in one day to tell us someone had offered him a job here, in Palm Springs. At some resort. I'm not sure exactly what kind of job—I think he was a waiter. Was that right?"

She looked at Hammond, who avoided her eyes. "Something like that," he said.

If she got the message in his evasion, she ignored it. Maybe, Stanley thought, she knew—or suspected—the truth, but no one corrected her.

"Well, anyway," she said after a pause, "he said Jeff could get a job, too, so Jeff joined him. They got paid pretty well it seemed. Of course, we hated to see them go, but we couldn't very well say no, could we? And they both sent their money home. Every week like clockwork, we'd get these money orders. And things did get better for Dorothy and me."

"I even put aside enough to buy us a car," Dorothy said. "That's how we drove down here today. It isn't anything grand, an old Datsun station wagon, but it runs good, and it makes everything so much easier. I don't know how well you know Los Angeles, but getting around without a car is a challenge. Just getting to the supermarket is difficult."

"So, as I said before," Elizabeth said, wrapping up her narrative, "you couldn't ask for two better sons. It's unbelievable that anyone would want to kill either of them, let alone both. Everybody loved those boys."

Which, Stanley thought, was true enough. Certainly the rich old queens at the Inn had been fond of them. And someone, maybe one of those old queens, had loved them overmuch. Loved one or both of them enough to kill. Deadly love indeed.

Chapter Twenty-Two

"I GUESS we need to rethink our opinion of those two young men," Stanley said. "Granted, they were nothing more than high-class hookers, but their hearts were in the right places, I'd say."

"Maybe. It's their dicks got them into trouble," Tom said.

"So often the case, wouldn't you say? I think their mothers were right; they certainly started out as good guys. To take care of their mothers, they traded the only things they had of value—their youth and their beauty. And I don't think either of them thought of themselves as hookers, not at the beginning anyway. But, you know, good and bad have a way of becoming established routines."

"What starts out to be just a temporary thing becomes the usual, you mean."

"Yes. It's like the stuff on the outside seeps inside. You wear a mask long enough, it becomes the face."

Tom's cell phone rang. To his surprise, the caller identified himself as Hernando Vega.

"I'd like to talk to you," he said. "Not at the Inn, please. Maybe you could come by my house?"

"It's late," Tom said.

"Not even eleven. And you need to hear what I've got to say." He gave careful directions, which Tom repeated for Stanley.

"Maybe," Stanley said when they were on their way, "he's going to confess."

The address Vega had directed them to was something of a surprise. The neighborhood was nice enough, if not as grand as some in Palm Springs, but the house itself was nothing more than a stucco-covered cottage dropped like a poor relation on a street of expensive-looking homes. It was not, like Nakamura's house, that the exterior was plain. It was downright dowdy, not much more impressive than the one in which Barry Palmer had lived.

"Doesn't look like the home base of one of the power movers in town," Stanley said as they approached the front door. It was in need of a paint job.

Almost the first thing Hernando Vega did, however, when he opened the door to them, was to shoot down any ideas they might have of his admitting to the murders. "I didn't ask you here to make some kind of confession, if that's what you're hoping for," he said, standing in the doorway. "I didn't kill anybody, and nobody's going to make me say I did."

"Just so you understand, we're not police officers," Tom said. "We're private detectives with absolutely no jurisdiction in this case. Which means whatever you want to tell us is okay. It's not official, and we can keep everything off the record."

"It doesn't matter," Vega said. "What I'm going to tell you can be shared with anyone you like. The more the merrier, as far as I'm concerned. Come in, please."

Like the exterior of the house, the inside was plain to the point of being cheap. He led the way into a sparsely furnished living room—a television atop a wooden table, a worn suede sofa, and two corduroy-covered chairs. A large spotted cat came from behind the sofa to greet him.

"Oh," Stanley said, "a desert lynx."

"You know cats?" Vega asked him, surprised.

"Not a lot." Stanley knelt down to pet the cat. "But I know a beauty when I see one."

"You can pick her up," Vega said. "That's Sheena. She loves people. They're a wonderful pet breed, the desert lynx. In some ways they're more like a dog, really, than a cat. She comes when I call her name, which most cats won't do, and she likes to play fetch."

"Sheena, Sheena," Stanley crooned, "you're the queen of the jungle, aren't you?" The cat came gladly into Stanley's arm and began to purr as he cuddled her.

"So," Tom said, bringing them back to business, "about that security guard, Mario. The way you reacted when you heard he'd been murdered, I'd say you had more than a casual acquaintance with him, didn't you?"

"I knew him, yes."

"Intimately?"

Vega looked at him for a long moment. "I'm not going to answer that," he said. "That wasn't what I invited you here to discuss."

"Fair enough. What did you want to talk about?"

"I wanted to inform you...." Vega hesitated briefly before he blurted out, "I've found Jesus. I stopped by the Baptist church tonight, on my way home. It happened all at once. An epiphany, I think they call it. I stood before the cross, and it was like this sheet of white light just descended on me, and I knew I was saved."

Tom was rendered briefly speechless. He and Stanley exchanged glances.

"Well, whatever works for you," Tom said. "But I don't know why you thought it was important to tell us that."

"But don't you see," Vega said, spreading his hands, "it means I'm innocent. The pastor was there. We prayed together, and he said it means I've been washed in the blood. I couldn't possibly be a murderer."

"I hate to break this news to you," Tom said, "but there's never been any shortage of murderers in the Christian religion. Or any other, for that matter."

Vega looked disappointed by their response to his announcement.

"And does this newfound religion mean you won't be patronizing the Winter Beach Inn in the future?" Stanley asked.

Vega's face registered his surprise. "Why on earth would you think that?" he asked. "What's one thing got to do with the other? Besides, you heard Frederick. In the future, I won't be paying for anything. I'd be crazy to pass that up."

THE SECURITY office was dark when they arrived back at the Inn, the gate open. Tom drove to the back lot, away from the fancier cars of the clientele. They made their way around the building to the side entrance. Although it was late, the pool area was still crowded.

"But everyone seems particularly subdued, don't they?" Stanley said.

"I imagine a string of murders could dampen your spirits," Tom said. "I'm surprised everybody's still hanging around."

"Not too surprising. The stud muffins are here, and where the stud muffins play...."

Tom's cell phone rang. He answered it and recognized Hammond's voice. "I got the ladies installed in a motel room, on the city's tab," he said. "Seems like the least we can do."

"Tough on them," Tom said.

"Definitely. But that's not why I called you. I wanted you to know I just heard from Doc Murphy."

"And?"

"He tells me that the Mario guy had a lot of cat hair on his clothes. Seems like it's a rare kind of cat hair too."

"Let me make a guess," Tom said. "The hair is from a desert lynx cat."

That was met with a pause. "Jesus," Hammond said finally, "how did you know that?"

"We've just been to visit Hernando Vega," Tom said. "And he's got a very friendly pussy."

"Rumor has it—"

"A desert lynx cat."

"Damn. I thought Hernando was hiding something. So, we've definitely got the dead security guard tied to Vega."

"There's more too. Vega has found Jesus."

"Ah. Well shit, then, that sure scratches him off my list of suspects," Hammond said.

"ONLY, I don't take Vega for our killer," Stanley said when Tom had shared the latest with him. They had gone into the club for a drink. It, too, was booming, the bars lined with lithe young bodies, the dance floor crowded.

"How do you figure? We know this Mario guy was spending time at Vega's house. The cat hair proves that."

"Yes, but that's no surprise," Stanley said. "For starters, Vega is a cheapskate. Frederick as much as told us early on that the starting rate for these boys is five hundred a pop, and Vega told us he gave Jeff Whiting two hundred. Which strikes me as the bargain of the month. Why Jeff went along with it, who can say, but Vega isn't dumb. He had to know he was getting a steal. And look at how he lives. He's a rich man and powerful locally, but his home is nothing to brag about. It didn't look all that much nicer than the one Barry Palmer lived in."

"Now there's a thought," Tom said. He took his cell phone from his pocket, started to dial a number, and saw the shake of Stanley's head. "Can I use the phone?" he asked the bartender instead.

The bartender set an old-fashioned princess-style phone atop the bar. Tom took it and dialed Detective Hammond's number. When Hammond answered, Tom asked, "The house that Barry Palmer lived in. You said you had looked at the lease. Who owned the house?"

Hammond hesitated briefly before he answered. "Hernando Vega," he said.

"One more question—make that two. How long had Palmer been living there, and what was the history of the house before that? Had it been renting regularly or sitting empty? Think you can find out?"

"I already know," Hammond said. "It had been empty for more than a year. He tried to sell it, but the market's been down. Not the best neighborhood, not a great house. He leased it to Palmer about eight months ago. For peanuts."

"That explains that," Tom said, hanging up the phone and shoving it back toward the bartender. "Probably Jeff Whiting did live there with Palmer, even though his name wasn't on the lease. Instead of paying them the full amount in cash, Vega was paying them in cheap rent, for a house he was having trouble renting otherwise. Solved two problems for him. Took a dog of a house off the market, and guaranteed that Jeff Whiting would play games with him for reduced rates. Maybe Palmer too."

"Like I said, a real cheapskate." Stanley was thoughtful for a moment. "I just thought of something else, maybe. We know that Mario was paying regular visits to Vega's house, the cat hair tells us that, and I think we can assume it wasn't to discuss real estate investments."

"You think Vega was getting serviced by Mario for a lot less than the boys here?"

"Mario wasn't a bad-looking sort. Not in a league with most of these guys, but to an old queen like Vega, and a real cheapskate, nothing to scoff at. Especially if, instead of a couple of hundred, you could get his pants down for forty or fifty."

"Or less," Tom said. "What if Mario was an illegal, and Vega knew that? He's got enough pull locally. He could probably convince Mario to come across for free."

"Not just a cheapskate," Stanley said, "a real sleazebag."

"So then, let's say Mario balks, he doesn't lower the zipper when told to. And Vega gets pissed and offs him."

"Only, Vega doesn't strike me as a man to act out of sudden rage. He's too scheming. He'd be vengeful if he didn't get his way, but it seems to me, he'd be more likely just to get Mario deported."

"Yeah, probably," Tom agreed, disappointed. He really hadn't liked Vega. He'd have been happy to pin a murder charge on him.

THE CLUB was still going strong, but it was after midnight by now, the end of a long evening. They finished their drinks and went back to the Joan Crawford suite. Tom took the key card from Stanley and opened the door. "I'll be glad to be finished with this place," he said.

"You know, it's funny, but I think I will too," Stanley said.

"It's all too much, isn't it? I mean, sure, luxury, a nice setup for rich old men, probably it even works out well for some of the young guys… like Frederick said, if you're stuck in a job slinging hamburgers…."

"It didn't work out for Barry Palmer or Jeff Whiting," Stanley said. "You know, Wayne, my decorator friend, he likes to say there's no point in lavishing money on the morally defeated, they only spend it on more defeat."

They had left the radio playing, and the music, something electric and jangling, greeted them as they came in.

"Hey, great," Stanley said, sitting to take off his shoes. "Let's dance."

"Stanley, we just left the club. If you wanted to dance…."

"I know, but here we can work on some new moves. Next time we're there, we can show those desert boys how it's done in the big city."

"You know I don't do that kind of dancing," Tom said. He took off his jacket and tossed it on the bed. Threw his holster with the Sig in it on top of the jacket. "Slow dancing is my style. A good old-fashioned two-step, I'm a pro. But this stuff…."

"Well, you could do it, if you put your mind to it. You're just thinking about your hip, but that doesn't have to slow you down any. You have a great sense of rhythm, and Lord knows you can move your body. Come on, let me show you."

He turned up the volume on the radio and, tossing his shirt aside, began to dance in a frenzy, hopping from one foot to the other and waving his arms and hands to the beat. "It's easy, it's just a matter of letting yourself go. Try it."

Tom remained where he was, unmoving. "Stanley, stop dancing," he said in a soft but firm tone of voice.

"Oh, come on, don't be a stick, you can do this, you just—"

"Stanley, for crap's sake, freeze." Louder, firmer. Like a Marine sergeant. "Now, damn it!"

The urgency in Tom's voice got through to him. Puzzled, Stanley nevertheless froze in place. Tom reached out slowly with one hand and turned down the radio until the music was little more than a murmur.

Not until then did Stanley hear what the music had concealed—a faint, almost papery rattling sound. He rolled his eyes downward. A snake, gray-green in color, had slithered out from under the bed and lay coiled no more than two feet away from his bare feet, its head raised, its tongue darting in and out as if in rhythm to the music.

"Tom…." Stanley's bladder threatened to let go. He had a sudden fear he would faint, would topple right over on top of the snake, its head swaying, eyes like onyx fastened on him.

"Don't move. Not a muscle."

"Oh, sure, that's easy for you to say…."

Tom slowly leaned toward the bed, careful not to do anything too suddenly. He seemed not to move at all, but somehow his hand found the Sig, slipped it from the holster, brought it up to his chest. He held it in both hands, sighting down the barrel, holding his breath—and fired.

The snake leapt into the air and fell back upon the carpet, writhing and flinging its rattling tail about. Its head was gone.

Stanley made a great jump, into Tom's arms. "Oh, Tom, that's… that was a rattlesnake."

"At a guess I'd say one of your green Mojaves. They seem to be everybody's favorite around here, rattlesnakewise."

"How did it get in here?"

"Good question." Tom looked around the room. Voices could be heard from outside, and a few seconds later someone banged on the door. Tom threw it open to find Frederick standing outside, his expression a combination of anger and fear.

"I heard a gunshot," he said. "What on earth…?"

Tom nodded toward the snake on the floor, its body still wriggling spasmodically, its rattle only a faint whisper. "We had company," he said.

Frederick stared for a second or two. Then he stepped into the room and closed the door after himself. Before it closed, however, Tom and Stanley had a glimpse of a quickly gathering crowd, young men and old, faces puzzled or alarmed.

But one of them, Tom thought, knew what had just happened. He tried to read the faces, but they were gone too quickly as the door was shut.

"This must be kept absolutely quiet," Frederick said in an icy whisper. "If the guests thought snakes can just slither into their rooms at will, this place would be emptied in an hour."

"Well, pardon me," Stanley said, indignation overcoming the fear he'd felt a moment before, "but it looks to me as if snakes can get into the rooms—and maybe people ought to know that."

"Snakes do not just walk into hotel rooms uninvited," Frederick said. "Or crawl, for that matter."

"I can tell you for sure this one did not knock."

"What he's trying to say, Stanley," Tom said, "is that the snake didn't get in here of its own accord."

"Oh." Stanley deflated. "Are you saying… you think someone…?"

"Someone wanted us dead," Tom said. "Or scared, anyway. And if we happened to die from rattlesnake bites, out here in the desert—not phony ones like Barry Palmer's, but the real thing—would anybody think it was homicide?"

"I certainly would," Frederick said. "The very idea, rattlesnakes in our rooms. It would put us out of business in an instant. Oh!" His hands flew to his cheeks, his eyes wide circles. "You don't suppose…. Is *that* what this whole madness is all about? Someone is trying to drive us out?"

"Could be," Tom said. "It's no secret that you're well protected locally, so if someone wanted you gone, legal maneuvers probably wouldn't do it. But there's bound to be people who disapprove. If they could raise enough of a stink, drive away your customers—"

"Clients," Frederick corrected him.

Tom ignored the correction. "It would be one way to shut you down. We've been thinking of individual motives for killing those three young men, but what if they were just pawns in a bigger game? What if you, this place, were the real target?"

"I'd never even imagined that possibility," Frederick said.

"Well, you'd better start imagining it. And while you're at it, start thinking about who might want to do that."

CHAPTER TWENTY-THREE

TOM PHONED Hammond to tell him about the snake in their room.

"Someone thinks you're getting too close," Hammond said. "They think you know too much."

"I wish I knew what we know," Tom said drily.

"Maybe we know more than we realize," Stanley said. "I think we need to take a step back, get away from it all for a bit."

"Why don't we get away from this place, spend tomorrow sightseeing," Tom said. "Maybe it will give us a new perspective."

Stanley was more than happy to get away from murder and murderous snakes and have Tom to himself for a bit. As time passed, he felt less and less enthusiasm for playing detective.

"What I did for love," he hummed to himself, already looking forward to the day ahead.

BREAKFAST WAS early, after which they hit the road. They explored an Indian canyon, and, discovering a pristine waterfall in another canyon that they had all to themselves, cavorted nude in it until an aging couple—leftovers, clearly, from the hippie era—found them.

"Rad," the man said when he saw them, and in minutes they were naked, too, and splashing about. Tom and Stanley socialized for a bit, until the woman began to take rather obvious notice of Tom's physical attributes, and the man began to cozy up to Stanley. The boys decided it was time to move on.

Joshua Tree National Park was only a short drive away, and they were in luck. The trees did not bloom every year, but just now their spindly branches were covered with creamy white blossoms. The desert cacti were already in bloom, brilliant red and yellow flowers. The desert, grooming itself for its most colorful season.

From there they drove through the nearby town of Twentynine Palms, which offered nothing of interest other than groups of young, buff men—in civilian garb, but easily identifiable as Marines from the local base. Tom hardly noticed them, but Stanley thought a single gay man might enjoy a brief visit, if only for the lovely scenery. Maybe he would mention it to Chris.

It was late in the day when they returned to the Inn. They had agreed with Frederick to keep mum about the snake in their room. Apart from Hammond, they had told only Chris and sworn him to secrecy.

"Frederick's put out the story that you fired the gun accidentally while cleaning it," Chris told them.

"Makes me sound like a putz," Tom said, "but the alternative is going to clear this place out, and we don't want that to happen till we've got things sorted through. Whoever our murderer is, he's someone in this crowd, and I'd like to keep him here."

Which meant, however, leaving the Sig in the room when they went to the club. "Otherwise, it's going to spook everybody," he said.

"It's really not a problem, though, is it?" Stanley said. "I mean, whoever put a snake in our room isn't likely to dump a bunch of them in the club. Talk about pandemonium."

Tom settled for jeans and a body shirt with no jacket, so that everyone could see at a glance he wasn't packing. When they first came into the club, some of the guys looked sideways at him, as if expecting another shooting. By the time they had been there half an hour, though, people seemed to have gotten over their nervousness.

They saw Johnnie Nakamura across the room, but he only nodded in their direction, and Tom thought he caught a glimpse of Randy Patterson on the dance floor, but when he looked a second time, Patterson had disappeared.

"I'm hungry," Chris said. "How about dinner in the dining room?"

"Nah, you go ahead," Tom said. "Stanley and I found a place downtown that we liked. I think we'll go there again."

THEY HAD again left the truck in the rear. They came out of the club by the back door and started along the walk to the parking lot. It was not quite seven but already dark.

Tom debated with himself about whether to go back to the room for the Sig. Probably, he decided, he wouldn't need it while they had dinner. It would be hard for anyone to plant a snake in a restaurant.

They had gone no more than a few feet, however, before he realized they were not alone.

"Uh-oh, trouble," he said, stopping.

Three men, Asian gangster-types in black suits, got out of a dark Mercedes and came toward them on an intersecting path. They were grinning coldly, eyeing Tom and Stanley with evident delight. Their expressions said clearly that they meant business, the kind of business they would apparently enjoy and Tom and Stanley probably would not.

Tom took a quick look around the parking lot. No one else about.

Three on two wasn't the worst odds—he'd fought worse ones many times—but Stanley wasn't a fighter. Stanley liked to say he was a devout coward, but that wasn't true either. Being scared didn't make you a coward. Stanley was a stand-up kind of guy, especially if his partner was in trouble. Not so long ago, he'd killed someone to save Tom. So he could be plenty ballsy. Stanley might look like a flighty queen—hell, he was a flighty queen—but he was tough, too, in a way hard to define, and that was the best compliment Tom could apply to anybody.

But he wasn't a fighter. Which meant Stanley was more likely to get hurt than to hurt one of them. And Stanley's safety was always Tom's top priority. If anybody meant to hurt Stanley, they had to get past him first.

He briefly considered running, not to save his own skin, but to get Stanley away from here—but he doubted they could outrun these guys, who had a car with its motor running just a few feet away. Worse, if you ran and got caught, it not only made you look like a coward, but a fool as well.

Or, if there had been time and room in which to do it, he'd have told Stanley to get into the truck, but the gangsters were between them and the truck, so that wasn't an option either. He flicked another quick glance around. The next best thing was the empty doorway beside them.

"Stanley, get behind me," Tom said. "In the doorway there."

"I don't think—" Stanley started to argue. Stanley liked to argue, and usually at the worst times, to Tom's way of thinking.

"Just do what I say. That way," Tom said, "if these guys take me down, you can still tear them to pieces."

Stanley actually laughed, sounding not at all scared, and stepped behind Tom into the doorway. He knew he ought to be scared, but he had great faith in Tom's ability to deal with this kind of situation. He had seen Tom in action before, and these guys hadn't. Boy, were they in for a surprise.

The gangsters separated. One of them stayed back, and the other two came forward, moving in at angles. With the doorway and the building behind Tom and Stanley, the would-be assailants had every possible escape route covered, if anyone tried to escape. Meaning they had every reason to suppose they had Tom and Stanley trapped.

Tom glanced for only a second at the third man, hanging back. That one hadn't moved, which meant probably he was like some kind of supervisor, or maybe he was the instructor and he wanted to see if his pupils had learned their lessons properly. In any case, for the moment he was not a problem.

But when Tom looked again at the other two, they had just become bigger problems than they had been the moment before. Each of them had come a step closer—and both of them had knives in their hands now. The overhead light glinted off shiny blades. *Tantō*, he thought. Short, thrusting knives, but they could slash and cut, too, as Nakamura had informed him.

"Oh fuck me," Tom muttered under his breath. He hated knife fights. Most especially he hated the ones where the other guys had knives and he didn't.

In his experience, defending yourself against knives involved one primary rule—don't let them cut you. Most important of all, don't let them cut you in the gut, but getting sliced anywhere was not a good idea. Once you started bleeding, you began to slow down and lose strength. A good street fighter with a sharp knife could keep you dancing until eventually you just fell over from the loss of blood. These guys looked like they knew how to use them. And there were two of them.

He wished now the Sig wasn't back in their room. *Had these punks somehow known that?*

He had some good weapons, though. He was a seasoned brawler, he was strong, and he fought hard. His fists were huge and his arms were long, very long. He backed up against Stanley, shoving him back into the doorway, and put one foot up against the doorjamb behind him, next to Stanley, bracing himself with his heel for purchase.

Then he waited. They would almost certainly come at him together, one from each side, coming in like an arrow, using the angles against him, planning to overwhelm him.

If he were arranging things, that's how he'd have set it up. That was something he had picked up on his own in street fighting over the years, but studying the art of samurai had brought it home to him in a new, a more refined, way—*kami-hasso*, the samurai called it. Becoming one with your enemy. Entering not just into his mind, but his body as well. He concentrated, trying to meld with them.

Nobody had spoken, but street smarts told him when there were two of them advancing, somebody had to lead the parade. If they were going to attack simultaneously, one of them had to give the signal. He guessed it would be the one on the right, who was a little taller and a little older. If he was wrong, he was fucked for sure.

He wasn't wrong. The tall one gave an almost imperceptible nod with his chin, and they both came in together, fast, knives held in slashing pattern.

Tom had been watching for the signal, though, and was ready for them. In situations like these, the attackers never expected to be attacked. Aggression could be an effective weapon, too, and Tom knew how to use it. When they charged, he pushed off with his foot from the building and charged at them. It took them by surprise and threw them off slightly, spoiled their choreography. He went right inside the hesitating knives, got each of them hard with an elbow to the face, felt teeth come loose on either side.

That left both of them dazed, but still on their feet. Tom spun around and caught the shorter guy with a punch to his ear, snapping his neck and making him lose his knife. It hit the pavement with a metallic clatter.

Tom didn't wait to see how that played out, but spun again and drove a knee hard into the taller one's belly, knocking the breath out of him in a noisy, "Whoof!"

He spun again and went back to the short one. A kidney punch dropped the attacker to his knees like a sack of potatoes. The tall one moved faster than he should have been able to, though, coming at Tom and swinging his knife in a high arc even as Tom was turning back.

If the knife had landed where it was intended, between Tom's shoulder blades, the fight would have been over, but the guy stumbled as he charged. The assailants had been focused entirely on Tom for the immediate present and had forgotten Stanley in his doorway, but Stanley was not as helpless as he sometimes looked. Plus, in his own way, he felt as protective of Tom as Tom did of him.

He saw they were concentrating entirely on Tom, and taking quick advantage of their mistake, he danced out of the doorway as lightly as a butterfly, put out one foot, and tripped the man charging Tom. As the assailant fell forward, Tom delivered a solid uppercut to the jaw, and he went down too.

The one who'd hung back shouted something in what sounded like Japanese and turned toward the Mercedes. The shorter assailant tried to crawl to the knife he had dropped, but Stanley twirled around, the way he did on the dance floor, jumped into the air, and came down hard on the man's hand. Bones cracked and the man screamed in pain.

Somehow the two gangsters managed to get to their feet and ran toward the car. It was already rolling when they jumped in.

"Baby, nice moves," Tom said, grinning and brushing his hands on his trousers.

"Well, sure, everybody knows I'm a terrific dancer, the hip-hop queen. So, we're just going to let them get away?" Stanley asked.

"No, no, you run after them and stop the car," Tom said. "I'm going to stand here and catch my breath."

"Hmphf," Stanley grunted. He stood hands on hips, watching the dark car skid around the corner of the parking lot and disappear. "What was that all about, do you think? Who were they?"

"Yaks," Tom said.

"Yaks?" Stanley did a double take. "You mean, like those Tibetan cows?"

"Yakuza. Gangsters," Tom said, and added, "Japanese gangsters."

"Japanese?"

Tom nodded.

"But that would mean…."

"Exactly," Tom said. "My guess is they're not local, but Hammond will know if he's got yakuza hanging around town. If not, it means they were imported, probably from Los Angeles, hired by someone Japanese. Someone with enough money and influence to pull that off."

"Nakamura," Stanley said. "He could do it. He probably already has them on his payroll. Especially if they're expensive and hard to come by. But why sic them on us?"

"For the same reason he'd put a snake in our room, or have one of them put it there, more likely. To scare us off."

"Well, I'll admit he's scared me—but not off. It only makes me want to know the rest of the story."

"Me too. I think it's time we take a good hard look at Mr. Johnnie Nakamura, samurai."

"Pretend samurai," Stanley said.

Chapter Twenty-Four

"And I broke somebody's fingers," Stanley wrapped up his telling of the incident.

It was after dinner. They were in Chris's room.

"Shoot. I miss all the excitement," Chris said.

"You are welcome to my share next time," Stanley said.

"So what do you think it meant, these guys trying to ambush you?" Chris asked Tom.

"I think it means we need to get into Nakamura's house somehow," Tom said. "If I can think of a way to do it without getting ourselves arrested."

"I think I know how that can be managed," Chris said with a Cheshire-cat grin.

"What have you got in mind?" Stanley asked. "Tell the truth and shame the devil."

"That house man of his, Yoki, he was interested in little old me. He gave me the eye while we were there for lunch the other day. I feel sure I could distract him."

"You sly puss," Stanley said. "I didn't even see this happening."

"Oh, please, you weren't supposed to."

"You know what this means, don't you?" Tom asked.

"Of course I do. It means I've still got the old magic," Chris said, fluffing up his hair and striking a pose.

"Umm, that too. But I was thinking like, maybe you could get him out of the house for an hour or so."

"So you could do your usual break-and-enter routine?"

Tom grinned. "Legally, it's better if you don't know what we're going to do. That way you're not an accessory to anything."

Chris pondered for a moment. "Maybe not out of the house, but I think I could keep him occupied in his room. It's over the garage, by the way. He did manage to tell me that… when he was giving me his phone number."

"Might work," Tom said. "If he doesn't hear us…."

"Once I get him in the sack, he won't be listening for prowlers," Chris said. "I double damn guarantee that."

IT WAS easy enough to arrange. Chris called the houseman with Tom and Stanley leaning over his shoulders to listen.

"Tomorrow is cook's day off," Yoki said. Chris winked at Stanley. "You could come by in the morning."

Tom mouthed the words "what about your employer," and Chris repeated them aloud.

"The master is never home during the day, unless he has made a date for lunch, and he never does that on cook's day off. Anyway, I happen to know, tomorrow he has an important meeting at his office. The house will be empty."

"Sounds great," Chris said. "What if I come, say, about eleven?" He eyed a question at Tom, and Tom nodded.

"Yes, eleven will be perfect. I will fix lunch for us," he said, and added with a faint giggle, "after."

"If you've still got the strength." Yoki laughed again, louder this time. Chris hung up the phone. "Bingo," he said.

"Mata Hari strikes again," Stanley said.

THE GARAGES were in the rear. Chris drove around and parked there so his car would be out of sight—just in case. He took the stairs to the apartment two at a time, but before he could knock, the door opened.

Yoki stood framed in the doorway, wearing a Japanese robe of muted blue shades. Chris handed him the small potted plant he'd brought.

"A cactus?" Yoki said, surprised.

"Eddie said flowers have meaning for the Japanese. He suggested a cactus."

To his surprise, Yoki tittered. Chris thought at the moment he seemed very much like a little boy.

"What?" Chris asked.

"The cactus is the symbol of sex, of lust."

Chris laughed too. He'd have to have a word with Eddie. He stepped past Yoki and slipped out of his shoes, not bothering with the paper slippers on offer—if things went as he planned, he'd just have to take them off again in a minute or two.

He turned back to give Yoki a hug, and saw that the robe had fallen to the floor in a pale blue puddle. Yoki was splendidly naked, his almond-colored skin gleaming like marble. His excitement was fully evident. He didn't look at all like a little boy now.

"Ah, yes, you did mention lunch," Chris said, opening his arms. Playing detective had never been so appetizing before.

Tom and Stanley parked at the curb half a block back. Tom glanced at his watch. "We'll give him twenty minutes to get things going," he said.

"Make it ten," Stanley suggested. "Chris works fast."

When the ten minutes were up, they left the truck where it was and walked the rest of the way, donning rubber gloves as they went. It took Tom no more than seconds to pick the lock, and they were inside, Stanley's heart beating a fast tattoo inside his chest. The house was eerily quiet, no ticking of clocks, no muted music. Even the air-conditioning was silent.

Stanley hated this part of their work, was always convinced that someone was going to be waiting in ambush for them, or would come in behind them and catch them in the act. Tom, though, was as nonchalant as if he were shopping at a department store.

"Isn't that the room where he keeps his samurai collection?" Stanley asked, indicating the door.

Tom studied it for a moment. Their time was limited, and Nakamura had been too open about inviting him in there to see his treasures.

"We'll skip that one for now," he said. "Seems an unlikely place to me."

"An unlikely place for what? What exactly are we looking for?" Stanley asked in a hoarse whisper.

"Don't know till I find it. Anything that would tie him to the three murders." He glanced again at his watch. "How long, do you think?"

"Twenty minutes."

Tom's eyes widened. "That's all? Twenty minutes?"

"For round one. Five for Chris to get his breath back, and about twenty-five for round two."

They started with what was obviously Nakamura's office. It held two desks. Tom took one and Stanley the other. The desktop was essentially bare, but the drawers were full. The top one held pencils, ballpoint pens, a stapler and a box of staples, scotch tape, index cards. He tried the one below it—address labels, envelopes, canceled checks. The third held bills, receipts, tax forms. He picked out a file that appeared to be business papers, leafed through it, paused to read one.

"He's got a place in Los Angeles too," he said aloud. "Looks like a condo, downtown."

"I thought nobody lived in downtown Los Angeles?"

"That's all changed since they put in the Disney center. There's a Four Seasons Hotel downtown too. Lots of luxury condos."

"Copy the address. I might have to drive into town," Tom said.

Tom turned on the computer and found it, as he had expected, password protected. He tried different words—Nakamura, samurai, even *katana*, but the computer continued to shut him out.

He'd have liked to take it with him. Hammond undoubtedly had techs who could break the code, probably in a minute or two. He couldn't do that, though, considering this was an illegal entry, no matter how you sliced it. He tried without success to think of some way he could convince Hammond it was legit. They'd need a search warrant, and the coincidence of the Japanese gangsters wasn't likely to be enough to get a judge to sign one.

Same with the telephone. He ran through the preprogrammed numbers, found nothing that stood out. Probably, though, Nakamura carried a cell phone with him. That's where the important numbers would be.

Other than the address of Nakamura's Los Angeles condo, the desks offered nothing of interest, nor did most of the house. They went from room to room, quickly, methodically, mindful of the time rushing by, but with no success.

"Aside from that samurai room, it looks as if Mr. Nakamura has no significant interests in life," Tom said.

"But he doesn't strike me as that kind of guy," Stanley said. "I'd have pegged him for a man of varied and probably passionate interests."

"A lover?"

Stanley had to think about that. He had never really imagined Nakamura in sexual terms, and yet, now that he thought about it, he rather supposed he was probably something of a dynamo sexually. Not an attractive man, in Stanley's opinion, but a man with an inner intensity. He was most definitely not the lie-there-and-let-it-happen sort. And in all probability, a top.

"Yes, a lover, and probably a very good one, if you like the type," he said aloud. To which Tom only grunted.

"Doesn't do anything for me," he said.

"Me neither—but I can think of a queen or two…."

They were just about to conclude they were wasting their time, Tom all too conscious of the fact that they were running out of minutes, when they found another locked door at the opposite end of the house from the samurai room.

"Interesting," Tom said, taking his picks from his pocket. "Everything else is so open, so on display. Have to wonder what it is he's got hidden here."

He made short work of the lock and swung the door open.

"Bonanza," he said, pushing the door wide for Stanley to see.

"Zowie," Stanley said, his eyes going wide. He found himself staring into a modern-day torture chamber.

Much of what was on display, he had seen before, of course, and what he had not specifically seen, he had heard of, certainly. Slings and manacles and whips and chains—they weren't that unusual in the gay world. He had friends who were into the bondage and the S and M scenes, although it had never been his thing—in his opinion, pain hurt, period. He had often described his own tastes as Basic Sucking and Fucking 101.

The noose hanging from the ceiling in the middle of the room was new to him, however—erotic asphyxiation, he thought immediately.

"Jeff Whiting," he said aloud. "I'll bet this is where he was killed."

"I'd say this is where they played together. But it's only circumstantial. It doesn't really prove anything," Tom said. "And Whiting was hand strangled. That could have happened anywhere."

"If we could find…."

"Take a look at that table next to you. What do you see?"

Stanley peered down at the empty tabletop. "Uh, nothing, actually," he said.

"Right. It's been wiped clean as a baby's bottom. And I'd bet money so has every other surface in this room. Even if Hammond had his techs dust, I'm guessing they wouldn't find a single print." As if to emphasize his words, he ran a latex-clad finger across the surface of a shelf. It left only a faint smudge.

"We're not going to find anything here. He's too sharp for that." Tom frowned and glanced at his watch. "And it looks to me like it's time we moved out. What do you think?"

Stanley glanced at his own watch. "Right about now, I'd guess Chris and friend are finishing a shower together. After which they'll fix some lunch...."

"Here?"

"Maybe. Not having seen that apartment, it's hard to say. Does it have a kitchen, or not? If not...."

"If not, they'll be coming down here." Tom sighed. "Which makes hanging around too risky. And a waste of time. There's not even any drawers or cabinets in this room to check out. This"—he indicated the torture room—"is interesting. It tells us about Nakamura's tastes, and we already knew about Whiting's. We can take it for granted they were an item. But it doesn't prove anything, and Nakamura is too cagey to have anything incriminating in this house, even behind locked doors."

They let themselves out of the house and walked back to the truck, Tom careful to lock doors behind them, Stanley breathing easily for the first time since they arrived. Tom pulled a U-turn and started back to Palm Springs. Out of habit, he checked the rearview mirror, and for just a second or two, he thought he saw a faded green pickup several vehicles behind them, but then it disappeared in the flow of traffic. He glanced up a few more times, but didn't see it again.

"Something wrong?" Stanley asked.

Tom shook his head. "Just getting a little spooky, I think." He took a last glimpse in the rearview mirror, but there was no sign of a green pickup. He had imagined it.

Chapter Twenty-Five

Since it was his day off, Yoki was rather surprised in the late afternoon when his employer buzzed him, meaning he wanted to see Yoki in the house. Yoki had been lounging about in his robe, savoring the memory of Chris's visit earlier and contemplating when they might arrange a repeat. Chris had said he only expected to be in town for a few more days, which meant probably he would be gone by the time next week's day off rolled around.

Still, Nakamura-san was often away for the day. It would surely not be too difficult to arrange an afternoon session. It need not be cook's day off either. Cook never came out to Yoki's apartment over the garage. Indeed, in nearly two years, Chris was the first one to set foot inside.

Yoki dressed quickly in what he thought of as his valet uniform—black trousers that fitted him like a second skin, and his pristine white tunic. Perhaps Nakamura-san had brought someone home with him for cocktails. That happened rarely, but it did happen.

When he came into the house, though, he found his employer alone, dressed in a yellow silk kimono. So, he had not just come in; he had been here for some time, long enough to change from his business suit into the more comfortable robe.

"Nakamura-san," Yoki greeted him, bowing respectfully from the waist. "Forgive me for being slow to respond to your summons. I did not expect to hear from you."

"No, I am sure you did not." Nakamura stood in the center of the large living room, his hands inside his kimono. His face and his voice were stern. Yoki felt a twinge of concern. He made it a point of honor always to please his employer. Nakamura-san did not look happy just at the moment, however.

"Is my master displeased?" he asked, bowing again.

Instead of answering that question directly, Nakamura-san said, "You had company today."

Yoki looked a bit embarrassed, but no longer felt greatly concerned. It was nothing, then, really. Perhaps he should have mentioned this visit in advance. He knew his master was very jealous of his privacy. In the future he would ask permission beforehand, just to be safe. He liked his job and the man for whom he worked. His pay was generous, and the apartment provided was a very comfortable one.

"Yes," he said with a smile. "A friend stopped by for some time. I hope that I did not exceed the bounds of my service by inviting him to come see me. I thought, since it was my day off—"

"And this friend," Nakamura-san interrupted him and asked almost as an aside, "it was only one friend, was it?" Yoki nodded, puzzled. "Is this friend someone I might know?"

"You met him, yes. Mr. Rafferty. Chris. He was here for lunch, what, three days ago. We… well, we rather caught one another's eyes on that day, so when he called to ask if we might meet—"

"Ah, yes. Christopher. He came for lunch with Tom and Stanley. The San Francisco detectives."

"Yes. And with Eddie." Yoki found himself growing uncomfortable. Something in the way Nakamura-san had pronounced those words— clipped, harsh. *San Francisco detectives.* "They are friends, the four of them. Tom and Stanley and Chris and Eddie."

When his employer continued to glower at him with what was surely an angry expression, Yoki said, "Perhaps I should have asked permission to have Chris visit me. But I did not mean to offend. You have never forbidden me to have friends up to my apartment."

"To your apartment? No, of course not. What you do there is your own business. I told you that when you first came to work for me."

"Then… that is where we were, the whole time. We…." Yoki blushed. "Well, we played about for a bit, and we took a shower together, and afterward I fixed some lunch. But we never came down here, to the house. I swear it. I would not bring someone in here, into your home, when you were away."

He paused. Nakamura-san continued to stare coldly at him. Angrily. Yes, he was angry, Yoki could see that clearly. *But over what?* Frightened anew, Yoki burst out, "Why do you look at me in that way? What have I done that was wrong?"

"And while you were entertaining your new friend, Mr. Rafferty," Nakamura said in an icy voice, "where were his friends?"

Yoki looked momentarily puzzled. "Eddie and…?"

Nakamura made a dismissive gesture. "Do not be a fool. I am not concerned with Eddie. He is of no consequence. It is Tom and Stanley to whom I refer."

"Why… I have no idea where they were. I never saw them. It was just Chris who came…."

"I can tell you where they were, Yoki, exactly where they were while you entertained Mr. Rafferty. They were here, in my home."

"But… but that cannot be…."

"Indeed it is so. They were seen. Tom Danzel and Stanley Korski were seen entering this house, minutes after Mr. Rafferty went into your apartment. And they left only a short time before he did. What would you estimate that span of time to be? An hour, perhaps? A bit less?"

"Oh, no, I cannot believe…." Yoki was aghast now, his mouth hanging open, his eyes bulging.

"It was enough time, certainly, to search to their heart's content, to seek out my most private secrets, would you not say?"

Yoki gasped, covering his face with his hands. "I cannot believe…. I trusted him. I thought he was genuinely interested in me…."

"As I am sure he was. And why should he not be? You are an attractive young man, Yoki. I am sure that your guest enjoyed your little interlude very much. But it was not your physical charms alone that brought him here. You do understand what I am saying, do you not?"

Yoki began to cry, tears coursing down his cheeks. Suddenly, with a loud groan, he dropped to his knees and crawled clumsily toward his employer, head bent. He took hold of the silk of Nakamura's kimono and buried his face in it.

"Oh, master, master, forgive me," he cried. "I am so ashamed. I have betrayed you."

"Yes, Yoki, you have," Nakamura said above him, standing statue still. A lengthy silence was broken only by Yoki's abject sobs.

Finally, Nakamura said, in a low voice, "You know what you must do now, to erase your shame, to atone for your betrayal." It was a statement, not a question.

Yoki lifted his tearstained face. Moments before, his master's hands had been inside the folds of his kimono. Now he held a small sword in them. The *wakizashi*. The knife of atonement. The blade glittered like ice in the late day sun.

Yoki's eyes widened in fear. "Master… you do not mean…?"

"It is the only way," Nakamura said.

Chapter Twenty-Six

Tom and Stanley stayed late at the club, waiting for a glowing Chris to join them. "Maybe we can arrange a repeat," Chris said when Tom told him of their lack of results.

"Sounds like fun, but don't do it on our behalf," Tom said. "I'm thinking of other possibilities."

They left Chris at the bar and went back to their room just a little tipsy, and enjoyed a long and satisfying bout of sex. After which Tom slept like the proverbial log and woke famished.

"Let's go out for breakfast," he said while they showered together. He soaped up Stanley's back and scrubbed it thoroughly, making sure he reached all the sheltered places.

"You don't like the café here?" Stanley gave him a quick kiss and climbed out of the shower, handing Tom an oversized bath towel.

"No, it's fine. I just get tired of the same old." Tom dried Stanley's back, and Stanley returned the favor. In the bedroom, a red light was blinking on the telephone.

"We've got a message," Stanley said, slipping into a pair of jeans and pulling a polo shirt over his head.

Dressed, Tom phoned the desk and was told there was a package for him.

Since the incident with the yakuza, Tom had changed his mind about leaving the Sig behind in their room. Things had gotten a little too hairy for that. He donned the shoulder holster and wore a light windbreaker to cover it. Better to be a little overdressed in the desert heat than have to deal with any more ambushes.

It was another perfect desert morning. Already they could hear the voices of men, young and old, gathered around the pool, but they went in the opposite direction to the lobby.

The clerk saw them coming and handed Tom a plain manila envelope as he walked up.

"Who left this?" Tom asked, taking the package.

"He didn't give a name. An Asian gentleman in a dark suit. He said it was something you needed to see. He said you'd understand."

Tom took the envelope from him. He had a bad vibe about this. Anonymous packages weren't usually good news. Could be some kind of explosive device, or that stuff, what did they call it, anthrax. He held it in his hands for a moment, wondering. Should he get in touch with Hammond, have his experts open it? He gave it an experimental shake. Something rattled faintly inside.

"Do you think…?" Stanley asked.

"Too flat for a rattlesnake," Tom said. And too light to be a bomb. It weighed almost nothing. Coming to a decision, he undid the clasp and turned the envelope up. Three photographs slid into his hand.

"Ah, shit," he said, staring at the photos in dismay.

"What?" Stanley asked.

"You don't want to see," Tom said, but Stanley was not so easily put off. He snatched the photos out of Tom's hand and looked at them.

There were three of them, showing the same scene in a sequence of events. In the first one, Nakamura's house man, Yoki, knelt naked on the floor, a silk scarf tied over his mouth, apparently to stifle any screams. He held a long, curved knife blade in both hands, its point pressed against his bare belly.

In the second picture, the blade had sunk in almost to the hilt. Yoki's neck was taut, his mouth straining against the silk scarf, his eyes wide with shock and pain.

In the third photo, he had toppled over onto the floor, his guts spilling out of the gaping wound in his abdomen.

"That's… that's barbaric," Stanley gasped, letting the photos fall from his hand. They fluttered to the marble floor. "That bastard killed him."

"No, Yoki almost certainly killed himself," Tom said. "This was the way to restore his honor. It's called *seppuku*. He had disgraced himself, shamed his master."

"By letting us get into the house? But how did Nakamura know we'd been there?"

Tom shrugged. "Video surveillance, maybe. I looked, and I didn't see anything, but these days electronic equipment is a lot more sophisticated than it used to be."

He was thinking of that glimpse he thought he had gotten on their way back, of a green pickup truck tailing them. But why would cowboy

Randy Patterson be spying on them for the Japanese businessman? They seemed an unlikely pair to be in cahoots.

"Or maybe he just left some kind of trip wire so he could tell if anyone had been inside. Maybe nothing more than a hair on a doorframe, to show him it had been opened. He knew, is the important thing. Enough anyway to grill the houseman."

"Who probably caved pretty easily," Stanley said. "He wasn't the warrior type. He was just a sweet kid."

"It's my fault. I screwed up," Tom said. "I should have realized Nakamura would expect us to take a closer look at him after the yakuza attack backfired on him. He'd have known then that he was our number one suspect. And he must have known we'd hit his house. I should never have let Chris drag the houseboy into it. This was inevitable, given Nakamura's samurai mindset. He'd have accepted nothing less from Yoki."

"I still say it's barbaric," Stanley said hotly. "And stop blaming yourself. You didn't do this. He did."

Tom ran his hands over his eyes. A fourth young man dead, and they were no closer to pinning down the killer than they had been before. Nakamura seemed the likeliest suspect, but there was no real proof. These photos showed young Yoki killing himself. No jury would convict Nakamura of it. As for the other deaths, there were too many questions still unanswered. What was Randy Patterson's part in all this? And could they really write off Hernando Vega?

"Now what do we do?" Stanley asked.

"I want to nail this bastard, if only for this."

"Good plan. But how exactly do we go about doing that?"

Tom considered for a moment. "I'm thinking about that condo in Los Angeles. We've been looking around here in Palm Springs. He'll expect us to continue. This is where the murders have taken place, after all. He likely wouldn't expect us to turn our attention to LA. But now that I think of it, that's where I should have been looking in the first place. If there's any guilty secrets to uncover, that's where they're going to be."

"Great. When do we go?" Stanley asked.

"I'm going this afternoon. You're staying here."

"But why?"

"First off, you'll be making our presence here known. If Nakamura or his spies see you, they'll think I'm close by. He knows how protective I am of you. He'll never imagine that I'm leaving you on your own.

Second, you'll be out of mischief here. No arguments. And I want you out of that room of ours. You'll move in with Chris."

"That's the first place he'll think of."

"That's okay, as long as he thinks I've just gone to the store for something. And just to be safe, I'll have Hammond send someone to keep an eye on you."

"Oh, Chris," Stanley said suddenly, stooping down to pick up the photographs he had dropped. "He can't see these. It would kill him."

"If he tries to arrange an encore with Yoki, he's going to find out."

Stanley took another look at the photographs, and wiping a tear from his eye, he shoved them back into the manila envelope.

"I'll discourage the encore," he said. "But I want to see that SOB pay."

"He's going to, don't worry."

Chapter Twenty-Seven

"Keep your cell phone turned on and charged up," Tom said. "I'll call you if I learn anything. And if anything looks the slightest bit fishy to you, call me. Meantime, stay close with Chris and Eddie. There's safety in numbers. Plus Hammond's sending a plainclothes detective to keep an eye on the three of you."

"I still wish I were going with you," Stanley said.

"This is more a one-man kind of operation," Tom said. "You just concentrate on staying out of mischief. I'll be back by evening."

Of course, the bodyguard Hammond sent them could not have been more obvious. Everyone else out by the pool was in bathing suits or, for the older men, tropical shirts and trousers, while the detective, seated at the table next to Stanley and friends, wore a suit, the jacket necessary to conceal the gun under his shoulder. He was sweating profusely in the Palm Springs heat. People noticed him.

"We might as well be wearing fairy wings," Chris said in a whisper. "Everybody's looking at him."

"There's an old expression: only the dead fish swims with the current," Stanley whispered back. "In case you haven't noticed, some of the glances our friend there is getting are downright lustful."

Chris and Eddie looked around. Stanley was right. "Maybe we should claim him for our own, move him over here with us," Eddie said.

"He is cute, sort of. In a loutish way," Chris said.

"That's because he is a lout," Stanley said. "He looks to me like he flunked sandbox."

Chris laughed. "I even gave him the smile. You know, *the* smile, and I got no response."

"Maybe," Stanley said, "that just means the years are passing you by."

Chris snorted his disdain. "The years may have passed you by, but I assure you I have made note of them and taken every precaution."

Stanley took another good look at their bodyguard. "He's straight," he said. "No, I mean, seriously straight. He's even pretending not to know he's being cruised. How much straighter can you get than that?"

They had just finished a first round of Cuba libres—plain cola for the detective. Eddie waved to the waiter for another round. At the next table, the detective's cell phone rang. He spoke into it briefly, disconnected, and leaned over to Stanley's table.

"That was my sergeant," he said. "Something's come up. I have to leave for a few minutes."

"What about us?" Stanley asked. "You're supposed to be looking after us."

"I'll be back in ten minutes, fifteen tops. You stay right here." He glanced around. "Lots of people. Nothing can happen to you here, okay?"

When he had left, Chris said, "Frankly, I'm glad he's gone. It would be different if I could get a tumble out of him. I still say he's kind of attractive, though."

"Oh, get real, the only attractive part is dangling down his left thigh."

"You noticed that too?"

"Well, it would be hard not to notice, and we're not the only ones."

"Unfortunately, it's obviously not going to do me any good." Chris looked around. "And he's not helping our social standing here either. We couldn't look more conspicuous if we tried."

"And heaven knows we have never tried to be conspicuous," Stanley agreed with a relieved laugh. "Look, I forgot my sunscreen—it's back in the room. I'm going to go get it before I turn into a potato chip."

"You want me to come with you?"

Stanley shook his head. "No, it's straight there and straight back. Don't let my drink get warm."

Stanley had gotten almost to the door of the Alice Faye suite when Randy Patterson suddenly came into the corridor from the bar, hurrying straight toward him.

"Stanley," Patterson said, "come with me, quick."

Stanley couldn't have been more surprised. "Come with you where?" he asked suspiciously.

"There's a bunch of gangsters out by the pool, hunting for you."

"I was there a minute ago—"

"They just came in. Japanese yakuza, and they look plenty mean."

Stanley hesitated. "Maybe they're not looking for me," he said, but without conviction.

Patterson snorted. "They aren't here to cruise the pretty boys. Come on, we'll go out the back way, through the kitchen. My truck's right outside in the alley. We can disappear before they figure out that something's gone wrong."

Stanley hesitated, reluctant to go with Patterson. Hadn't Patterson been tailing them? Hadn't he searched Barry Palmer's house? "I'd better call Tom." He took his cell phone out of his pocket.

"Call him from the truck," Patterson said. He took Stanley's arm, all but dragging him in the direction of the kitchen. Stanley weighed his options. He couldn't go back to the pool, if the yakuza were there, and he couldn't stay here, either—if they came looking for him, he wouldn't be hard to find. Maybe Patterson was right—not about the truck part of it, but maybe he'd be better off outside. Probably they wouldn't think of looking for him in the alley.

"What about Chris and Eddie?" he asked aloud.

"I didn't see Eddie, but Chris ducked out the minute these guys showed up. I think he slipped into the bar. But these guys aren't interested in them. It's you they want to see."

Stanley remembered the yakuza who had ambushed him and Tom before. Only, Tom wasn't with him now, and if these were the same guys, one of them was probably holding a grudge over some broken fingers. People could be very touchy.

Stanley came to a halt. "I should say something to Chris at least."

"No time. I'll fill him in once you're out of here."

Stanley's instinct was to resist. Tom had told him to stay put. But Tom hadn't been expecting the yakuza to show up here looking for him either—and he truly did not want to tangle with them again, not on his own.

"Plus, I promised Tom I'd kind of keep an eye out," Patterson said. "He'll be seriously pissed if I let anything happen to you."

Stanley glanced in the direction of the pool in time to see a dark-suited man step into the doorway. For the moment he was blinded by the bright sunlight outside and the darkness here, but it would be no more than seconds before he spotted Stanley.

"Okay," Stanley said, hurrying across the room, head down, eager now to be outside. The club was empty but for a bartender polishing glasses and one couple dancing romantically to a slow number. Stanley went through a beaded curtain and was in the hallway that ran past the restrooms to an exit door at the rear.

"This way," Randy said, taking Stanley's arm and shoving the door open.

"Only," Stanley said, stopping again, "how did you know those guys were looking for me? I mean, they could have just been hanging around."

"Better safe than sorry," Randy said. He put a hand at Stanley's back and shoved him through the door. Stanley stumbled into the alley and saw a dark Mercedes sitting just outside, motor running, doors open. He'd seen that car before....

"Oh, crap," he said. When he attempted to step back, however, he found one of the yakuza right behind him, blocking any escape. The other two came at him from each side, grabbing his arms and propelling him toward the open door of the Mercedes. He was shoved roughly into the back seat, one of the gangsters on either side of him, the third behind the wheel. The doors slammed shut.

When he looked past the man next to him, out the window, Stanley saw Randy standing in the open doorway, looking after them, his face perfectly blank. The truth was inescapable. Randy had set him up.

Once they got on the 111 and he saw road signs for Palm Desert, he knew where they were going. And, really, it was perfectly clear, wasn't it?

Who would have Japanese gangsters doing his bidding, if not a wealthy Japanese businessman and onetime movie star? B-movies, he reminded himself.

But what did Mr. Nakamura want with him? *Surely he doesn't think I'm going to commit* seppuku *to satisfy his samurai honor?*

He looked out the window of the car at the passing desert. The yellow sage was in bloom. A mesquite seemed to claw angrily at the sky. A swirl of dust rose up about it like a swarm of hornets and settled back to the ground again.

Another thought popped into his mind—their police department bodyguard's disappearance had been awfully convenient. Someone, apparently, had pulled some strings.

He had a pretty good idea who too.

CHAPTER TWENTY-EIGHT

BACK AT the pool, Chris glanced at his watch. Stanley had been gone a long time, it seemed to him. The waiter had brought yet another round of drinks—and their bodyguard still hadn't returned. Things were not looking good, in his opinion.

"I'm going to go look for Stanley," Chris announced.

"Maybe I'd better come with you," Eddie said.

"Might be a good idea. Tom said we should stick together. I should have gone with Stanley to the room." Mentally he was kicking himself for not going with him, but it had seemed safe enough when Stanley suggested it—straight there, straight back.

It was evident when they got to Chris's room that Stanley wasn't there. "And here's his sunscreen that he came to get," Chris said. "It doesn't look like he even got this far."

"Would he have gone to the bar?" Eddie asked.

They stopped there, but no Stanley. Randy Patterson was nursing a drink. Chris asked him if he had seen Stanley, but Patterson grunted a negative and drained his glass. It did not appear to be his first drink.

Now what? Chris wondered. He took his cell phone from his pocket and dialed Tom's number. The phone was out of service. Well, it would be, wouldn't it, if Tom were doing one of his breaking and entering routines.

"I guess we go back to the patio and wait for Detective Hammond's man to return. Then he can call his boss and get some advice."

"Do you think…?"

"I think something is definitely rotten in Denmark."

"STANLEY," NAKAMURA greeted him. "So good of you to pay me a visit."

"Like I had any choice," Stanley snapped. "What's this all about, anyway, Nakamura-san?" The last syllable toxic with sarcasm.

"Oh, I think you know. You and Tom had begun to look a bit too closely in my direction. Searching this house was a mistake. It told me how you were thinking."

"So, speaking of mistakes, sending your gangsters to rough us up told us how you were thinking."

"Yes. That perhaps was not wise. I did not appreciate what a warrior your partner is."

"Plus you killed Yoki. That sweet young man."

"Indeed I did not. Yoki chose the path of honor. It is the samurai way. He knew what was expected of him. Speaking of your Tom, where is he? He seems to have vanished. My men reported that he was not at the Inn with you."

"Believe me, you'll see him soon enough. As soon as he's heard you had your goons snatch me, you won't have to worry about finding him. He'll find you."

"Exactly what I wish for. Come with me, Stanley."

Stanley looked over his shoulder, but the trio of dark-suited gangsters was still there, preventing any hope of escape. And there was no chance of getting to his cell phone. But who would he call anyway? By now, Tom was in Los Angeles, at least two hours away. Okay, given the way Tom sometimes drove, an hour and a half. Still too far to do him any good. He had no choice but to go where Nakamura led him—which was exactly where he had expected, to the locked room at one end of the house. The S and M chamber.

"I believe you saw my playpen the last time you were here," Nakamura said, unlocking the door and ushering Stanley inside.

Stanley paused inside the door, looking around. "This is where you and Jeff used to play, isn't it?" he said aloud.

"Exactly. Interesting little specimen, young Jeff," Nakamura said. "Sit down, Stanley." He pointed to a plain wooden chair in the middle of the room.

"You're indecent, you know that, don't you? Not to say immoral."

"That is only your definition. To the Japanese, decency is public, morals a private matter."

"If you think I'm going to kill myself—"

"Kill yourself?" Nakamura laughed. "Oh, no, Stanley, *seppuku* was not what I had in mind."

"But you are going to kill me, aren't you?"

Nakamura paused then and looked long and hard at him. "I had thought...." He hesitated. "Tell me, Stanley, suppose I did not. Suppose I spared you. Would you be grateful? Would you be willing to become my *kōhai*?"

Stanley didn't know the word, but he thought he got the gist of it well enough. He was astonished. This man who could have the pick of the beauties lounging about the pool at the Inn was propositioning him?

Nakamura interpreted his silence as meaning he was considering it. "I could set you up in your own little *bettaku*, a love residence. I am a wealthy man, wealthy and generous. And a man of exquisite tastes, as you know." He paused and said in a lower voice, probably, Stanley thought, intended to be persuasive, "Some say I am an excellent lover."

"I have a lover."

"But if he were gone...?"

"He won't be. You're dreaming. Tom is as tough as they come."

"Still, I am thinking, Stanley... perhaps a lover is not what is best for you. The sort of young man you are. Perhaps you would be happier with a daddy. I do not mind playing that role in a young man's life. I rather enjoy it, to be honest."

Stanley flashed back on his own father, his real "daddy." What a twisted relationship that had been. There had been a time when it had been loving—or he'd thought it had been, at least. His mother had been distant, vague, and then she had died in an automobile accident—but he and his father had been close. When he had been a boy.

It was the gayness that changed everything, his homosexuality. If he had been willing to keep that hidden, to stay in the closet, their love might have survived. Once he came out to his father, though.... But was that really love, what they had known, if in order to have it, he had to pretend to be someone other than who he was? He had thought not, had initiated the conversation that was the death knell for their relationship. They had lived together for a time after that, but there was no longer any affection between them.

In time, his father had been confined to a nursing home. Stanley visited him as often as he could, but his father rarely spoke to him, rarely even looked at him, and when he did, it was with loathing.

"No," he said aloud, giving his head a shake, "I don't want a father figure."

Nakamura actually looked disappointed. "Ah, so," he said, "my offer does not interest you, then?"

"Not in the least."

"That is unfortunate. It could have been your salvation."

"My salvation?" Stanley snorted his disdain. "You're pathetic, you know."

"You may think so, but thus far the gods have smiled upon me."

"*Natura deficit, fortuna mutatur. Deus omnia cernit.*"

"I'm afraid my Latin is crude...."

"Nature fails us, fortunes change, God beholds everything from above."

"Ah." Nakamura nodded, considering. "Then he sees what I am about to do. If he did not want it done, he could strike me with lightning, could he not?"

He took some electrical wires from a shelf near where he stood.

"What are those for? Are you planning on torturing me?"

"No. I'm going to make you into a human bomb."

"A bomb?" A shudder went through Stanley's body.

"Yes. Oh, I am not going to blow you up here—I would not want to take out this house. That would mean destroying a very special collection. And even if I am to lose it personally, I could not do that to my treasures. But yes, I am going to blow you up. In due time."

"Tom was right. He said you were a snake. Why don't you rattle your tail for me?"

Nakamura laughed. "You have a great sense of humor, Stanley. I shall miss that. But it is funny you should mention snakes."

"Oh, that was you, too, wasn't it? The snake in our room?"

"My friends put it there, yes. I thought it might discourage you from seeking further." Nakamura approached him with the wires. "I am going to attach these to you. Take off your shirt, if you please."

Stanley leaned away from him. "You aren't putting that stuff on me. I am not going to be your bomb."

"There is an alternative. If you look at that desk over there, you will see a syringe lying atop it. If you would prefer the syringe...."

Stanley looked at the syringe. He had a good idea what was in it. "Okay," he said, tugging his shirt over his head, "start strapping."

"A thousand pardons, Stanley." Nakamura began to tape the electrical wire to Stanley's bare chest.

"Yeah, sure, I get it, this hurts you more than it does me."

"You say that in jest, but it is probably true. When the bomb goes, you most likely will not feel a thing, but I will be sadly aware of what has been lost."

"Yes. Your ass when Tom gets hold of you."

"You think he will kill me?"

"I'm sure of it."

Nakamura shrugged. "Perhaps. And perhaps that is as it should be. I think it may be that mankind needs the periodic shedding of blood. Like those ancients who worshipped at the cult of Mithras. I am sure you know about them. Maybe we, too, need from time to time to descend into the grave."

Stanley watched the electrical wire being wrapped around his chest. "What was it Arendt said, about the banality of evil? I guess the next thing will be sticks of dynamite? This is so Dick Tracy, you know."

"I am afraid I do not know this Mr. Tracy."

"He's like Tom, with a square jaw."

"Ah, I see," Nakamura said, in a voice that indicated he did not. "But no, not dynamite. We are a bit more sophisticated than that. There will only be these two small packages." He taped them to Stanley's chest using duct tape. "Separated, like this, they are harmless. When combined, the results are swift and explosive. The electrical wires are just the means of combining them. So it can be done at a distance, you understand."

"So you won't get hurt, of course."

Nakamura stepped back to look at his handiwork. "You misunderstand, Stanley," he said, satisfied. "I am a samurai. I have failed. My role in the deaths of those young men will soon be made public. It is not my plan to survive, only to die with dignity. But you will die first. You and Danzel-san."

Chapter Twenty-Nine

Tom hated being separated from Stanley. He'd always heard about distance making the heart grow fonder. In his case, it made his balls start aching. It was funny, they could sleep together every night in the same bed, and most of those nights he was content with just holding Stanley close and waiting for the inevitable signal from Stanley that he was ready for something more.

When he was away from Stanley, however, his dick got testy. He couldn't stop thinking about sex, and the mere thought of a crack, even the crack of dawn, had him pole-vaulting.

He had called his old friend Inspector Bryce before he left Palm Springs, to see what Bryce could find out about Randy Patterson. He was coming into downtown Los Angeles now, and he called again to see what Bryce might have learned.

"LAPD found a Randy Patterson who was a bit player in movies," Bryce told him. "Beyond that, there's not much. No arrests, not even a traffic ticket. Meaning, he's very clean, or someone with a lot of pull has cleaned up any record."

The information struck a jarring note. "What kind of movies?"

"Ah…." Bryce paused to read something. "Samurai flicks, it looks like. Rising Sun Studios, if that means anything."

"I'm not sure."

Tom thanked him for his help and disconnected. And puzzled over what he had learned.

Now, what was that about? Randy Patterson had lied to him about the movies, had said he'd never gone that route. But why? Most Hollywood types, they got a minute on-screen, they told you about it endlessly, like they were in line for an Oscar.

Why had Patterson wanted to hide his movie "career"?

The building in Los Angeles where Nakamura lived was about what Tom would have expected—sleek and modern, fifteen floors, not far from the city's rejuvenated Japantown. He coasted slowly past the entrance and saw a uniformed security guard in the well-lit lobby.

He drove on for a few blocks, changing streets, looking for a commercial block. He found one over two streets, and a block after he'd found it, saw a flower shop. He parked illegally and went inside, making a bell over the door jingle.

The shop appeared at first to be empty, but the bell's summons brought a pretty young Japanese woman through a beaded curtain at the rear. She smiled brightly and said, "Good evening, sir, may I be of assistance?"

He glanced at a cooler with a glass door, shelves of blossoms inside. He didn't know much about flowers, but roses he could recognize. "Yes," he said. "I'd like some roses. A dozen of them."

Her smile widened. He guessed roses were pricey.

"Do you have any particular color in mind?" she asked.

The only roses visible in the cooler were deep red. "Red ones, I think," he said.

"Very good, sir. Did you want them arranged?" When he looked blank, she said, "In a vase. With, perhaps, some baby's breath and...."

"No, just wrap them for me."

She smiled and bobbed her head and took the container out of the cooler. She laid a sheet of green tissue on the counter and carefully counted out a dozen roses, which she placed on the tissue, and wrapped the paper neatly around them in a cone, stapling it discreetly on the back side before she put the bucket of roses back in the cooler.

"Would you like to write a card for them?" she asked, indicating a revolving rack of miniature cards next to the cash register.

"No," he said, and then changed his mind and spun the rack slowly, looking at the available choices: happy birthday, happy anniversary, congratulations.... He found a blank one and pulled that out. She handed him a pen from the desk.

"Would you write it for me," he said, and added in explanation, "no one can read my scribbling."

She bobbed her head and picked up a pen from the counter. "Very good, sir." She had clearly been trained in the principle of the customer is always right.

"With love," he said, "from Tippi."

When she looked a little uncertain, he spelled it for her. She wrote it in a small, neat script, slipped the card into an envelope, and offered it to him. He nodded to the flowers, and she tucked it among the blossoms.

He drove back to the apartment building and parked in the delivery zone out front. Inside, he paused in the lobby to look at the tenant list on the wall next to the elevators. Saw Nakamura's name listed on the fourteenth floor. Only one neighbor.

"Help you?" the guard asked.

"Flowers for Mrs. Animoto." Tom looked surprised, as if he hadn't seen the security man there until now. He held the roses up for the guard's inspection.

The man stood up from his desk and reached out a hand. "I'll take them," he said.

"Deliver them personally, that's my instructions."

The security guard gave him a long suspicious look. Tom maintained a façade of innocence.

"I'll call her and tell her you're on the way up," the guard said, relenting.

"Spoil the surprise."

"Some people don't like surprises," the guard said flatly. He dialed and spoke briefly into the telephone.

She was waiting at her door, looking both pleased and puzzled, when Tom stepped off the slow-moving elevator. He saw her and walked toward her, holding out the flowers for her to see.

"Roses? For me?" she said.

"From Tippi," he said, handing her the bouquet.

"Tippi? But I don't know anyone named Tippi."

Tom shrugged. "I don't take the orders, ma'am. I just deliver."

"But I…." She looked addled.

He glanced up and down the empty corridor and lowered his voice to a confidential tone. "You want my advice, ma'am? They're very pretty flowers, expensive too. Someone paid for them. And I was paid to deliver them to you. If I were you, I'd take them inside, put them in some water, and enjoy them. Let Tippi figure out what went wrong."

She looked down at the roses and then smiled at him. "Yes, they are pretty, aren't they? Well, I suppose...."

"Good afternoon, ma'am," Tom said, before she had time to think it through any further. He backed away, half turned as if he were on his way to the elevator. She smiled again, timorously, shook her head, still bewildered, and stepped back into her apartment. The door closed softly after her.

Leaving Tom alone in the hall. He figured he had maybe fifteen minutes before a suspicious security guard got to wondering what was keeping him and came looking. Not much time, but maybe enough to see something.

He went to Nakamura's door, slipped his lock picks from his pocket.

Chapter Thirty

The apartment inside was dark. He shined his penlight around a living room furnished in sleek modern—glass, chrome, lots of black leather. He was about to leave the room when he saw a row of framed photographs atop the dresser. He crossed the room and shined the light on them—and found the cowboy from Palm Springs, Randy Patterson, smiling up at him.

He flashed the light on the other photos. There was one of Nakamura and the dead wife, one of the wife alone. Patterson was in all the others, nine or ten of them. Alone, or with Nakamura in two more. In one, they stood side by side, and in the other, Nakamura had his arm around the younger man's shoulders.

Another of Nakamura's boyfriends, which neither of them had thought to mention? Or… he picked up the one of the two of them together, the one where Nakamura had his arm about Patterson's shoulders. Patterson was looking at the camera, unsmiling. Looked downright sullen, in fact, but Nakamura was beaming down at him with an expression on his face that could only be pride.

Seeing them together like this, close, Tom saw what he hadn't noticed before—the family resemblance. It was slight. The boy must have taken after his mother—not the late Japanese wife, obviously, but the clerk in the studio mailroom that Patterson had talked about. Who dated some second-stringers. Like, maybe a second-rate actor in samurai movies. The mail clerk who got pregnant and raised the boy alone, but with financial help from the father.

But he'd seen it before, all the hints; he just hadn't put it together. He'd attributed the cowboy's dusky skin to the desert sun, but there had been a tint to it already. And the oddly tilted eyes, not exactly Japanese eyes, but maybe he'd had some surgery to hide his parentage—that wouldn't be surprising for a bastard with a Japanese father.

And on that score, staring at the picture, there was no doubt in Tom's mind. The cowboy Randy Patterson was Nakamura's son. The pride with which Nakamura was beaming down at him was fatherly pride.

He had to think that out: there was something somebody had said that was nagging at the back of his mind. Time was running short, though. He put the picture back on the dresser and left the room, moving quickly now.

The door next to the bedroom opened into some kind of den or study. When he flashed the light around, it bounced back from a pane of glass. He stepped into the room, flashed the light at the glass again, and something moved. Gray-green bodies slid around one another, raising their heads toward the light, tongues flicking, tails rattling.

Green Mojaves. Three, four, five—it was hard to count, the way they were twisted up together. Enough of them, for sure. Probably enough venom to wipe out half of Palm Springs.

Tom stared and thought of Nakamura, back in Palm Springs. And his son, Randy Patterson, in Palm Springs. And Stanley, alone. In Palm Springs. Stanley, who was a magnet for trouble.

He let himself quickly out of the apartment, ignored the clunky elevator, and took the stairs down, two and three at a time.

"What kept you?" the guard asked when Tom burst into the lobby.

"Had to tie my shoestring," Tom said and ran past him without pause, out of the building.

THE MIDAFTERNOON traffic out of the city was barely crawling. He dodged in and out as best he could, but he was almost to San Bernardino before he began to make any time. When he did, he flipped open his cell phone and called Hammond.

"I'm on my way in. It's Nakamura. He's our killer."

"Yeah, we know that now. Only trouble is, he's a couple of jumps ahead of you, sorry to say," Hammond said.

"Meaning?"

"Meaning, he's got your boyfriend."

Something tightened in Tom's chest. "Stanley?"

"Unless you got another one I haven't met. Says if you want him, you'll have to go one on one. I don't think he's talking boxing gloves. Oh, he says you've got two hours. One of them is about gone."

There was a silence on the phone, so long a silence that Hammond finally said, "Danzel? You still there?"

"Call the patrol boys," Tom said in a voice of cold steel. "I'm just passing San Berdoo on the interstate. Tell them I'm coming in pedal to the metal. Big red Ram, they can't miss me. Tell 'em to clear me a path or stay out of the fucking way."

"What if some cowboy tries to catch you?"

"He'd better be in an F-16. The Ram's supercharged."

"Danzel, don't—"

"Call them," Tom said, and ended the connection.

Chapter Thirty-One

He caught the first patrol car just before Highland Springs, about thirty miles out. The cruiser was parked by the road when Tom roared by. The patrolman came after him, pulled into the left lane to try to get past him, but couldn't top Tom's speed, and Tom wasn't interested in slowing down. The highway patrolman settled for trailing after him, lights flashing and siren wailing. Ahead of them a pair of cruisers was already clearing a path down the highway, running flat-out.

There was another car waiting for them at the exit from the interstate. He heard Tom and his trailing cruiser coming and was already rolling when the Ram careened onto the Gene Autry, tail end swinging wide, tires smoking as they fought for a grip on the pavement. Behind him the patrol car fishtailed, almost lost it, the driver getting it back under control just at the end.

Even with the escort, it was impossible to maintain flat-out speed on the city's streets. They dropped to ninety and went in a convoy, one front, one behind, cars pulling over, faces staring.

Hammond heard them coming and was waiting outside the police station when Tom skidded to a sideways stop, one cruiser before him, one after. The lot was filled with black-and-whites. A horde of policemen, uniformed and plain clothes—must have been just about the entire force—watched wide-eyed as Tom leaped down from the truck. He recognized Sandy from the lobby, and Hammond's fellow detective. Anticipating the shootout at the OK Corral, probably. Tom ignored them, went straight to Hammond.

"Where is he?" Tom demanded. "I'm going to kill that son of a bitch."

"Maybe," Hammond said. "He's up there."

"Up where?" Tom followed the direction of his glance.

"San Jacinto. Up at the top. Emptied the place out, sent everybody down. Says it's just him and your buddy there now. And you, when you get there. And you'd better come alone. No guns either."

"Where do I catch the bus," Tom said.

"It's a gondola. We'll take you to it. But I don't advise going up there."

"I'm going up. That fucker thinks his rattlesnakes are mean, wait till I bite him on the ass."

"Thing is, he's got a bunch of explosives strapped to your buddy. That's how he managed to get the place cleared out in a hurry."

THE GONDOLA to the top of the mountain departed from the Valley Station. Hammond drove him there, a parade of police cars following in a caravan. A large crowd had already formed—locals, sightseers, tourists who had been rousted from the park above, more cops—it looked like a thousand people, milling about, talking excitedly among themselves. They grew silent, staring, as Tom alighted from the police car. A park ranger was waiting for them and came out to meet them.

"That son of a bitch took over my station," he said. "He had a bomb strapped to his hostage, said he'd blow the whole place to bits if we didn't evacuate. Man, this is so fucked. Nobody takes over my station."

"The hostage, how was he?" Tom asked.

"Scared. Looked pretty cool, though. He told the perp, 'You're gonna wish you hadn't messed with Tom Danzel.' Got some balls on him, I'd say. The perp duct-taped his mouth to shut him up."

"He got that right, at least. That's about the only way to shut Stanley up," Tom said dryly. He stripped off his holster and the Sig.

"Better keep the jacket," Hammond said. "It's cold up top." It was already cooler here at 2,643 feet than in the city. "Plus, I've got an ankle holster, we'll fix you up with a backup—"

"I won't need a gun," Tom said.

Chris and Eddie were already there in the front ranks of the crowd. Chris ducked a cop trying to hold him back, but Hammond waved for the cop to let him through. Eddie came in his wake.

"Tom, you can't go up there," Chris said.

"He's got Stanley. I'm getting him back."

"He's a samurai."

"An old samurai. Not even a real one, a movie actor samurai, and washed-up besides. And I'm Tom Danzel."

"You can't fight a samurai, even an old one, with what you've learned watching a handful of videos. If you go up there, he's going to kill you. Then he's going to kill Stanley anyway."

"He's right," Eddie said. "Even the worst samurai will win against an untrained fighter. He'll slice you in half before you even know what hit you."

"Better listen to your friends," Hammond said. "This guy is just going to kill both of you. Look, maybe we can get some guys up there with a heli—"

"Like he wouldn't hear that coming, he wouldn't know what you were going to do? He'd kill Stanley in a heartbeat the first chopper he hears."

"Okay, there's trails beyond the station. We can take some guys up to Idyllwild, that's higher up. They could hike down, take him by surprise."

"If we had a couple more hours. I don't think we do. I think he wants me up there, and he's going to be seriously pissed if I don't show up, and soon. And when he gets pissed, Stanley's going to pay the price."

"Well, shit...." Hammond looked flummoxed.

"Look, I appreciate your concern, but here's what I do. I kick ass. I'm going to kick his. It doesn't matter if we're talking swords or boxing gloves or water pistols, the bottom line is still the same. He's got Stanley and Stanley is mine. I get him back. And I kick ass. End of game."

It was still afternoon, but it suddenly seemed to Hammond as if it were evening. Everything was washed in red the way it sometimes was with the great desert sunsets—but he blinked and realized it was only the blood red in Danzel's eyes. This guy was seriously steaming.

All at once, Hammond smiled. He wished he could be up there on the mountain with them when Danzel got there. He didn't know what was going to happen, but of one thing he was dead certain—it was going to be bad. Very bad.

Tom started up the steep path to the Valley Station. After a moment everybody fell in behind him, like he was leading a parade. The elevated station sat on a platform that rose on concrete ballast. It had been constructed so that the flash floods that sometimes roared down the canyon wouldn't budge it, nor the fifty mile an hour winds.

A gondola waited for him at the station. "You'd better let the car operator take you up," the ranger said.

"He wants me alone. Show me how to operate this thing."

The operator gave him a quick course and happily exited the car when Tom told him to. In a couple of minutes, the car had begun its ascent, Tom standing in it alone, staring straight ahead.

There weren't many things in life that scared Tom Danzel. Heights was one of them, though he kept that fact to himself. Stanley had suggested, on their drive in, that they take the ride up to the top for the fun of it, and Tom had nixed the idea. Ten-plus minutes dangling helplessly in the air was about as far from fun as anything he could think of.

Worse, to his way of thinking, was that the damned car didn't just go straight up, it rotated 360 degrees as it climbed. Great if you wanted to enjoy the unrestricted views of the canyon and the valley below. He didn't. He kept his eyes glued firmly on the mountain ahead. The only sound was a faint whistle of wind and the hum of the motor that turned the car.

It arrived at the first of the towers, bumped, accelerated over the tower, and dropped slightly with a free-fall-like sensation. Tom exerted all his willpower to keep the car on the cables.

The walls of the canyon outside were close enough he could have identified the plants struggling to grow there, if he'd had a mind to. Another tower was coming up. He leaned into it, bracing himself for the sensation of free fall when they had passed it. The gondola accelerated. Tom made himself breathe. Slowly. Deeply.

It felt like an eternity later when the car climbed into Mountain Station. It unlocked from the main cable and glided back and forth between rubber bumpers on either side. Snow glistened beyond the windows. The thermometer outside registered 35 degrees.

The car stopped. Tom stepped off it onto the landing gangway. It was cold, a shocking contrast to the desert heat below. His breath made little clouds.

Nakamura was waiting for him. Tom had seen him before he arrived, standing at the platform, watching the gondola approach. For the last few yards, he and Tom had stared stonily at each other. Behind him, Stanley was tied to a chair from one of the restaurants.

"Maybe you want to kiss him goodbye," Nakamura said when Tom stepped out. "You will not set the bomb off by doing so."

"You've got a detonator."

"This thing? Oh, that was just so that I could clear everybody out. I do not need it. The explosives are on a timer now. You have thirty minutes before they blow." He looked at his watch and corrected himself. "Thirty-one minutes. But you will not be around to hear the explosion."

"There won't be one," Tom said. "So, how do you want to do this?"

Nakamura lifted an eyebrow. "Why, with swords, of course. I thought you were into all things samurai. There is a sword right there on the ground in front of you."

Tom picked it up and glanced down at it. It was the *katana* Nakamura had shown him that day at his house. Seventeenth century, Edo—that a ronin might have carried. "Nice sword," he said, a little surprised. He'd have expected the man to give him something second-rate, just to fuck with him.

Nakamura read his mind. "A samurai does not cheat," he said.

"You're no samurai. You've been exposed. You've shamed yourself. Killing those boys out of nothing more honorable than sexual heat. A true samurai would commit *seppuku*."

"What makes you think I do not intend to? But a samurai kills his enemy first. You have about twenty-eight minutes left now before the bomb attached to your little boyfriend goes off. You will not be here to see it, though. And when I have dealt with you, then *seppuku*."

"So you say."

"You think I am evil because I killed those boys. Jeff was an accident. Of the worst kind. If I have ever come close to loving anyone, it was him. But the sex that we had, it was a sickness in him. He was the one who wanted it that way. I would have been content just to hold him in my arms, he was so beautiful. The perfect little *gaijin*. One time he asked me for five thousand dollars. I do not even remember what he told me it was for. I brought it to him in one hundred dollar bills and tossed them on the floor in front of him. He sat on the floor making little piles of bills, delighted. I do not think he even was aware that I was there. He was never more adorable to me."

"It didn't stop you from killing him."

"That truly was an accident. He had to be choked when he ejaculated. That was the only way he could reach orgasm. What happened was probably always inevitable."

He thought about that, shook his head sadly. "After that, the rest was inevitable too. Barry knew Jeff had gone to spend the night with me. He knew what we did. When Jeff did not come home, he got suspicious. There was a video of Jeff and me. You could not see my face, but Barry did not need to. He knew who it was. So he tried to blackmail me. I had no choice. He was the enemy. The samurai does not hesitate to deal with enemies."

"And the security guard?"

"Mario? He was the one who let Randy erase the security recording. Unfortunately, sooner or later, the guard would have put the pieces together, and then he would have to tell someone. I could not have that. It had to be done."

"So does this," Tom said.

"Yes." Nakamura's voice was sad. "This, too, was inevitable from the beginning, I fear. You were fated to come into my orbit, just as you have done. I knew, once you talked about Jeff, about the fake snake bites on Barry, that you were getting too close to the truth, that eventually you would figure things out. I sent the snake to your room. And the yakuza to try to scare you off. I wanted to spare you. I hoped that you might just leave...."

"I don't scare off."

"No. I can see that."

"Maybe you're the one who should be scared," Tom said. "Look, one of us is a fake samurai. You've never fought a real fight, just pretend, and I've spent years on the streets, brawling with all kinds of tough guys. Which of us do you think ought to be nervous?"

"I know all things samurai. In those movies, I was not just acting. I did not come up here to pretend."

"I didn't come up here to jaw either."

"No, of course not. Time is running out. For Stanley, certainly. And it is foolish indeed for me to suppose that you could ever comprehend the samurai way. No *gaijin* can."

"What I comprehend is, one of us is going down, and it's not going to be me," Tom said in a confident voice.

He fitted the looped *saya*, the wooden scabbard, over his shoulder, took a step forward, and halted. Better to leave some distance between them. Beyond Nakamura, he could see Stanley. His mouth was taped shut, and his eyes were wide, tears trailing down his cheeks.

Tom took no more than a glance at him, however. He couldn't afford to let anything distract him now. Rage, fear, all emotions were distracting, they led to sloppy fighting, they left one vulnerable. The samurai put all that aside when he fought. He would too.

He was facing a pro, maybe an aging pro, but a pro nonetheless, and he was fully aware that he himself was a rank amateur. He was fast and he was strong, and he had been in a lot of fights. He was good at tuning in to the other guy, but he had never fought with a sword, and Nakamura had, if only in those movies. And this wasn't going to be just a couple of guys throwing punches. This was all or nothing.

Kami-hasso, he told himself. Become one with his opponent. He watched Nakamura, eye to eye, till it felt as if he could see right into Nakamura's brain, detect the impulses as they ran from brain to muscle.

Instinct told him when Nakamura was about to draw, and Tom drew with him, but he was not quite as fast. He was glad now that he hadn't come any closer. Nakamura could have chopped him down in one swift motion, and the fight would have been over.

Tom had made up his mind in the ride up here that he would be the aggressor. That was the way he fought, and anyway, time was against him. His odds were going to get slimmer as the minutes ticked by. He went into a kind of trance, everything else fading from sight but the man before him.

He lunged forward, but Nakamura slipped like an eel out of the sword's path and, shouting "Ai," came back with a fast cut to the side that should have sliced Tom open. Somehow Tom managed to turn that away with his own blade, but so far this wasn't looking good.

"You are better than I expected," Nakamura said, and he seemed to relax, but Tom sensed that his relaxing was only a ruse, and when Nakamura suddenly attacked, a straight thrust at Tom's face, Tom had already leaned away from it. The tip of the sword came a fraction of an inch short of his throat.

From his experience in facing shooters, Tom felt certain that Nakamura, too, was experiencing what was most often described as tunnel vision, focusing so intently on the threat right in front of you that everything outside of that tiny space vanished. At San Francisco PD, they had trained officers to take a quick sidestep, in hope that they might disappear for a few seconds from their enemy's vision, give them a life or death chance.

Tom moved quickly to the right and attempted one of the classic moves from the old samurai flicks, *yokogiri*, a sideways cut he had sometimes practiced, like playing air guitar. Nakamura dodged, but not fast enough. The sword nicked his arm.

The sight of his own blood enraged Nakamura. "Damn you," he shouted, his anger flaring, and he swung his sword in a barely controlled diagonal cut, which would have quartered Tom if it hadn't just missed him. Before Tom could counter, Nakamura came at him again from the left.

Tom turned inside the thrust, but Nakamura recovered faster than he would have thought possible. Tom roared and made a futile slice at the air, but Nakamura had already pirouetted away from him, and this time Nakamura's sweeping blade, left to right, cut into Tom's left arm, deep, almost to the bone. Tom smelled his own blood, and in seconds the wound had begun to hurt, bad. It wouldn't take long for the cut to weaken him, bleeding the way it was, and once that happened, it was all over but the singing. If he was going to beat this guy, he had to do it soon. Sooner than soon. It had to be now.

With his enemy wounded, however, Nakamura was encouraged. He unleashed a blur of sword strokes, so fast and so hard that it was all Tom could do to fend them off, let alone retaliate. The air rang with the music of steel on steel. Tom backed up a step, and then another, looking for any opening and finding none.

Tom's defenses had begun to falter, and he was getting rapidly weaker. His cuts with the *katana* were nothing more now than wild swings. Nakamura sensed his opportunity and went for the kill.

"This," Nakamura said through clenched teeth, "we call the *yakiba*. It comes in through the bone of the hip, shatters it, and travels downward. Good bye, *gaijin*." He came in under Tom's ineffective sword, his own blade slicing the air.

Something went wrong, though. The sword cut into Tom's hip as intended, but instead of amputating everything south of there, as it should have done, it stopped hard, with so violent a torque that Nakamura almost lost his grip on the haft.

He recovered, but not fast enough. With every ounce of the strength he had left in his right arm, Tom brought his own sword up in the classic rising cut he'd seen in every one of the movies, from left to right. It wasn't a perfect samurai cut, which would have gone clean through the spine, rending the body in two, but it was enough. Nakamura, his eyes wide with astonishment, toppled to the ground.

Tom's hand went to his hip, where the steel insert had stopped Nakamura's blade. The cut was clean but shallow. It was bleeding, but not a geyser, meaning he hadn't lost an artery. He stepped over the fallen Nakamura, tossing his sword aside.

"You have to finish me off," Nakamura hissed through clenched teeth. "It is the samurai way."

"Hell, I never said I was a samurai. You want the job done, do it yourself," Tom said. He went to where Stanley waited, bound to his chair, and carefully pulled the tape from his mouth.

"Baby, you do get yourself into more shit," he said with a relieved grin.

"Tom, the bomb," Stanley gasped.

"Oh, that. Hell, we've got almost two minutes left before that contraption is set to blow." He used the blade of the sword to cut the wire free and gave the bomb a wide toss. Three seconds later, it exploded. Rocks and sand debris flew into the air.

"Well, maybe not two whole minutes," Tom said, dodging a clod of dirt.

He got Stanley free, and they clung to each other tightly for a moment, until Tom said, "Uh, I'm bleeding badly, baby. I think we'd better head down the hill." While Stanley tore a strip from his shirt and wound it around Tom's arm, Tom fished his cell phone out of his pocket and dialed Hammond.

"Jesus, you're still alive?" Hammond answered in a surprised voice. "We heard that explosion, and we thought…."

"No, we're both still intact. But I'm going to need a medic. I've got a couple of good cuts."

"What did you do?"

"I kicked ass."

"What about Nakamura?"

Tom glanced at where Nakamura lay. He'd managed to raise himself up enough to take Tom's advice. He had finished the job, falling on his own sword. The blood was rapidly forming a pool beneath him, steaming in the cold air.

"He won't need a medic," Tom said.

Exclusive Excerpt

A Tom and Stanley Mystery

Does murder follow Tom and Stanley around, or do they follow the murders?

After a hospital stay, Stanley is invited by Father Brighton to convalesce at St. Marywood, an isolated monastery on the ocean cliffs of Big Sur. Upon arrival, Stanley finds Father Brighton dead. The order's doctor writes it up as a death by natural causes, but those seem to be quite prevalent at the monastery. The recent demise of a young brother who fell from the cliffs is described as an accident, but Stanley's nose is twitching. Plus the order's finances have taken a sudden, mysterious turn for the better. Is something rotten at St. Marywood?

Stanley and Tom can't resist digging around, even if it means testing their tumultuous relationship against a gaggle of handsome, young, virginal, and—they are told—gay men.

Coming Soon to
www.dsppublications.com

CHAPTER ONE

LIKE A shaft of copper gold, the late-afternoon sun pierced the curtained windows. The plum tree that stood outside cast a feathery silhouette across the floor, as delicate and precise as one of those paintings the Chinese do on silk. Someone had turned the air-conditioning off, and with the windows sealed, the atmosphere was hot and humid, making Stanley Korski drowsy. His eyes drifted closed… only to fly wide when the stranger appeared.

Stanley had been thinking about death so frequently of late that it was almost no surprise to look up and see him standing in the doorway of the hospital room—a robed figure with a cowl that half obscured his face until he pushed it back.

Still half-asleep, Stanley said, "Only, aren't you supposed to be carrying a scythe?"

"A scythe…?" For a second or two, the dark-robed man looked puzzled. Then he grinned, a smile that took years off his otherwise weatherworn face. "Ah, you've been contemplating your mortality, I suspect," he said.

"Yes," Stanley agreed. "Or the lack thereof. So assuming you're not the grim reaper, you must be a monk. But why is a monk coming to visit me in the hospital?"

"I'm a friar, actually."

"Oh, I see. And the difference is…?"

"Monks stay in their monastery. They retreat from the world. As you can see, friars get out and about."

"Including hospital visits, it seems."

"Sometimes." The visitor paused, appearing to consider how best to explain his presence. "You must wonder what I'm doing here?"

"Well, I truly hope it's not to administer the last rites."

The friar laughed. "No, have no fears. It's nothing of that sort." Again, that slight hesitation. "I'm an old friend of your friend Chris. Chris Rafferty."

Which seemed, to Stanley, a non sequitur. He screwed up his face, thinking, *Chris is so very… well, so very sociable, to put it nicely.* His thoughts ground to a sudden stop. Wait, Chris was a friend. One didn't like even to think critical thoughts about a good friend. "Really? I don't recall…."

"At one time," the friar added.

"He never mentioned a friar." Which was what Stanley had been puzzling over. Even Chris, who could be very "oh, that doesn't matter" about such things, would hardly have failed to mention a man of the cloth. "I've heard about practically everything else over the years, but never anyone in a brown frock."

"It was a long time ago," the visitor said. "Before I joined the order."

"Please tell me he didn't drive you to it," Stanley said with a laugh. "He can be a pill at times, no one knows that better than I, but I've never heard of anyone so broken up over him they would retreat to a monastery. Or a—well, what do you call your places, anyway?"

"Technically, they are friaries, but to be honest, we usually just refer to ours as a monastery."

"Hmm. That is confusing, you know," Stanley said, laughing to take any sting out of his remark.

This time the friar actually laughed with him. "Yes, I'm sure it is. Don't worry, it'll all come clear in due time. And as to Chris, no, I can't blame him for driving me to anything. Though, yes, it was the nature of our relationship that made me turn to the order, in a manner of speaking."

"Which is a remark surely designed, I think, to make one curious. At least, it did to me. Make me curious, I mean." Stanley lifted an eyebrow. "I hope you're going to elucidate."

"I'm afraid it's not a very original story. I was a priest, and I was gay, but I wasn't a happy homosexual."

"Ah." Stanley nodded. That he could understand. "Gay does not always mean happy."

"So very true. And I think, if truth be told, at the time I was more gay than priest. All that guilt."

"I understand. I suppose we all go through a period of guilt. It's part of the initiation ritual, I believe."

"Yes, I think you're right." He paused briefly. "At any rate, in my case, it poisoned my relationships—even with Chris, though I did love him greatly. I was older than him. At the time, he was still quite young. And very beautiful."

"I never knew him when he was in the cradle, but he must have been a beautiful baby," Stanley said. "I remember a picture—with a bearskin rug—already flaunting himself, and he was no more than an infant."

The friar's laugh was easy and fell pleasantly on the ear. "No, he was not quite that young when I knew him, but young. In his teens. His late teens, to be honest, but still, too young for me to consider taking our relationship that next step further, though at the time, I thought he was willing."

"She always was a hussy."

The smile again. "I suspect his interest in me had as much to do with father fulfillment as it did with sexual attraction. But he was a lovely young man, and I was not exactly a paragon of virtue. I wanted to do more, I can confess that now, but I felt as well that it would be wrong— wrong for him, certainly."

"Well, if it's any consolation, he turned out a slut anyway."

That earned him another laugh. Stanley decided he liked the laugh—and the man. "He speaks well of you too," the friar said.

"Which means, if you can say that, then you must have stayed in touch over the years."

"Does it?"

"If you know him to speak of me. We are longtime friends, but obviously I didn't meet him until after your time together."

"You are right, of course. And, yes, we have stayed in touch. Although not perhaps as much in touch as I would have liked…."

Stanley raised an eyebrow, but the father went on with only a slight pause. "But we have over the years exchanged the occasional card, and even a phone call or two."

"Close but distant, in other words. That's not as rare as one might suppose."

"Exactly. So when I had a problem, I called Chris, just to get his advice. And he suggested I come see you."

"He told you I was in the hospital?"

"No, I went to your office originally, but the girl there told me you were here, in the hospital. So…."

Which was a puzzling remark. So far as Stanley knew, his partner, Tom Danzel, was in the office. And he'd heard Tom called many things since they'd first met—had in fact given him a few choice labels himself—but no one, to the best of his knowledge, had ever called Tom a "girl." At least not and walked away with a full set of teeth.

His visitor, however, was still speaking. "…not just any problem, mind you, but the sort of thing that couldn't quite be resolved where I was, that needed outside eyes…."

"What kind of problem?" Stanley asked, his eyes narrowing. He'd straighten out the business about the office in due time; for now, he was too intrigued by the nature of the friar's visit. Friars didn't just pop in for hospital visits, not in his experience—though admittedly his experience with friars had been practically nonexistent. No doubt Chris could tell him more. "What kind of problem are we talking about, exactly?"

The friar had remained standing in the doorway, but now he came the rest of the way into the room and motioned toward the wooden chair next to Stanley's bed. "May I?"

"Of course, Father…?"

"Brighton."

"Like the beach."

"Just so. My mother was English and very fond of the seaside. When she met my father—well, never mind, it's a long story, and not really relevant to my visit here today."

He seated himself on the chair, pushing his cowl back from his head. He was older than Stanley had at first realized. On the gray side of sixty, Stanley guessed, though still handsome. *The English rose fades early*, he found himself thinking, *but slowly*. Father Brighton's hair was silver but full—the order, whatever it was, didn't require tonsure, then—his sensuous mouth making Stanley think he must have been hot indeed when he was younger. Wouldn't Chris have just had his eye on a studly priest? He was going to have a serious talk with that hussy, lusting after a man of the cloth, and he himself apparently little more than an infant at the time. Once again that image of a naked baby on a bearskin rug popped into his mind.

"Just how long ago was this—I'm not sure what to call it—this flirtation of yours?"

"Oh, quite a long while ago—and I'm not sure flirtation isn't a bit strong. I had designs. I don't think Chris shared them especially. And though, as I say, we have remained in touch, it's been since then a very casual sort of thing. It took a bit of effort, to be honest, even to track him down. It turned out he had moved since I had last written him."

"Which brings us to your visit here… and your problem…."

"I had in mind saving that for later."

"Later? Is there going to be a later? This isn't just a onetime visit?"

"When Chris told me you were a detective and mentioned your illness, it occurred to me that you are going to need some time to convalesce when you get out of here. An opportunity, if you will, to kill two birds with one stone."

"I've been in this bed for over a week now. I don't think I much like that simile—or is it a metaphor?"

"Certainly just a figure of speech, and you're right, not an apt one, all things considered. What I've come for is to offer you the perfect place to convalesce, just down the coast a bit, near Big Sur—sea air and mountain vistas and lots of quiet."

"Sounds lovely. Does it have a name, or am I simply to refer to it as Eden?"

That laugh again. A deep, ringing baritone that suggested all kinds of manly things to Stanley, and none of them pertinent to a priest. *Or a friar*, he corrected himself. Something, at any rate, which ought to negate seductive thoughts.

"Saint Marywood," Father Brighton said. "Though I'm not sure Eden would be so awfully remiss. It is a lovely place. Except there are no apple trees."

"Is it a monastery, this lovely Saint Marywood?"

"Yes. Or friary, if you prefer, though I've always thought that a bit pretentious. Anyway, friary is ordinarily used to indicate the mendicant orders, and we don't beg for alms. We are self-sufficient. More or less so, at any rate."

"Then I'll stick with calling it a monastery. Where, I take it, I will be surrounded by monks. Quiet monks, presumably, since you mentioned that especially."

"Friars. And reasonably quiet, yes, but not entirely. Meals are silent, but otherwise some of the young men are quite vocal. And, I might mention, not all of them are as old as I, if that tempts you."

Which it did, and Stanley thought the friar rather knew that without being told, but still, he wasn't one to give up his secrets so easily. "I have a boyfriend."

"So I am told. Tom Danzel, your partner in that detective agency, isn't it? That's what Chris told me, at any rate. But surely there's no harm in looking. Which, I should probably say, is about all that could be expected to happen anyway, notwithstanding their predilections. They do take vows."

"Celibacy?"

Father Brighton nodded somberly.

Stanley gave an exaggerated pout. "Well, that doesn't sound very promising. All those girls in dresses and no one allowed to kick up their heels. Or raise them, so to speak."

"I wouldn't want to give you a false impression. But in another sense, you could be said to have your cake and eat it too. Or feast on it with your eyes, at least. I can promise you that, certainly—a feast for the eyes, one that I myself savor often, to be perfectly honest. I gave up certain of my activities pursuant to my vows, but the predilections remain, do they not?"

"Well, I'm not dead yet, so…. Wait, what are you suggesting? Predilections? Are these monks—"

"Friars."

"Friars, then. Are they all gay?"

Father Brighton smiled somewhat impishly and nodded. "Someone once said that queers make the best monks."

"And friars too, it would seem. And they are all young men?"

"Most of them. The past is more likely to be an encumbrance to the young."

"Still, monks—excuse me, friars…. I can't help thinking it seems such an unlikely choice for a young man to make."

"Something about the passion, I should think. And the asceticism. Mind you, as I say, there is that vow of celibacy."

"Which is never broken?" Stanley sighed. What was the point of young men with their passions flaming like a fire on the hearth if you had no hope of employing a poker?

Father Brighton shrugged. "Some things are left up to the individual conscience. I'd be less than honest if I didn't say I think it sometimes happens. As Plutarch put it—"

"The wildest colts make the best horses," Stanley finished for him.

Father Brighton beamed at him. "Exactly. You know your Romans."

"Better than I know my friars, obviously. I've been intimately involved with one or two over the years—Romans, I mean, never a friar. So what you're saying is that a few of the colts are still frisky?"

"Most of the brothers are still colts, certainly, young men in the prime of their lives. And while they do work in the local schools, as teachers—friars serve in their communities, you see—they are also much of the time somewhat isolated, so it's not surprising if they sometimes stray from their vows. That's to be expected, I should think. But I have to be honest, I also think such instances are rare."

Stanley thought about that for a moment. "And this is why you didn't really want to bring the police into this, whatever this problem is."

"In part, yes. I think ideally we'd want someone of a certain sensibility. You can understand that, surely?"

"I can. But I may as well tell you, I'm done playing detective." Stanley sighed.

Father Brighton raised one eyebrow slightly. "If you'll pardon my saying so, you seem troubled."

"Hmm. Not troubled so much as weary. Of... well, lots of things. It's too long a list to go into here."

"But not that partner you mentioned—Tom, as I recall."

"Tom? No...." Stanley paused, thinking for a moment, and said, more emphatically, "No."

"If you'll forgive an old man for spouting advice, let me say, Stanley, from where you stand—"

"Lie," Stanley corrected him. "I've been very much horizontal of late."

"And it becomes you, if I might offer a comment. But what I started to say is, the road before you looks deceptively long, but it's not. It's far, far shorter than you could possibly imagine. If you've found love, cherish it. Squeeze all the happiness and love you can into every moment. They have a habit of fading away all too soon, those moments."

"Were you saying that I look attractive horizontal? And you sound as if you're troubled yourself."

Father Brighton laughed again, his expression changing in an instant from somber to happy. "Yes, to the first part. As to the other— perhaps, as you put it, I am just a bit weary too."

"And there is that problem you mentioned...."

"Which I shall not burden you with after all, I think. Since, as you say, you are no longer playing detective."

"I don't think it was ever really my cup of tea, and I've already informed Tom, my partner, that when I get out of here, I'm not going back into the business. We always seem to end up with murder on our hands, and in my experience, murder nearly always involves dead bodies. Just out of curiosity, by the way, is that the sort of problem you're having at your friar place—a spot of murder?"

"No, no, nothing so dramatic as that."

"And you don't want to tell me about it while you're here?" Stanley hated to be left in the dark, especially regarding other people's business.

"Well, if you aren't coming to Saint Marywood…." Father Brighton shrugged and said—perhaps a little too brightly, Stanley thought—"And really, it's not all that pressing."

Pressing enough to talk to Chris and, at his suggestion, drive from Big Sur—four or five hours, wasn't it?—to make a visit here to the hospital. Despite his promises to himself that he was done with detective work, Stanley found himself mildly intrigued. He'd all but made up his mind he was through with all that. Still, he felt a slight quickening of his lately sluggish pulse.

He was about to pursue the matter a bit further, but the doctor, whose name Stanley never could remember, appeared at that moment in the doorway. He wheezed—as was his frequent habit—and looked past the friar, directly at Stanley.

"If it's not a convenient time…," the doctor said in a voice that indicated he thought it ought to be.

"I was just leaving." Father Brighton got up quickly from the wooden chair, but on his way to the door, he paused to look back.

"The offer of convalescence remains, regardless of that other matter," he said. "It's a lovely place, really."

And there's still that unexplained problem, Stanley thought, more tempted than he wanted to admit to himself. "I confess, it is attractive."

"If you change your mind," Father Brighton said, "you are certainly welcome, for as long as you wish. And Chris will know how to reach me."

When he had gone, the doctor walked over to Stanley's bed. He wheezed again, glancing down at some papers in his hand and back up to Stanley. "I'm happy to say the tests have confirmed our most recent diagnosis. Not leukemia at all, just a rather atypical mononucleosis. But you did have me worried for a time."

"Hmm, strictly speaking, I think you were puzzled," Stanley said. "I was the worried one."

The doctor rewarded him with an unamused smile. "Yes, well, in any case, you'll need a few days more—"

"I was hoping to go home."

"You will need a few more days of rest," the doctor said emphatically. "We'll see how things stand in a day or two."

"Or lie. Which I've been doing for days, and I must say, notwithstanding that some seem to find it attractive, it does get boring."

"Your boredom won't kill you."

Stanley was not quite so sure. He remembered Chris, who was a nurse, saying, "If the disease doesn't kill you, the doctors may do the job."

This doctor, whose name Stanley still couldn't recall, had scarcely wheezed his way out of the room when a young woman came in. *They must be selling tickets*, Stanley thought. He hadn't had more than one visitor a day since he'd been here, not counting Doctor Wheeze, and now it seemed like he was on the Gray Line tour.

"If you're Stan, these are for you," his newest visitor said, holding out an arrangement of yellow and white daisies in an emerald green jar.

"Stanley." He hated being called Stan. It sounded so… well, something he wasn't, even if he couldn't quite put a name to it. Macho, maybe.

"Stanley," she corrected herself with a bright smile and a generous display of teeth. "I'm Delightful."

"Yes, I should say you must be," Stanley said, setting the flowers on the nightstand. Or if not delightful—and that took some knowing, didn't it?—she was, without question, comely. Lustrous auburn hair framed a perfect oval of a face—a very pretty face it was too—and fullness of bosom and hip was accentuated by a wasp-sized waist. Stanley had a vision of male heads snapping about as she passed, of shops and homes emptying as surely as they had emptied of other occupants for that Pied Piper. His partner, Tom, had been a dedicated skirt chaser until he had embarked on the as-of-yet-not-clearly-labeled relationship with Stanley. Tom would surely be salivating. And running with the rats. Probably at the head of the pack.

The potential object of salivation beamed at him, once again flashing perfect teeth. "You're wondering about my name. Everybody does. The answer is quite simple, though, really. My parents were hard-core hippies," she said. "So they named us accordingly. My brother is Willing."

"I think I may have met him," Stanley said. "Charming creature, as I recall."

His visitor laughed. "And I was christened Delightful. But everyone calls me Dee. Dee Collins. I'm your girl Friday."

"Leaving Saturday through Thursday unaccounted for?"

She gave him a generous grin, tossing those auburn curls this time. More men were surely abandoning the shops, or at least their hospital rooms. An intern passing the open door happened to glance in and, seeing Dee Collins, paused briefly to give her what the French call an *oeillade*, which Stanley had always thought sounded more elegant than a leer. To her credit, Ms. Collins did not notice—or did not show she noticed, in any case. Stanley had the impression that she did not miss much, certainly not where men were concerned.

"Well, those too," she replied. "Or Monday through Friday, in any case. Tom hired me." When Stanley only looked blankly at her, she added, "Tom Danzel."

"Yes," Stanley said, his face carefully free of expression, "I know the name. And what exactly did Mr. Danzel hire you for?"

"I told you, I'm your girl Friday. He says you aren't coming back to the office, and he needed someone to manage things there. So"—she spread her hands wide—"I'm it."

"Like a game of tag," Stanley said. "And odd man out." He knew his partner. Tom was a faithful kind of guy, but temptation when it came to him probably wore a miniskirt that barely reached past the waterline and had black-encased legs that seemed never to end. All the sorts of things Tom would be sure to notice. *Oeillade*, indeed. He immediately thought of one or two things he did not care to have her manage—his partner foremost among them.

He tossed the covers aside and swung his own unencased legs to the floor. "Actually, that bit about my not coming back to the office is still up in the air. Doctor Huffenpuff says I can go home today, but I will need to convalesce for a bit. If you would be so kind, Delectable, my clothes are on a hanger in that closet just behind you."

"Delightful." She took a hanger from the little closet and handed Stanley his sweats.

"Exactly. As it turns out, I've got the perfect place for resting up. We are going to spend a couple of weeks down the coast. Sea air and mountain vistas and lots of long brown skirts."

"We?" She looked appropriately puzzled.

"Oh, I haven't informed him yet, but Tom will be going with me. It will be like a vacation."

"But…." Her smiling expression became one of dismay. "But what about the office?"

"That, it seems, will be in your hands—your surely competent hands, I should think." He raised an eyebrow and gave her a mocking smile. "I'm going to put my knickers on now. No peeking."

Victor J. Banis is the critically acclaimed ("the master's touch in storytelling" ~*Publishers Weekly*) author of more than 200 books and numerous shorter works in a career spanning nearly a half century. A longtime Californian, he lives and writes now in West Virginia's beautiful Blue Ridge.

Website: www.vjbanis.com

More Mystery from DSP Publications
DAVID C. DAWSON
THE DEADLY LIES
a Dominic Delingpole Mystery

Sequel to FAPA Award-winning *The Necessary Deaths*
The Delingpole Mysteries: Book Two

Dominic and Jonathan are on their romantic Spanish honeymoon, and things are perfect… except Dominic has kept a secret from his husband. He's failed to tell Jonathan that he plans to meet his former lover, Bernhardt, who is speeding on his way from Germany to present Dominic with a mysterious gift.

But Bernhardt is killed in a suspicious car accident. Shortly before he dies, he sends Dominic a bizarre text message that will take the newlyweds on a hair-raising adventure.

Lies upon lies plunge Dominic and Jonathan into an internet crime that could destroy the lives of millions of people. What is the mysterious Charter Ninety-Nine group? And will their planned internet assault force Dominic to choose between the fate of the world and the life of his lover?

www.dsppublications.com